The WEIGHT of a THOUSAND FEATHERS

BRIAN CONAGHAN

BLOOMSBURY

LONDON OXFORD NEW YORK NEW DELHI SYDNEY

For John Patrick Conaghan

BLOOMSBURY YA
Bloomsbury Publishing Plc
50 Bedford Square, London WC1B 3DP, UK

BLOOMSBURY, BLOOMSBURY YA and the Diana logo
are trademarks of Bloomsbury Publishing Plc

First published in Great Britain in 2018 by Bloomsbury Publishing Plc
This paperback edition first published in Great Britain in 2019
by Bloomsbury Publishing Plc

A catalogue record for this book is available from the British Library

ISBN: HB: 978-1-4088-7153-9; PB 978-1-4088-7154-6;
eBook: 978-1-4088-7155-3

2 4 6 8 10 9 7 5 3 1

Typeset by RefineCatch Limited, Bungay, Suffolk

Printed and bound in Great Britain by CPI Group (UK) Ltd, Croydon CR0 4YY

To find out more about our authors and books visit www.bloomsbury.com
and sign up for our newsletters

# of a
THOUSAND
FEATHERS

WINNER OF THE AN POST IRISH BOOK AWARDS TEEN &
YOUNG ADULT BOOK OF THE YEAR 2018
SHORTLISTED FOR THE CBI BOOK OF THE YEAR AWARD 2019
LONGLISTED FOR THE CILIP CARNEGIE MEDAL 2019

'Conaghan is a sublime storyteller who can make the reader
hang on his every last word'
The Times Children's Book of the Week

'An emotional rollercoaster of a book, written with so much
heart ... bounces off of the page ... A bold, life-affirming read'
Irish Independent

'A hard-hitting, heartbreaking tale ... One sentence after
another knocks the reader out'
Independent

'The characterisation is superb ... A remarkably brave story'
Irish Examiner

'Conaghan's lightness of touch and sense of humour shine
through this heartbreaking story, and each of the characters
lingers in the imagination
long after the final page'
Scotsman

'Although it's heartbreaking at times, there's also tenderness
and humour ... The tremendous empathy with which
Conaghan writes about young people is impressive'
Irish Times

THE BOMBS
THAT BROUGHT US TOGETHER

Seed's Salon

Mum is dead.

I find her propped up in her chair, hands resting gently against her lap. No rings, free from bling, just the way the little boy in me remembers. Her open eyes are like two sparkly saucers staring at the television; some chiselled-toothed guy is trying to punt an all-singing, all-dancing mop. £11.99 all in. Bargain.

I cuff her face four, maybe five, times, until my slaps morph into strokes. Long, soft ones. Her skin feels like December. I think about mouth-to-mouth, but there's no point. I stand tall and stare at her, my dead mother, as if she's an art exhibit.

Dead still.

Still beautiful.

I tighten my eyes, try to cry, then lean in, scroll her lids shut, kiss her wintery forehead and whisper, 'Goodbye, Mum.'

I've had that dream so many times, and it always ends the same way: me pecking her and whispering variations of *goodbye*. However, what made last night's dream different was *where* she died: it's rare she pops her clogs in the living room. Usually happens in her bedroom, in her own bed, surrounded by her own stuff. Because the bedroom is where Mum will go to live when she deteriorates. And she *will* deteriorate, because that's what happens with MS – it creeps up and bites sufferers on the arse when they're least expecting it.

So you're having zero symptoms?
Life chugging along as normal, is it?
What, you think you've defeated me? ME?
Well, let's just do something about that.
BOOM!
Here's another attack for you.
How's that for a relapse?
Now, get yourself back to Go.

MS is a slow burner. Waxes, wanes, skips along. Sometimes I wish she had the big C instead; at least the big C can be found, fought and defeated. Let's leave it at that.

It's Saturday. Last weekend of freedom before school restarts. Zero homework. But chores galore to do, as always.

I try as best I can to pamper Mum:

'Jesus, Bobby, I'm not a horse, be gentle.'

'I am being gentle.'

'Well, pretend I'm a baby then.'

'Way too creepy.'

'I pity the girl who gets you, Bobby Seed.'

'Oh, really, is that right?'

'Ouch! That's sore.'

'Sorry, brush slipped,' I say, smacking her dome with it.

Takes me generations to brush it. No joke. You could watch *The Sound of Music* during our session. I count the strokes, usually well over a hundred, until we're both satisfied. No way Mum could do a hundred strokes herself. Ten knackers her. She does try but then looks as if she's arrived somewhere on the back of a motorbike sans helmet.

'I'm telling you, Mum, you could definitely get a job in a farmer's field.'

'Oh, be quiet or I'll tell you where your real mother lives.'

'Just sit still.'

'I'm sure it's Her Majesty's Prison something or other.'

Mum's hair is like strands of silk. Still dark, still on the long side of short.

Wet.

Brush.

Stroke.

Sometimes she'll lob the odd grenade into the mix by requesting a plait. No bother, Mum, do I look like Vidal Sassoon? I keep telling her I'm more your pull-back-and-ponytail type of hairdresser though. In her youth she had hair like a black pearl. Her words not mine.

We find the action peaceful and therapeutic; allows for a physical contact that's full of quality. Space to relax and reflect. Actually, balls to that. She needs me, she relies on me and, well … she's my mother, isn't she? I know I'm *supposed* to love her, but it takes no effort. I love her from sole to summit. Life's not all darkness and thinking ill of the ill. We do laugh, honestly.

'Do your hairdresser, Bobby,' she asks.

Shirt tucked tight. Hair back and parted. Mannerisms exaggerated. Voice effeminate. I assume my position behind her.

'OMG! Your hair is total gorge, Anne.'

'Think so?'

'Know how many of my customers would kill for locks like that?'

'Many?'

'Too bloody many.'

Wet.

Brush.

Stroke.

'Going out tonight?' I ask.

'Few drinks with the girls just.'

'Up to Memory Lane?'

'Where else?'

'I snogged the barman up there once. Like a washing machine on full spin so he was. Thought I was going to pass out with dizziness.'

'Is he not married?'

'Erm … he said nothing to me.'

Wet.

Brush.

Stroke.

'Going on any holidays, Anne?'

'Magaluf with the girls just.'

'Oh, it's a pure riot over there.'

'You been?'

'Two summers in my early twenties.'

'Nice?'

'Can't tell you about it, they'll lock me up.'

'Sounds a hoot.'

'Pure MEN-tal. Oh, don't get me started.'

Mum's pretty good right now, but there've been loads of days when she's too shattered to laugh, too sore to speak. Then my brushing feels tired and tragic. But even then I know I'll miss these moments in Secd's Salon. Give me misery over nothing any day.

Danny Distant

While looking after Mum is physically draining, it's that little brother of mine who takes up tons of my emotional energy. Affectionately known as Danny or Dan by those close to him, i.e. Mum and me. To the cruel, he is Danny Distant; I'll spare any vile anecdotes. There's no official diagnosis for what Dan has – Mum didn't want one. She didn't want him branded like some swine awaiting slaughter. Danny is just different … idiosyncratic … distant. Not a crime. No need to pin a hefty life label on him, is there?

Danny compressed:

Three-year-old: no issues. Typical toddler.

Six-year-old: hadn't progressed beyond the world of the three-year-old. Eyebrows raised. Loads of furtive whispers.

Ten-year-old: hovered in six land … Oh, Christ, that poor boy!

And so on.

You get the idea.

Now fourteen, three years my junior, Danny teeters around the nine or ten mark. Sometimes older, sometimes younger. Depends on the day. But our Danny is made of greatness. I know it. Mum knows it. Think Bel knows it too.

I'm not the only nominee for the Social Bravery Award. Bel sometimes helps out, especially with Danny; she's my girl friend. Not *girlfriend*. She's a friend who happens to inhabit a female body. We're pals. Probably best pals. Although I think she'd like to move the goalposts on the whole pals act thingy.

Evidence? OK, here's the evidence: once upon a Friday (last week) we bought some nasty cider from the no ID required shop and bolted back to mine. We were thinking of starting a ritual called Drowning Our Sorrows Friday. This was to be our opening night; getting a bit tipsy and giddy would help take our minds off stuff. Bel has her own shit to contend with: cliché boozed-up father. He's got her date of birth tattooed on his knuckles. I know, enough said.

Anyway, cutting a dead long story short, we got cider-rattled and Bel tried to plank the lips on me. Then she threw out the L-bomb. I pretended to be drunker than I was, slapping her on the thigh and squealing: 'Shut your trap, Bel. You're totally pissed out your knickers.'

Conveniently that little episode has been forgotten, not a word spoken about it since.

Oh, what happened yesterday? I can't remember a thing.

Me neither.

I'm never drinking again.

Me neither.

To be honest, I'm still spitting a bit as all that lips and love shit could've put a massive dent in our palship. And Bel's the only real friend I have. Real gem.

It helps that Danny trusts her and has no problems allowing Bel to enter his world. It's a beautiful thing seeing both of them in action.

'If anyone at school calls me Danny Distant again, I'm going to dynamite their balls,' he says.

'Do those people love you, Dan?' Bel says.

'No. Stupid.'

'Do they even know what you're good at?'

'They don't know shit from shampoo.'

'But Bobby and me and your mum love you and we know you're amazing at most things.'

'I'm amazing at eating pizza.'

'Exactly. I bet none of those guys at school are.'

'They're idiots.'

'Agreed.'

'Dicks.'

'Probably.'

'Arsehole punchers …'

'Right,' Bel says. 'Get yourself off that couch and go get groomed online, or whatever boys your age do.'

She has that ability to drag him back into life. I take comfort in seeing her play both mother and big sister. We're both lucky to have her.

Anyway, Drowning Our Sorrows Friday is a non-starter for a glut of reasons, but mainly because boozing is like gargling on your own vomit: Bel's battling against becoming a chip off the old block, while I need to be my best Bobby Seed, you know, just in case.

I guess you could say we're just your archetypal damaged nuclear family. Although my brain tells me we're about to become more nuclear.

Pins and Needles

It kicked off with the occasional pangs of pins and needles in her feet, before moving steadily to her legs. I was twelve. Tingles frequently began creeping up the right side of her body. This went on for months. Mum told no one. She only visited the doctor when those black spots started to skew her vision. That's when she felt everything collapsing, she said.

My memory is different though. I'm fourteen. We're doing the big shop in Asda. For some reason Danny isn't with us, can't remember why. Maybe a school thing.

Trolley's bulging at the seams. Mum's pushing. I'm looking for things to have, eat, want. I usually persuaded Mum to let me drink a Coke while walking around, putting the empty can through the checkout at the end. (Shhh, didn't do this ever. I shelved it before we got there.

Not exactly aggravated robbery, but still. Mum never found out.)

'Can we have Pot Noodles for dinner, Mum?'

'No chance. Broccoli and kale tonight.'

'Don't even know what that is,' I said.

'It's brain food.'

'Aw, really?'

'Yup, and stacks of it is required since yours is so weak.'

'Why can't we have what other families have?'

'Oh, stop being a teenager, Bobby, or I'll abandon you in aisle six. Do something useful – reach up and get that cranberry juice for me.'

I'm on tiptoes, hand in the sky, pure Superman pose, when I hear a deflating puff of air from behind. Mum's slouched over the trolley.

'Mum! What happened? … Mum, you OK?' Didn't know whether to drag her off the fruit and veg mountain or leave her be.

'Help me up, Bobby.'

She's upright.

'Just felt really dizzy there for a second.'

'Here, drink this.' I handed her the Coke I was saving. 'Drink loads of it. Might help.'

She sipped. I could tell it wasn't going down well.

'Better?'

'Better,' she said.

The colour returned to her cheeks, but her expression screamed defeat.

'Mum?'

'I'm good, Bobby. I'm better.'

'Honest?'

'Honest,' she said. I didn't believe her. 'Did you get that cranberry juice?'

I launched my frame up again and scooped a carton off the shelf. Jammed it into the trolley.

'Mum, can I get a Starbar?' I imagined munching it, feeling the chocolate paint my mouth, knowing full well she'd say, 'No chance.' Mum thought apples were treats while chocolate bars were the devil's diet. But I always asked. She always refused. Our recurring joke.

'You can have what you want, son,' she said.

'Mum, seriously, are you OK?'

'Just tired, Bobby.'

'Anything I can do?'

'Maybe push the trolley. I don't have the energy.'

But the wheels made it easy to push, even with weight in it. I didn't say that. It was clear she couldn't shove it another yard. That trolley could've been overflowing with steam and she'd have been too weak for it.

'Course I'll push,' I said.

'Let's get you a Starbar.'

I no longer wanted one.

I wanted my mum.

I wanted her to take the piss out of me, embarrass me, put me in my place with the slice of a sentence. But that day I understood, a good two years after those pins and needles started nipping away, that I'd be getting a new mum, a totally different one. And my heart was broken. Torn to shreds in fucking Asda.

Teacher Tries Her Best

I can't get back to sleep after another dead mother dream. I wait for the sun to smile. Thinking a thousand tiny thoughts:

Should I have a fiddle?

When reciting the alphabet, why do I say L-M-N-O-P really quickly?

What's another word for 'thesaurus'?

If I had a sealed envelope with my death date written inside, would I open it?

Why us?

First week back at school after summer and all I want is to rest my head on the desk. Turn my bag into a pillow. This double life of domestic god and diligent schoolboy sure rips strips off your strength.

The teacher's up front rabbiting on about something: white noise. Bel's doodling and shaking her knee under the desk as if desperate for a pee. My head's heavy, a swaying tree.

I feel a dunt in the ribs. Sore. I guess I'd rather take a rib punch than a lip plant though.

'Hey,' I whisper. 'That was painful.'

'You were practically sleeping on me,' Bel says.

'Right, OK, but no need to –'

'Do I look like the Premier fucking Inn?'

'I'm a bit tired,' I say.

'No wonder, listening to this shit.' Bel nods towards the teacher.

'What's happening?'

'Some guff about poetry.'

I perk up because poetry is a kind of secret pleasure of mine. No one knows that I inhale it in the dead of night, that it answers many questions I have swirling in my head. I've even, you know, tried to, like, dabble myself.

'Pure nerd fest,' she says.

We snigger.

Teacher clocks it and marches up to us.

'Something to add, Bel?' teacher says.

'No, miss. Just chatting about what you were saying.'

'Really?'

'Really, miss.'

'So what was the last thing I said then?'

'Poetry stuff,' Bel replies.

Giggles from the class fill the awkwardness.

'This is an important year, Bel. I suggest you take it seriously.'

'Will do, miss. Thanks for the heads-up.'

Teacher dismisses Bel as a no-hoper, then focuses on me. Her expression relaxes. Soft focus. The face of pity.

'You OK, Bobby?'

'Just a bit tired, miss,' I say.

'It's to be expected,' she says.

Bel's eyes whack the ceiling.

'I think the poetry element of the course will be a strong point for you this year, Bobby.'

'Hope so, miss.'

Teacher gives Bel the sneer-face before turning on her high-rise heels. *Clickety-click.*

'Right, everyone turn to page sixty-six. "Poppies in October."'

After the long summer hanging out with Bel, making sure Danny didn't get the shit kicked out of himself for whatever reason – staring sternly at someone in his *you fuckin' want some?* manner or letting his tongue run before engaging his brain ('Look at that woman's giant arse!') – I thought that going back to school would be a breeze compared with the daily demands of being me:

Can you change these sheets, son?

Bobby, is my bath ready?

Where's all the Rice Krispies gone?

Have you taken the washing out?

There's clothes still on the line.

Is Danny eating properly?

This is cold!

This year is a biggie: exam year. Making-informed-decisions-about-the-future year. Getting-the-finger-out-the-arse year. Total stress. Naturally, being seventeen, I have no clue what to do when school's over, and I can't stop the constant motherly jabs on the issue.

'What do you want to be when you grow up, son?' Mum asks.

'As in *grown up* like a man?'

'Well, the jury's still out on that one, but let's imagine you're all grown up, and, yes, we can pretend you're a man too.'

'I'm honoured.'

'So, what are you thinking then?'

'Apart from being a priest?'

'Apart from that, Father.'

'Think I'd be suited to the astronaut life.'

'Well, I've always said you're a bit of a rocket.'

The chats never really develop beyond nonsense. Mum knows I'll be OK; she knows I'll make the right choices. She understands the gulf between teen life and adulthood is vast, so why waste those years trying to leap forward?

'Seriously, Bobby, what *are* you going to do when you leave school?'

'I'm thinking boxing trainer or lion tamer.'

'Good practice with our Danny. Go for it.'

That's generally how we play it.

I've always thought something creative is a possibility. Now, when I say *creative*, what I mean is writing. Hey, I can rattle off a short story or poem like the best seventeen-year-olds: angsty and lamentable. Any loot to be made in that game? Probably not.

Food. I like to eat. I enjoy watching *MasterChef*. Being chief cook for Mum and Dan, *MasterChef* is essential viewing. Mum finds it hard to swallow at times so soup is a staple on the Seed menu.

I read books. Librarian/editor?

I like clothes. Fashion designer/blogger?

I like money. Banker/accountant?

I like brushing hair. Hairdresser/up-stylist?

I like school. Teacher/student?

I like staring into space. Philosopher/dole sponger?

I like not having an illness. Doctor/nurse?

Not sure my talents stretch to any occupation.

Lunchtime, and Mrs Sneddon, the school counsellor, practically drags me into her office for 'a little chat'. Don't get me wrong, I like Mrs Sneddon – she genuinely cares about the students, no bullshit there – but sometimes she plays the role of God's true disciple, plonked into our school with a single remit: heal the infirm and needy. Ladies and gentlemen, and those unsure, I give you Bobby Seed!

'How was your summer, Bobby, love?' Mrs Sneddon calls

us 'love' and 'darling' and gets away with it, but imagine Mr Conroy, Mr McClair or Mr Melrose saying that. I see frogmarching, cameras flashing, blankets draped over heads. Careers and marriages shattered. Can't beat a double standard.

'Summer was fine, miss.'

'And your mum, how's she doing?'

'Same, no change really.'

'Well, that's good, at least she isn't deteriorating.'

Mrs Sneddon doesn't have to listen to the painful howls when Mum's muscles spasm uncontrollably. Mrs Sneddon doesn't have to witness the look of mortification on Mum's face when I'm fumbling around her listless body during 'bath time'. Mrs Sneddon doesn't have to hear the humiliation in Mum's voice when I'm reminded that the baby wipes are running low. No, Mrs Sneddon, Mum isn't deteriorating, but maybe I am.

'And what about your brother? Is he OK, love? Is he coping?'

'Danny's doing fine, he just plods on with life. Being back at school is good for him.'

'The school he's at is perfect, I know it well.'

'Yeah, he likes it.'

'He feels safe there?'

'Yeah.'

'And you, darling. What about you? How are you doing?'

'I'm doing OK,' I say, which is sort of a grand lie.

'It's all a huge pressure on you, Bobby.' I stare at my feet. 'Don't think we don't recognise this, love.'

'It is what it is, miss.'

'It's not easy being a young carer, Bobby.'

Tell me something I don't know.

'Yeah, well,' I say.

'It's OK, I understand.' Her hand rests on my forearm. I nod a type of fake thanks for her *understanding*.

See, child experts will tell you that I'm way too young to carry such a burden of responsibility on my tender shoulders. Their job is to make assumptions and evaluations. Really, what do they know other than what I'm prepared to tell them? I'll tell you what they know, shall I? Assumptions and evaluations. Teachers *feel my pain*. I can tell by the way they look at me, giving me a wide berth that no one else seems to get. Thinking they know the score. They don't. Thinking I can't handle it. They're wrong. Thinking I'm psychologically damaged by it. I wouldn't use the word 'damaged' to describe it. Funny how no one ever uses the word 'love' when discussing my case. I do what I do because she's my mum; she's the only one I have, so wouldn't mind holding on to her for a bit longer. That pure and that simple. Now, tell me this: do you need a PhD and a sack of certificates to work that out? I reckon some common sense and good judgement. Makes me laugh that they all think they know me. I could fill a book about what they *don't* know.

Thing is, I'm just your average seventeen-year-old: same

fears, same desires, same hang-ups, same, same, same. Dull, dull, dull. OK, hands up, there's the seventeen-year-old in me who's poles apart from everyone else as well. Unique. The seventeen-year-old who has to brush his mother's locks every day, sort out her medicine, sponge her clean three times a week, ooze positivity when all I want to do is punch the shit out of a wall or wail in the shower.

Same yet not.

'I understand,' Mrs Sneddon says again.

Worst thing anyone can say is that they understand what you're going through when, clearly, they haven't a scrap of understanding. Ever want to rile someone? Tell them you understand their pain: that'll work a treat. Unless somebody has walked an inch in my shoes they couldn't possibly understand what I'm experiencing. Yes, they might get the sadness or loss part, but it's the whole gamut of other emotions they're clueless about. Emotions that consume my every waking hour. Occasionally I flick out of them, reflect on other things, normal things, but it's too fleeting; I'm quickly yanked back into its clutches. Fear, obviously, is the worst. Fear of losing Mum, of me and Danny having to fend for ourselves. I fear a life of hovering above all the action because I've had to care for everyone else.

Then there's the head-numbing isolation. I don't get to experience what my peers are doing; I don't get time to hang about the streets or go to the cinema or attend some crap nightclub or sit in a mate's bedroom listening to tunes all night. No, I have stuff to do, stuff I can't share with anyone. Sharing isn't part of my grind. OK, Bel knows that Mum is ill and Danny is, well, Danny, but she doesn't know the inner workings of my mind, what I want, what I need. Bel doesn't know how tearful and resentful I often get, or how certain thoughts scare me to death.

Then there's the fact that I'm seventeen. Seventeen, for God's sake. My parents should be chastising me about my internet use. I should be teetering on the margins of criminality, having furtive meetings with online strangers; I should be full of angst and nervous energy and spending insurmountable periods in the bathroom. But I'm too buggered for that. Life equals exhaustion. So what's the point in blurting out all this to Mrs Sneddon? She *understands*, right?

'I want you to have a look at this, Bobby,' she says, handing me a folded A4 leaflet.

'What is it?'

'You don't have to read it now. Take it away with you, look at it in your own time.'

I open the flaps. It's from the Department of Education, but has the logo of a group calling themselves Poztive. How cool, hip and down-with-it are they?

'Now, you don't have to make any quick decisions this minute,' she says. 'Mull it over first, OK?'

I scan. Read bits. Look at some smiling teens. Lots of teeth.

'Erm ...'

'Now, I know what you're thinking ...'

'I'm not sure about this, miss.'

'Just thought I'd let you see. No one is forcing you, love.'

'I'm not really into the whole self-help thing.'

'It's not self-help, Bobby. It's a type of peer-group meeting.'

'It all seems a bit circle time to me.'

'That's not a bad analogy.'

'That's what I was afraid of.'

'It's about shared experiences with people your own age. You might get something from it.'

'Yeah, apathy or eczema,' I say.

'Some people can be energised by these groups,' she says, pointing at the leaflet. I wince.

'Not for me.'

'Well, I'll just leave it with you for now, love. You make up your own mind about it.'

'Thanks.' I stand. 'Why are you offering this to me now?' I ask.

'Because it's a new initiative,' she says. 'Solely targeted at young people your age, people who might be facing issues outside the realms of being a carer – you know what I mean, Bobby?'

Couldn't possibly have a clue who she's talking about.

'Right,' I say, tucking the leaflet inside my school blazer pocket.

'I applied on your behalf. I hope you don't mind, sweetie?'

'No, I don't mind, miss.'

The bell rings.

'OK, you best be getting off.'

'See you later, miss.' I pull the door towards me.

'Bobby?'

'Yeah?'

'Any thoughts on what you're thinking of doing?'

'I've got double biology, miss.'

'No, I mean when you're done with this place.'

'Not completely, but it'll definitely be something in the sewage industry.'

Mrs Sneddon giggles.

'Go on. Get out of here. Sewage! Would you ever listen to yourself.'

On the way to biology I feel the leaflet rubbing against my nipple. I'm late. I smarten the pace. The leaflet attacks my nipple with vigour. I hate being late for class, having to stand there while some jumped-up power-hound teacher gives you a bollocking. I enter.

'Sorry I'm late, miss,' I say.

Mrs Lennox is a teacher to be feared in the school. She's on the total-nuts spectrum. Bel says she's a people hater and would rather live on an island, fawning over plants and frogs.

I spy Bel behind Mrs Lennox's shoulder. She's wearing an *oh-you-are-so-dead* face, revelling in my tardy transgression.

'Bobby!' Mrs Lennox blurts.

I'm like, what? Seventy-eight seconds late. What's the stress?

'I was with Mrs Sneddon, miss. In her office,' I explain.

'That's no problem, Bobby.' In a nanosecond, Mrs Lennox's face changes from reinforced steel to squidgy putty. 'We've barely started.'

Honestly?

No belittling in front of the class?

No insulting my intellectual capacity?

Nothing?

Suddenly I feel myself wanting to be scolded. I don't need special treatment. I want to be on par with every other dick-head and downbeat.

'Right,' I say, and make my way to a clearly exasperated Bel, who mouths, '*You fucker.*' I raise a victory eyebrow.

'Perk of the job,' I whisper. I might enjoy fleeting moments of special treatment, but I don't crave the full-time sympathy vote.

'Section six, Bobby. We're starting the Krebs cycle.'

I open my book and scratch my chest.

Bel slowly leans into me.

'I hate you, Bobby Seed.'

'My nipple is killing me, so a little kindness, please.'

'I hope it falls off.'

Positive Thinking

Before you attend your first Poztive meeting we'd love to hear a little about YOU.

1. *Tell us about your daily routine as a young carer*
2. *Tell us what your plans and/or ambitions are*
3. *Tell us about your hobbies and pastimes*
4. *Tell us about anything else we might find interesting*

1.

I get up around 6.30–7, have a quick shower, get dressed then wake my little brother. I make sure he gets washed and dressed properly and has everything he needs for school.

Around 7.30 we have breakfast. I fix my brother cereal, followed by toast and apple juice. When he's comfortable in front of the TV, I go back upstairs to check on Mum.

I'll rouse her, prop the pillows and switch the radio on. BBC 5 Live or 6 Music.

Usually she needs the toilet so I help with that.

I return downstairs, look in on my brother, and get Mum her pills. Some days she's feeling strong and wants to get dressed and come downstairs, other days she's weak and prefers to remain in bed. I take her some jasmine tea. She enjoys a boiled egg and toast. Most days she wants nothing.

I might have to change the sheets, but not every day. Mum still tries to do this herself, but it's best if I take charge as this usually exhausts her.

I keep an eye on Mum's mood, making sure she is relaxed and happy.

I inhale a bowl of cereal and a glass of water.

I try cleaning as I go.

I sniff through my brother's school bag, make sure he hasn't forgotten anything.

I walk him to his school, point him in the direction of his first class.

I like school, but it's hard being away from Mum; I tend to worry the whole time I'm there, thinking of her safety.

The worry of death never leaves you.

I try blocking these thoughts out and concentrate on schoolwork. By midday I'm shattered.

After school we generally head to Lidl or Aldi to buy dinner or essentials.

Once home I make my brother change his clothes and do whatever homework he has. Always a struggle.

I ask Mum about her day, give her any medicine she needs, then I dive into my civvies.

I come downstairs and do general cleaning chores, just to make sure the house isn't a kip.

I'll scan the fridge and find a meal to cobble together, making sure it's nutritious and that Mum can physically eat it.

My brother is very fussy – he likes pizza, pasta and McDonald's. Veg is tough.

I get my brother to lay the table.

Another struggle.

And, if Mum's legs are in good nick, we all sit down together. These days she has hers in bed.

Once dinner is over, me and Danny do the clean-up.

I can't even tell you the struggle this is.

I go see if Mum needs anything and we chat for a while. She likes to wag on about my future or tell me how great music and stuff was when she was my age. She asks about my day, we talk general rubbish and laugh loads. This is our time in the day to forget about the obvious.

If I can catch some downtime (hate that phrase), I might read or write something.

Very relaxing.

Then all I want to do is sleep.

I get my brother ready for bed: teeth brushed, face washed, computer off.

My Lord, the struggle with that!

I help Mum to the toilet so she can get cleaned and prepared for the night ahead.

When I'm sure there is silence, I might need to put a wash on or do homework or something else.

After that I'm beyond being wiped out.

I go to bed.

Then the day starts again: worry, tiredness … and so on.

I put the pen down, shake my arm into life again, look at questions 2, 3 and 4 and think: *Someone give me a gun!*

In Arms

Mum's care while I'm at school is far from perfect. Some white coat comes to give her a laughable sponge-down, a bit of food (mush) and administer afternoon medicine. Then they bolt. No circulating the muscles. No fresh air. Zero craic. A twenty-minute in and out job. Gets right on my goat, so it does. But it's the NHS and it's free, so step away from the goat.

No sooner out the door when Danny's nipping at my ankles. See, I haven't told him her MS is worsening, that she's not going to miraculously leap out of bed one morning and treat us to a swift shopping spree in town. I didn't tell him because, well, because I prayed for this miracle too. Pure denial. But now he wants to know the score.

'What's happening, Bobby?'

'Nothing to worry about, mate.'

'Not telling makes me worry more.'

I wet my lips, straighten my shoulders.

'Thing is …' My voice wavers. 'Mum's developed a type of cold now, Dan,' I spout.

'A cold?'

'Yeah.'

'Like a runny nose and coughs?'

'Well, yes, but a bit worse than that.'

'Worse how?'

'Like a really bad cold that's hard to shake off.'

'So when is she going to get better?'

'Soon I hope, but I've got a feeling it'll be a while.'

'Next week? Next month?'

'Who knows. She's going to have good days and bad,' I tell him.

'Like me.'

'We need to be very patient with her, Dan. Don't demand too much, OK?'

'Roger that.'

A cold? How can I shrink Mum's declining state of MS into being a fucking cold? Maybe I'm trying to convince myself: head wedged up my arse with denial, ill-prepared for what's glaring. As big brother, I should have all the answers for Danny. Still, I need to protect him. But, as Mum taught us, truth lessens the weight and opens the doors; lying shackles you and darkens everything. I guess even truth has to be tempered with compassion; I mean, who benefits from Danny knowing what to expect until it's facing us square?

'When will it be gone, Bobby? When will she not have it?'

'She's going to have it forever, Danny.'

'That's stupid, all colds go away.'

'Not this one.'

'Will you get it?'

'Don't think so.'

'Will I?'

'No, and stop thinking like that, Danny.'

'I hate it.'

'Me too.'

'I really hate it, Bobby.'

'I know.'

'And I fucking hate those walking sticks she uses.'

'She needs them, Dan.'

'She's like an old granny.'

'Don't say that. Don't ever say that. She needs those sticks, OK?'

'I just want her to be like all the other mums. That's all I want.'

'Hey, come on, buddy.' I wrap my arms around him, squeeze his head into my chest. Try to control his convulsions.

'Why can't she be like all the other mums?'

'Don't cry, mate.'

'I just miss my mum, Bobby.'

And he says it over and over again.

'She's still here. She'll always be with us.'

'I want her every day. To go for walks or run around the garden or shout at me.'

'Me too, Dan.' I find it hard to say anything else after that. We hold each other until the well runs dry.

#1 ... incomplete

there's a rousing future
in us all
except, of course, those who don't
crave its coming

there's a rib-tickle
in us all
except, of course, those who don't
care for the howl

there's a vast reservoir
in us all
except, of course, those who don't
covet its rise

I wonder what riches await me ...

Teens Exposed

Working alongside the Social Work Department, we can offer respite support throughout the duration of the meetings with Poztive ... provide the bespoke care that your mother requires ... as part of our experienced and specialised care team ... ease your worries and burden ...

And so, against all my natural instincts and general sense of scepticism, I duly accepted their kind invitation and signed my anonymity away to the good people at Poztive.

A break from mundane young-carer land appeals big time; more stints away from home will work wonders for my adventurous side. The idea of being out without that shroud of worry is alluring. I ask Bel if she can do a bit of free babysitting for an hour or so each week while I go to the meetings. Make sure Dan doesn't drink bleach, and look in on Mum occasionally, easy stuff. She's only too delighted to escape her own gaff.

Seems everyone got here before I did. They're as mint as I am, cumbersome in their skin too. I know we're all spanking new but I can't help feeling the most virgin. Everyone twists their heads in order to get a right proper snoop. Now, I'm not usually lacking in self-confidence, but having that number of eyes on you definitely tests this. Their eyes scorch my body. The slamming door behind doesn't help.

Bang!

Me: Rigid.

Them: Shuffle. Turn. Stare.

They're sat in a small crescent shape. I'm rooted to the spot, watching them watching me, thinking: *Are my clothes cool enough? Am I oozing poverty? Is my hair in good nick? Do any of them like what they see? Do any of them fancy me?*

My shoulders relax. My breathing steadies. I want to advance, but something in me enjoys the attention. This is different from the attention I get at school: no faces of faux sympathy, no hangdog expressions among these people. Here I'm an equal, a possibility. Grab it while you can, right?

'You must be Bobby?' a voice says.

Comes from the person sitting in the middle of the crescent, isolated from the others. Clearly the leader. Older. Beaming face. Welcoming. Not one of us.

I lengthen my lips.

'Come, Bobby,' he says, 'join us.' Gesturing me towards

the rest of the group. Very cultish. My seat is at the edge of the crescent. Best in the house.

'You haven't missed anything yet,' the leader says. 'We're only getting started, getting ready for introductions.'

I flash a quick look at the others: glazed airs. They're uneasy. Seven young carers. Same age, sixteen or seventeen. One leader, male.

'In fact, before you came in I was just telling the guys here about our motto,' the leader adds. I nod. 'Which is?' he asks, startling some girl, who shifts uncomfortably in her seat, tucking her hands under her thighs and sliding her black Converse beneath her chair.

'Think positive … Stay positive … Be positive?' she mutters from under her veil of mortification. Poor girl would rather be in her room sifting through a friend of a friend of a friend's photos on Instagram. Couldn't blame her. Yet, here she is, purring Poztive's motto to perplexed strangers in an uber-negative tone.

'Excellent. Think poztive. Stay poztive. Be poztive.' The leader emphasises the 'z' sound as if it's a motto to live by.

The girl's T-shirt is of Nineties band The Sundays. I like her immediately. Wonder if her mum introduced her to them too. Kind of makes perfect sense to have The Sundays emblazoned across her chest. The place isn't awash with Friday afternoon or Saturday night people; this half-moon crescent is the perfect embodiment of Sunday folk: reflective and jaded.

'OK, guys, since it's our first meeting I'd like us to go round the circle for some quick introductions, and, if you feel like it, you can talk about who you're caring for,' the leader says. 'But no pressure, you can equally tell us your name and sit down.'

Really? We have to stand up? I'd call that pressure. I thought it was only the sex, drugs and booze addicts that did that. I feel like saying, *Look, we've done nothing wrong here, we're casualties in all of this. Our wounds are not self-inflicted. It's not our fault. Why do we have to stand up?*

'I'll kick us off,' the leader says, rising from his chair. 'My name's Roddy and I looked after my father from the age of twelve. Dad suffered from a genetic muscle-wasting illness that took away his ability to move. We did everything for him, and I mean *everything*, which I'm sure some of you here can understand.'

Roddy speaks about his dad in the past tense, while we're very much imprisoned in the present. Is there a need for full disclosure at meeting one, Roddy? Can we not just ease ourselves in?

I shoe gaze; the others do something similar. Roddy reconnects his arse to his chair. I feel slightly embarrassed for him.

'Right, so, why don't we start at this end?' he says, meaning I'm last. A girl, Erin, sheepishly rises and gives us her spiel about looking after her dad.

The Sundays girl is up next. I hunch myself up in my chair.

'My name's Harriet. I care for my mum. She suffers from seizures because of brain tumours, so somebody needs to be there at all times. The seizures will eventually kill her. That's a total fact.'

Talk about lobbing a hand grenade into the pot!

I'm like, *Far too much info, Harriet.*

But she's calm and unaffected.

Roddy mouths, '*Thank you, Harriet.*'

Awkward.

Then some guy stands, looks down towards Harriet. For a split second I think he's going to offer her further vomit-inducing encouragement.

'Dig the T, Harriet.'

Harriet is silent, but a slender grin appears on her face. Her band has been recognised. She's been recognised. A kind comment, I think. The guy then switches to everyone else, scanning his audience.

'Hey, friends call me Lou. I'm good with y'all callin' me that too. I'm here today because of my damn mom.' I think he's piss-taking when he says that. 'She deals with what ails her and I deal with that too. We deal together. But I guess y'all know what I'm talkin' about.'

'We do, Lou. We do,' Roddy says.

'Cool,' Lou says.

This Lou guy has an accent, a full-on American twang; he's getting away with saying things like 'I guess', 'dig', 'damn mom', 'y'all' and 'cool' without sounding like a pure dick.

'That's all I got,' he says, flopping down in his seat and running his hands through his dark locks. Could do with a grooming; in fact, everyone could be doing with a decent hairdo. And I might just know the hairdresser!

The guy beside me with short red hair and brown rectangular specs follows. A bit weedy. A bully's dream. Intelligent-looking guy.

'Hello, my name's Callum, much prefer Cal though. My mother has profound psychological issues,' Cal says, looking directly at the first girl to speak, Erin, who tightens her lips in solidarity. 'My father also has stage four bowel and colon cancer, which has intensified things at home somewhat. Obviously, we don't know how long he has.'

Jesus, Cal, thanks for that right hook, left hook double whammy.

'However, he still shows an impressive degree of fortitude. We all continue to fight the good fight.'

Cal remains on his feet and grins, clearly sending out a defiant message: his plight isn't going to dent his own happiness. Cal's clinging on to his individuality, battling back. 'That sums up everything.'

He sits.

Some guy called Tom and a girl called Clare pop up and down before I register what they've even said.

My turn.

Nervous pangs rip through me; it's hard enough getting me to share a packet of crisps, never mind sharing the defects of my life. I'm not a big fan of public speaking. Even at school I hate reading aloud – although I'm decent at it – or answering teachers' questions. The crux being I don't like the sound of my own voice, nor do I feel the need to be heard. But I guess sharing is one of the reasons we are here.

My throat is dry. I edge my body up and face the group. I look at Harriet, who smiles. I'm on the verge of saying something positive about her T-shirt, but it would be a lame imitation of Lou.

Lou beams, which actually increases my confidence.

Did he wink?

They all wait for my spiel.

'Hi, my name's Bobby. I'm seventeen. I care for my mum, who has MS. I also kind of care for my little brother, who's a cool dude.'

'Cool dude' doesn't sound right coming from me. Lou, yes. Me, no. I regret saying it. Regret trying to sound as if I want to be a … *cool dude*.

'Thanks, Bobby,' Roddy says as if urging me to sit. 'And thanks, everyone. I know sharing can be difficult.'

I hear people nose breathing. We stare at him, awaiting instruction. Tough gig this Roddy guy has. He continues, 'But at Poztive we are all about you guys – naturally, the loved ones you care for are important, vitally important, but being here is all about *you*, not them.'

'So we don't have to talk about the people we care for then?' Lou asks.

'Focus on *you* is what I'm saying.' Roddy gestures to us all. 'Discuss your likes, dislikes, books, music, films, fashion, whatever. It's your choice.'

Lou nods towards Harriet, who looks at the other two girls in the group. I stare at Lou. No eyes on me.

'And your role is to facilitate?' Cal asks.

'Exactly,' Roddy says.

'So, basically it's about shared empathy and catharsis?' Cal adds.

'In part, yes.'

'What does that even mean?' Clare says.

'Just that dudes like us can feel better about stuff, right, Cal?' Lou says.

'Something like that,' Cal replies.

'Well, I'm up for it,' Tom says.

'Me too,' Clare says.

'Sure, what else would we be doing?' Erin says.

'Exactly,' Tom adds.

I search deep for something profound, relevant or witty to contribute. I have nothing.

'I assure you, guys, things happen organically here,' Roddy says.

'I'm bringing a dictionary next time,' Harriet says.

Some of us laugh, not Cal or Erin.

'You'll get to know one another pretty quickly,' Roddy says. 'Especially after we have our residential.'

'Hey, wait a minute. Nobody said anything about a

residential. I mean, man, come on. What are we, Scouts or something?' Lou pipes.

Harriet sniggers, but shakes her head in agreement.

Me too.

I sense a mutiny stirring.

'So, a residential is like camping then?' Tom asks.

'I can't camp. My skin's bad,' Harriet says. 'No danger I'm crashing in a tent.'

'Look,' says Roddy, raising his voice slightly. 'It's not a camping trip, OK? The *residential* is a weekend in the Borders of this beautiful country of ours, where you guys get to stay in a stunning country estate. It's funded, meaning you'll all have a nice comfortable bed to sleep in and an *indoor* toilet. There won't be a tent in sight.'

'Like a mini holiday?' Clare says.

'More cultish retreat, I'd say,' Lou adds.

'I'd imagine it's about mind expansion and periodic relief,' Cal says.

'I'm well up for that,' Tom says.

'It's a weekend where you don't have to worry about getting up in the middle of the night to take someone to the toilet, or think about what to make for dinner, or how to organise the medicine for the day. That'll be someone else's problem for that weekend. It gives everyone a well-deserved break. Who wouldn't want that?' Roddy says.

A break?

What's that?

What wouldn't I give for a break.

Gradually the dynamic is changing. I can see it happening.

'Maybe … it would be … nice,' Erin says.

'It'll be brilliant,' Clare says.

'You serious?' Harriet pipes. 'Pissing in fields? Doesn't sound brilliant to me.' A shiny ray of sunshine among the dim shadows.

'Potential to be enlightening,' Cal offers.

'Don't know what that is, but I want some of it,' Tom says.

'I'm not totally down with it,' Lou says. 'What do you think, Bobby?'

He's asking what *I* think? Asking for *my* backup? He said my name.

Roddy looks at me.

In fact, they all look at me.

Somehow within the space of ten minutes I've become the group's designated silent one. The iconoclast. The pain in the arse.

A free weekend away from the grind sounds like a winning lottery ticket.

They wait for my reaction, as if I have the casting vote or something.

'Yeah, I could do that … I mean … it all sounds good to me,' I say.

Lou sharpens his eyes at me, holds my gaze. He doesn't blink. Have I said the wrong thing? His lips part, fashioning into a smile. I do believe I've just swayed him in the opposite direction. Lou's head nods slightly.

Did he wink?

'Right. Cool. I'm sold. So, when do we take off, Rod?' Lou asks.

'In a few months, after more group sessions,' Roddy says. 'And it's just Roddy, none of this Rod business, Lou.'

'So, basically we have to come here in order to go on the trip?' Lou asks.

'Basically,' Roddy says.

'That's a pure piss-take,' Harriet utters under her breath.

'No problem. I guess I can do that,' Lou says.

'Great.' Roddy springs off his chair. 'Right, let's have some merriment.'

I'm paired with Lou because we're 'of similar build'; we're given a piece of fabric and told that one of us has to blindfold the other. I tie it to Lou's head and stand directly behind him.

'OK, guys,' Roddy shouts. 'We're going to begin with a simple trust exercise. Those without the blindfold have to catch your partner when they fall.'

'This is kindergarten shit,' Lou says in his darkness.

'You'll be fine,' I tell him.

'Hey, Bobby, if you don't catch my ass you'll have a world of pain coming your way.' Lou isn't being threatening or aggressive, but he sounds apprehensive.

'I'll catch you,' I say. 'Don't worry.'

'Right, everyone start very close, and after each fall I want the non-blindfolded person to take one step back and allow your partner more space to fall into your arms,' Roddy says. 'Got it, guys?'

A barrage of 'Yes'es and 'Got it!'s fly back at him.

'Be cool now, Bobby. OK?' Lou says.

'Just fall back,' I tell him. 'I've got you.'

He falls.

I'm so close that I just ping him back on to his soles.

I step backwards and repeat. Easy.

Another step back and I feel more weight as Lou falls. My hands reach to his chest, buffering the impact of his body. We're certainly not of similar build. Lou has muscles, actual muscles – muscles certain women, and men, would go gaga over.

'Now do you trust me, Lou?' I ask.

'You're all I got, Bobby.'

We change positions. Suddenly I feel aware of my puny body, lacking definition or quality. A child's body. Lou catches me as if he's holding a baby at bay, throws me around like a boxer on the ropes. He enjoys it. So do I.

In the next activity one person sits on a chair while the other has to remove them from it without touching or threatening them.

'It's an exercise in quick-thinking psychology and verbal gymnastics,' Roddy says. I'm glad we get to keep the same pairings.

I sit first.

'Close your eyes,' Lou says.

'No touching, Lou,' I remind him.

'Ready?'

'Ready.' I glue my eyes shut.

I sense him circling me. Set to pounce. Weaving something. He leans in to me. I taste his breathing, feel the heat of it on my lobe.

'Bobby, if you don't get your ass off that chair I'm gonna put something in your mouth.'

I almost fall off the bloody chair.

'Really? That's what you're saying? You do know how inappropriate that sounds, don't you?' I say.

'Holy shit! You best get your ass off it and go tell Rod that I'm not playin' fair then.'

I cackle.

We both do.

'I'm serious, dude, you better get off that damn chair.'

Throughout the chair exercise we giggle like a couple of teens. But I suppose that's what we are, after all.

Now, if you'd have told me that I'd be playing infantile drama games with a group of strangers in a chilly hall I'd have run a mile, but, actually, I'm having a blast. That evening I experience something I haven't had for such a long time: fun. And some voices I wouldn't mind hearing again. It's liberating to have an hour or so free of Mum and Danny – which, if I think about it too much, is a full-on guilt fest.

When goodbyes are being doled out afterwards, my heart clouds over. My body recalibrates itself. The carefree switch in my head flicks to OFF. I think about whether Danny has done his homework, if Mum minded being 'watched' by Bel for a while after the carer/nurse bolted, if her medicine has been administered and if her tunes were the right ones. I wonder if the house is a kip.

All I want to do is lie on my bed, tuck my arms behind my head, look at the cracks in the Artex and think, just think. But I guess that's a luxury not afforded to me.

On the walk to the bus stop the wind attacks my face and I morph into care mode again.

Ryan Gosling Goes to Bingo

Danny's deep into some Netflix series when I get home. Bel's flaked out on the couch, glued to her phone. Babysitter from hell material. Both ignore me.

'I'm back,' I say.

Silence.

'Anything happen while I was gone?'

The say nothing.

'Erm … hello.'

'Shhh, Bobby,' Danny says. 'I'm trying to watch *Horrid Henry*.'

'And I'm trying to read my Twitter feed, so button it,' Bel says.

'Right,' I say. 'All good?'

'No probs,' Bel says.

'Mum OK, Dan?'

'Think so, she's up in bed.'

I stand in the middle of the living room, arms wide. Expecting more.

'That's it?' I say.

Bel removes her face from her phone.

'Oh, sorry, honey. Hard day at the office? Your dinner's in the oven. Here. Let me get your slippers.'

'Hilarious, Bel.'

'Shhh, you two. I'm honestly trying to watch this.'

'Pause it for a sec, Danny.'

'God's sake.' He presses the pause button. 'I can't do anything in this house.'

'Just tell me what's been going on,' I say.

Bel and Danny share a glance.

'Like what?' Danny says.

'Yeah, like what?' Bel adds.

'Don't know. Anything interesting happen? How was the carer who came? Anything to report about Mum?'

'Bobby, you haven't been to Ibiza for two weeks,' Bel says. 'You've been out gallivanting with a bunch of saddos, talking shit for an hour. Nothing went wrong.'

'So, no one missed me then?'

They look at each other again as if in cahoots about something.

'What did you have for dinner, Dan?' I ask.

'Pizza.'

'Again?'

'One was in the freezer,' Bel says. 'Popped it in the oven, ten-minute job. Easy. He loves pizza, don't you, Dan?'

'Pizza's magic.'

'Did you do the dishes?' I ask.

'You weren't here,' Danny says. 'I was waiting on you.'

'For what? To do them for you?'

'Keep your bra on, Bobby,' says Bel. 'I was just about to do them before you came in. Couple more tweets to post first.'

'Fine, what about the carer sent by the Poztive organisation?' I ask.

'He was up with Mum. Then wasn't up with Mum. Then went home just before you came back,' Danny says.

'That's about the size of it,' Bel says. 'But enough about our extravagant evening. Tell us how you got on.'

I inhale, about to enlighten them. Bel starts:

'Was it shit? I bet it was. Was it full of pure deadbeats and fat girls? Bet it was. Did you want to slit your throat with a rusty nail? I would've. Was anyone crying? Hope you weren't in floods, Bobby. Were you? Did you turn into a spacecadick?'

'It was OK, actually,' I say.

'Really?' Bel says.

'Yeah.'

'You're lying,' she says.

'I'm not.'

'You are.'

'Honestly, I'm not.'

'I can tell when you're lying, Bobby Seed. It was a total nightmare, I can tell.'

'Wrong.'

'Well, whatever. I still don't believe you.'

'It's true. It was good.'

'OK, don't wet yourself with joy,' she says.

'Bobby?'

'Yes, Dan.'

'Can I go with you next time?'

'Erm … I think it's only for carers … for people over sixteen. Afraid you're too young, buddy.'

'Ugh, it's craptastic being my age. We get nothing exciting to do.'

'Is Mum still awake?' I ask.

'Not sure,' Danny says.

'Haven't heard anything,' Bel says.

'I'm going to check on her. Why don't you get the dishes done, Danny?'

'But I'm watching Netflix. It's not fair, I never –'

'It's OK, Dan, I'll sort them out,' Bel says. 'Unpause and go Netflix yourself into brain-freeze oblivion.'

I give Bel the thumbs up and mouth a '*Thanks*'.

*

I peek my head around the bedroom door. Mum's lying on her side, semi-asleep. The pills do that. I wipe away frothy drool that's running down the side of her mouth.

'Hi, Mum.'

'Oh, it's you, Bobby.'

'Well, don't get too excited.'

'No, it's just that I was expecting Ryan Gosling.'

'He decided to go to the bingo instead,' I say.

'Fool.'

'Something about a better class of woman there.'

'Yeah, well, he doesn't know what he's missing here.'

'I'll say.'

'Anyway, enough about me and Gosling. How was it, son?'

'It was fine.'

'Did you want to strangle yourself?'

'Have you turned into Bel all of a sudden?'

'She steals all my best lines, even from my bed I'm a cultural influence. What can I say?'

'Maybe say … nothing.'

'Well, tell me. Did you go into strangulation mode?'

'No.'

'Shame.'

'It was better than I expected though,' I say.

'Did you have to stand up and tell them all about your sick mother, and how she completes you?'

'Oh, shut up, will you.'

'I mean, look at me, how could I not?'

When she grins her eyes sparkle: two misty blue diamonds illuminating the room.

'Mum?'

'What?'

'I had a lot of fun.'

'Did you?'

'I think I actually enjoyed it.'

She reaches up, strokes my face, an energy-sapping manoeuvre.

'I'm so glad, son. You deserve to have fun. You deserve it all.'

'The people were nice, Mum.'

'I'm very proud of you, you know that?'

'You're getting sentimental in your old age,' I say.

'It's the drugs, they make me feel drunk occasionally, so I haven't a clue what I'm saying half the time.'

'I bet you don't. Anyway, how was the carer they sent?'

'Oh, he was gorgeous. Looked like Jim Morrison pre-fat days.'

'Mum.'

'What, you don't believe me?'

'Finding it hard to.'

'Rumbled.'

'So?'

'He was a little plump. Smelled like a woman. Soft hands,' she says.

'He give you any dinner?'

'I wasn't hungry.'

'Mum, you have to …'

'It's hard to swallow today.'

'Any dizzy spells?'

'As in, I was tripping?'

'I'm still your child, remember.'

'We all have our burdens.'

'Right, want me to help you up, come down to see Danny and Bel?'

'I'm going to sleep, I think. I'm exhausted, Bobby.'

'Need the toilet?'

'No.'

'Water?'

'Got some.'

'OK, better go. Ryan is waiting at the bingo for me,' I say.

I straighten the covers, spar with the pillows, part hair away from her eyes and kiss her forehead.

'Night, Mum.'

'See you in the morning.'

I wait until her eyes are closed, watch her nose take in air, follow the rise and fall of her stomach. I make to go.

'Bobby?' she croaks.

'Yeah?'

'I'm glad you liked the meeting, son.'

'Me too.'

'I think you should keep going.'

'Think so too.'

Teens Get Acquainted

The next time we meet we're invited to talk about how we see our future, jobwise. Apparently that's what you ask when you engage sixteen and seventeen-year-olds in conversation. Talk about lack of imagination.

'I'm inching towards forensic physician,' Cal says. Not sure what this is exactly, but it has Cal's prints all over it.

'I'd really like to be a nurse,' Erin says.

Lots of earnest head movements.

And then it's my turn. A change of tack badly required, I think.

'I'd really like to be a ceramic plate designer,' I say.

Confused looks quickly mutate into tacit understandings. Harriet clocks on first: she declares her want to be a horse whisperer.

Check me out, Mr Trend Setter.

'And I want to be a fortune cookie writer,' says Clare.

'I want to be a model,' Tom says, although I'm not sure he's at the piss-take.

It's mad but Roddy actually believes it all.

I can tell that Lou is getting agitated with Roddy's fake curiosity in our futures. He sits stewing like a wasp on a windowpane: puffing passive-aggressively. That's the thing with being a young carer: we're stressed, anxious, tired, seeking compassion and YOUNG. For example, I get away with being a sulky pain in the balls because it's problematic for people to challenge my behaviour. I get away with being, well, a teenager.

After someone mentions chocolate consultant in a sentence, Lou mutters, 'Come on, Rod, give us a break here.' Roddy pretends he hasn't heard … sure he hasn't! I catch Lou's eye. He gives me a little nod, kind of makes me blush; in fact, my face is flaming up.

I feel remorseful for trivialising the exercise, so I stick my hand in the air. I tell the group I don't actually know what I want to do, but they're having none of it. They want me to keep the joke going, to provide them with laugh material; they need a bone.

'But if I must – I mean, if someone had a gun pointed at my temple and I had to choose something – then I hope one day to find a cure for what my mum has,' I say.

Welcome to Bobby Seed's Balloon Deflating Class! I think Erin's going to break down. Cal and Tom stare at their laces.

Clare tugs at her nails. Lou thumbs his appreciation. Thanks to me, resident fun-sucker, most of us now feel ashamed for undermining the exercise. And this fun-sucker just mic-dropped everyone back down to earth with a clattering boom. I want to shout: *My fault entirely – hands up – one hundred thousand sorrys*. However, my attempt at taking it seriously is also a grand lie because there will be no cure for Mum's illness. Why waste a life searching for something that doesn't exist, eh?

Not wanting to alienate myself further, I decide on a different approach.

'But if I couldn't do that, I'd like to be some kind of writer,' I say. 'Poet or something.' I sense the scud of humiliation sweep over me. Why did I mention the P-word?

And we're back in the game!

'You write?' Lou asks.

'Badly,' I say.

'You write poems?' Clare asks.

'Really badly,' I say.

And Lou? Why hasn't he told anyone what he wants to do?

'And what about you, Lou?' Roddy finally asks him.

I'm genuinely interested in what Lou has to offer, especially since he's so disparaging towards the exercise. I prick up my ears. Lou leans back. His chest swells in his denim jacket, fully buttoned. I try not to stare, hard not to.

'It's a futile question, dude,' he says.

'How so?' Roddy says.

'Well, for one, I don't wanna confine myself, do I? I mean, who wants to be doin' the same thing for eternity? Not me, that's who.'

The group is pin-drop quiet.

'A lifetime of work is self-imposed imprisonment,' Lou says. 'What it is, is psychological torture.'

I want to offer my backing because in many ways I like his way of thinking; he has a point, even though he's being a bit of a killjoy about it. Rich coming from me.

'You really believe that's the case, Lou?' Roddy says.

'Look, man,' Lou says, scanning the rest of us in the room, 'for people in our situation, thinking about the future ain't quite as appealing as it is for other folk.'

'You think?' Roddy says.

'We equate the future with fear. It's not something for us to get too excited about, Rod …'

'It's Roddy.'

'Yeah. Our future symbolises the inevitable, and that inevitability, well, that means grief, pain, heartache or whatever.'

'That's a bleak outlook, Lou,' Roddy adds. 'If you don't mind me saying.'

'Bleak is right. You said it, dude. You said it.'

There's no laughter behind hands, no sly looks or sniggers. I find myself agreeing with Roddy. I want many things in life but a bleak future isn't one of them. Don't get me wrong; if that's your bag, go for it. Reach for them bleak old stars up there, just don't drag me along for the ride. Count me out.

Me? I'm hoping for a brighter beat. My outlook needs to be filled with bright colours. It has to be. Bright colours only.

*

When Roddy wraps it up for the night, everyone scarpers as if the last class in school had finished. Hoards bolting for the freedom gates. I guess we all need to relieve whoever's doing the caring duties. But Bel doesn't need me to rush home. Sure, her and Danny are probably creating their own graphic novel or shooting the shit out of legitimate targets on one of Danny's Xbox games. Basically, I can stroll. Look in a bookshop window. People watch. Not think about Mum.

I go for a piss and leave the building. Inhale air into my lungs. Function halls smell of varnish and disinfectant, so it's good to breathe again.

As my chest expands I hear a vroom sound from the back of the building, assume it's Roddy vrooming off to drink his nightly glass of wine on a tattered settee, ready to unwind after his daily toil of helping the hopeless. Good job well done and all that.

The bike, a cool-looking scooter, shoots past before I have a chance to wave a goodbye; it then circles and comes to a halt in front of me. Up pops the visor and out gleams these eyes.

'Hey, Bobby,' Lou says.

'Lou!' I say, hoping to sound confident.

'I gotta spare helmet if you wanna ride somewhere?'

My heart trots. I am flustered by Lou's offer, unsure if he's being friendly or simply posturing. It's hard to tell.

'Erm … well … erm … like …'

'Come on. Jump on. Beats ridin' the bus, right?'

'Do you have a licence for that?' I say, wishing the words hadn't left my mouth.

'What do you mean, *do I have a licence*? I'm seventeen, for Chrissake,' Lou says, as if he's just landed here from an American teen flick. Ever since I heard his voice I've kind of envied it: his accent propels him from the humdrum.

'Oh, you're seventeen. I thought …'

'Dude, you wanna ride or not?'

'Erm, I suppose so.'

'Cool.'

'Thanks,' I say, rushing down a few steps towards the bike. 'That'd be great.'

Lou swings his leg over and dismounts, flicks the bike stand and opens up the little box at the back, where he produces the spare helmet.

'Here.' He hands it to me. 'See if it fits.'

I force it down over my head.

'It's fine,' I say, my face scrunched up and distorted inside it. Kid's helmet? Lou kicks the stand down and sits on the scooter.

'Hop on.' I hop on.

As he turns to face me our helmets click.

'Where to, dude?'

I tell him what direction to take.

Off we scoot.

I don't know the protocol of being a backseat passenger. Should I loop my arms around him or hold on to the metal frame behind my lower back or just try to balance without touching anything? I pluck for the uncomfortable option, metal frame, as it seems totally inappropriate to man-hug Lou on our maiden voyage.

I briefly put my hands on my thighs, but for my first time on a scooter it's a bit unnerving. Scary really. The neon lights in the streets flash past far too quickly for my liking. I try to stay composed, not allowing my terror to be transmitted. How uncool would that be? I can't tell if Lou's peacocking his scooter skills to impress me or this is relatively normal scooter behaviour. Either way, all I visualise is the pair of us spreadeagled under a bus, blood streaming down my face with my leg pointing in the opposite direction from where it should be.

While Lou's trying to make idle conversation I'm focusing on staying alive. I belt out monosyllabic answers. To be honest, I can't quite hear him. During one particularly sharp turn I coil my arms around his torso. Totally instinctive, no joke. I feel his stomach, taut and stiff, under the coarse denim of his jacket. I'm unsure if it's my sudden grasp that's caused him to tense up.

'RELAX, MAN,' he yells from under his visor.

'Sorry, I didn't mean to,' I say, which he doesn't hear.

We hit another spiky turn before Lou puts the brakes on. We've stopped somewhere I don't recognise. Well, I recognise it all right because it's in our area, but it's a place I've no reason to be at. And it isn't my house.

'This isn't where I live, Lou,' I say.

'Yeah, sorry about that, Bobby, I just need to make a quick pit stop.'

'What?'

'I have to see my man in here, dude,' he says, getting off the bike and removing his helmet. 'A quick in-and-out job.'

'Want me to come ... ?'

'No, best if you wait here, guard the bike.' He runs his fingers through his hair until it's fully slicked back on his head. 'It's a vintage Vespa.'

'Oh, OK,' I say, not knowing the difference between a vintage Vespa and a vintage hairdryer. 'So you want me to stay here and guard the bike then?'

'I'll be two minutes, max,' he says.

I don't get a chance to reply. Lou's already heading up the path towards *his man*'s front door, helmet bouncing on his hip. I peel off my own helmet and stand awkwardly in front of the bike, praying no yobs turn up intent on getting their feral mitts on a vintage Vespa.

Thankfully it is less than two minutes before Lou re-emerges. His word is good.

'Job done,' he says, skimming the road left and right. 'OK, ready?'

'Ready,' I say.

Lou looks at his watch.

'Shit, it's late. I'd better get you home.' I'm thinking that maybe it would've been quicker to have caught the bus after all, but I do understand the frantic twist in Lou: I have the same thing happen if I think Mum isn't coping without me. I guess I'm very aware of my responsibilities.

When we remount the scooter Lou reaches back and grabs my arm. 'You'd best hold on, Bobby, I'm now officially in a goddam hurry.' He yanks my hands on to his waist. I finger the pockets of his denim jacket. If I wanted to I could put my hands right inside them. I don't. Of course I don't. But that's not to say the temptation isn't strong. And I am as tempted as hell.

#2 ... incomplete

let me watch you from afar
at my safe distance

do you see me seeing you
in my reflections?

it's all impulse and ruminations

but

if called
i'll come charging

if invited

        i'll shatter safety and shorten distance

don't be far away

        come here

Junk Food Friday

'If you tap that pen off your teeth again I promise you're getting punched,' Bel says.

Something is bothering me. My mind is ambling. Unable to focus.

'Shhh,' I say. 'I'm trying to work here.'

'Don't lie, you hate maths.'

'Not true.'

'And you're pure crap at it.'

I look at her. She's not wrong. On both counts.

'You're one to talk, Bel.'

'Erm, hello, I'm crap at everything,' she says, as if proud.

'Education isn't for everyone. Maybe you could be a teenage mother. Bet you're not crap at pushing a buggy in the rain.'

'I'm serious, Bobby. I will attack.'

'Have you finished the exercise?' I ask.

'It's me you're talking to. No.'

I tap my pen again.

'Seriously, Seed,' Bel spits.

'Can we talk about Drowning Our Sorrows Fridays?'

'No sweat. Go.'

I explain what she already knows, that I'm not much of a drinker. So with my responsible mature-teenage hat on I tell her it would be wholly negligent of me to continue with our Friday boozing sessions. I also want to avoid any pissed kissing temptations. It's not that I don't find Bel attractive. I do. She's totally gorgeous in the sense that she doesn't know how gorgeous she is, which adds to her overall gorgeousness. Such an alluring quality. If I pushed it, there's no doubt that we'd be love's young dream and I'd be the envy of just about every hormonal guy in school. But, here's the rub: I'm simply not drawn to her in that way. My loins don't spin when she's around. No slight on Bel. No slight at all. It's just … I don't fancy girls.

Bel doesn't throw a mad hissy fit when I suggest our Drowning Our Sorrows Fridays should be a thing of the past. No hissy fit, but her response knocks me sideways.

'Well, I didn't want to say, Bobby. I thought it was completely irresponsible of you in the first place. With your mum up there and that, know what I mean?' She shrugs her shoulders and flicks her eyes skywards.

Gobsmacked isn't the word; you could have put a full

fist into my gaping mouth. It was HER IDEA in the first place.

'And with Danny in the house as well. I mean, if the council or police had got wind of us drinking, you'd have been fucked, mate.'

I'm pretty sure I could've squeezed two fists in after that.

'But –'

'I don't even like cider,' she says.

'But, Bel –'

'I was only doing it for you, help perk you up.'

'But –'

'To help you take your mind off everything.'

'Bel …'

Oh, what's the point?

'We shouldn't lose our Fridays though,' she says.

'I agree.'

'So what you got in mind?'

Nothing like being put on the spot

'Why don't we just get a takeaway instead?' I suggest.

'A takeaway?'

'Yeah, Indian or pizza or something.'

'On Fridays?'

'Every Friday.'

'Sounds totally mediocre.'

'I think it's a good idea.'

Bel's eyes become smaller and tighter: she's morphing into deep creative mode. 'We can call it …' You can tell her brain's in overdrive, clocking up umpteen title permutations. Her lips move at the same speed as her thoughts. 'We can call it … We could call it … We should call it …'

'Junk Food Friday?' I blurt.

'Yes, Junk Food Friday.' She points at me. 'That's good. I like that.'

'I'm glad.'

'You finished the exercise, Bel?' the teacher shouts from his desk.

'Nearly, sir.'

'Well, head down and get on with it,' he says. 'You OK, Bobby, need help?'

'No, I'm fine, sir,' I say.

'Good to hear. Good to hear.'

We stick our heads closer to the desks.

'So, it's decided? That's what we'll call it?' I whisper.

'Junk Food Friday it is then, agreed?'

'Agreed,' I say, but I can't help thinking that she's just nicked my idea and will be passing it off as her own.

December

My birthday isn't until December. My eighteenth. The biggie. The one where I go to sleep a boy and wake a man. Mum wants us to celebrate it NOW. September! This isn't the effect of the pills toying with her senses.

'I'm not talking about limos and rap music, Bobby. I'm suggesting the three of us spending some time out of this house.'

'A holiday?' I ask.

'Tried. Unfortunately the *world* is fully booked.'

'That limits your options.'

'I'm talking about going out for food or something.'

'Like dinner?'

'Wow! You sure you're turning eighteen?'

'Yes, Mum, but not until *December*.'

'You say December but that day they left you on our

doorstep I do recall frost. I just put two and two together and plucked out December.'

'You should really be writing these down, you know.'

'Actually, you could be a February baby, but, really, who knows?'

'Look, is it not a bit weird to celebrate someone's birthday almost four months before it actually occurs?'

'It is your eighteenth.' Mum taps her head. 'Or is that my son from a previous relationship?'

'Seriously, your talent is totally wasted, you know that?'

'Recognition at last.'

'And, anyway, *your* birthday is before mine. It's in a few weeks.'

'OK, let's celebrate your *non-birthday* then, how's that sound?'

'Eh?'

'Let's just go out.'

'Why didn't you just say that in the first place?'

'Where's the fun in that?'

'Can we wear nice clothes?' I say.

'You can even shower if you want.'

'Really?'

'I insist on it.'

'Where will we go?'

'Danny will be with us so that narrows it down to ...'

'Say no more.'

Conversations like this lead me into a false sense of

hopefulness. You forget for a few minutes. You're not worrying if there's a prescription you were meant to pick up today or if Dan has clean clothes for tomorrow, you're just kind of chewing the fat and plodding on as if everything's normal. Your mind isn't on your troubles at all. Until, that is, it smacks you full force on the jaw and jolts you right back into its clutches. A bit like getting admitted to a nightclub then getting lobbed out before the coats come off. It could be anything, a subtle grimace of pain on Mum's face, the frailty of a movement, lack of clarity in her words, and BANG! Suddenly we've all returned. Illness. Disease. Sickness. Ailment. Disability. Mum wanting to go out celebrating is a positive thing; Mum wanting to celebrate birthdays prematurely worries the life out of me.

'Help me up, Bobby,' she says, rising from the chair. 'Bit tired. I'm going to lie down and listen to music.'

'I'll help you upstairs.'

'I can manage.'

'OK, I'll escort you then,' I say. 'I'm heading up anyway. Homework.'

'Such a gentleman. Your mother will be so proud when I tell her.'

I could've carried her. I don't suggest it. She doesn't ask. We do the usual: I hold the bottom of her back and she grabs my arm. One step at a time, slower than five decades of the rosary. No rush, now.

'How's school going, son? I didn't ask.'

'It's fine. School's school.'

'Are you still in the thick group?'

'They don't do that any more, don't think they're allowed.'

'Well, they should bring it back,' she says.

'What?'

'At least you know what you're working with then.' Her face blooms; she nips my arm. If either of her sons had been disposed of into some thick group, I can imagine the old powerhouse Mum marching right down to the school demanding revolution.

'Just keep walking and try not to speak.'

'Won't be long,' she says.

Won't be long for *what*? Getting into bed or the not speaking part?

'We haven't been out for ages,' she says, after I get her settled. 'It'll be nice to spend some time together.'

'I know, it's been yonks.'

'I'll try not to embarrass you both.'

'Shut up.'

'I'm serious,' she adds.

'Yeah, so am I, shut up.'

'I don't want to embarrass you or Danny, son. I don't.'

'Mum, stop saying that. How would you embarrass us?'

'You're a teenager, Bobby.'

'And? So?'

'So teenagers don't go out with their mothers. Teenagers

hate their mothers. Teenagers just want money and the internet. In fact, they want to live in the internet.'

'You're so down with teen life, it's impressive.'

She holds out her hand. I take it. She brings mine up to her lips. Her eyes soften.

'You've such a beautiful soul, Bobby Seed, know that?'

'Mum!'

'You don't know it, but one day you will and so will everyone else.'

She kisses my knuckles.

'Right, go and get your homework done before I take my slipper to your arse.'

A final hand kiss.

'Night, Mum.'

'Night, son.'

Dumb and Dumber

'You know I really appreciate this, Bel,' I tell her.

'Sure, what else would I be doing?'

'Well, not looking after our Danny for a start.'

'I'd just be at home watching some Neanderthal pisshead shouting at snooker on the telly. Believe me, Bobby, this is like being given a free pass.'

'Right,' I say. 'I'd better go or I'll miss the bus.'

She grabs my cheeks and squeezes them between her hands.

'I want you back at a reasonable time, young man, and I'll be smelling your fingers when you do, so no smoking.'

'Promise, Mum.'

Bel takes a step back, folds her arms in comedy fashion.

'Look at you, you're so handsome.'

'Shut it.'

'My baby's all grown up.'

'The carer will be here in ten minutes. Mum's good, she's listening to the radio. Danny's up–'

'Stairs playing on his Xbox,' Bel interrupts. 'I know, Bobby. I know.'

'Right.'

'Well,' Bel says, 'he tells you he's playing on his Xbox, but, come on, he's fourteen. We both know what he's doing up there all the time.'

'Do you have to?'

'Someone's got to slap you into reality.'

'I'd better shoot.'

As soon as I open the door to leave I see him. There at the end of the path. Modish, hip, trendy. Whatever the word is, he has it in droves. My helmet's resting on the seat behind him. *My* helmet?

Lou waves.

'Fuck's that?' Bel asks.

'Oh, that's Lou. He goes to the meetings too.'

'Why is he just waiting there like some weirdo Knight Rider?'

'Knight Rider was about a car, Bel.'

'And I care because?'

'He's just here to give me a lift, I think.'

I haven't a clue why he's turned up. I presume it is just to give me a lift.

'What, he was just passing by?' Bel says. 'In a cul-de-sac?'

'How am I meant to know?'

Lou vrooms his vintage Vespa.

'Well, you better go before your chariot rides into the sunset without you.'

'Laters,' I say.

I look at Bel. She isn't impressed, her face jammed between scowling and sneering. I return Lou's wave and begin walking. With each step, everything inside tightens. But I'd be lying to say there isn't a flutter of excitement there too. My stomach's among the butterflies. Yet for some reason I feel a pang of guilt. I glance back at Bel, but she's already closed the door.

Play it cool, Bobby.

Steady as you go, son.

Don't do anything too dickish.

Lou removes his helmet, claws his hair into shape and flashes me a white grin. I echo his smile.

'Thought you might like a ride,' he says.

'How did you know I'd be here?'

'I dropped you off, remember?'

'No, how did you know I'd be home?'

Lou grabs the spare helmet, chucks it.

Did he wink?

'Hunch, Bobby. Just a hunch.'

'I'm glad you're here. I'll take the lift.'

'Cool.'

I force the helmet down over my head and straddle the

vintage Vespa. I don't need to look: I know Bel's twitching behind the blinds.

'Ready?' Lou says.

'Yeah.'

Rev that engine, Lou, let's open these wings and fly to where the breeze catches us.

Lou slaps his hips. 'Hold here and don't squeeze so much this time.'

'OK.'

I rest my hands on him, his hips. Exactly where he instructs me to. All bones. I feel the leather of his belt. I could coil a finger in the loop of his jeans if I wanted. We move off.

'I really appreciate this, Lou,' I shout.

'Eh?' he shouts back. 'Louder!'

'THANKS FOR THIS.'

'NOT A PROBLEM, HAPPY TO HELP.'

As he speeds up my grip intensifies.

'CHEERS,' I shout.

'RIDIN' A BUS IS SUCH A PAIN IN THE ASS. THIS IS MUCH QUICKER.'

'IT'S GREAT,' I bellow. 'It's so great.'

Lou's body shelters my face from the wind. I smell him. Same deodorant as the one I use, convinced of it. He seems quiet today, which makes for some pretty awkward silences.

'HOW'S YOUR MUM, LOU?' I shout.

'EH?'

'YOUR MUM, HOW'S SHE DOING?'

'WHAT?'

'YOUR MUM, IS SHE –'

'WHAT? CAN'T HEAR, DUDE.'

'NOTHING. IT'S OK.'

At traffic lights, Lou leans into me.

'You say something?'

'Just asking how your mum was doing. Doesn't matter.'

'Mom's Mom, nothing changes. You know that, right?'

'Yeah.'

'You comfortable?' he asks.

'I'm totally cool.'

Totally cool. Really, Bobby? Really?

'HOLD ON TO ME, I'M GONNA PUSH IT OUT A BIT.'

I stiffen my grip; my hands creep around to his stomach. He twists the throttle towards him. We bullet along the road. Neon lights shoot past. The Vespa sounds as if it could leave the ground at any minute, ET style. I'm wedged between exhilaration and shitting it.

'THIS ROCKS, RIGHT?' Lou shouts.

'TOTALLY ROCKS,' I screech.

First and last time I'll use that phrase ... for obvious reasons.

Harriet flicks us the finger when we ride past her near the entrance. Erin waves, as does Clare. Cal gives us some sort of military salute. We pull up. I get off. Lou kicks the Vespa on to its stand.

'God, I need to get myself one of those things, Lou,' I say.

'Pretty damn good, eh?'

'Thanks again.'

'Pleasure.'

But the pleasure's mine: it bursts out of my pores. I think it's the first time that someone has picked me up from my front door. Gone out their way to do that. And you only do that for people who are nice, right? For people who've made an impression on you, right?

'No, I really appreciate it.'

'I'll take you home afterwards.'

'You don't have to, I can get –'

'Consider it done.'

'Don't you have to get back as soon as though?'

'As you know, this thing flies when it needs to. I get home in plenty of time.'

Right-handed, Lou ruffles his hair; left-handed, he sorts it. I fix my own locks into life. His hair is cascading and compliant, while mine sits like a weary Brillo pad after scouring burned pots. He slaps his gloves inside the helmet and we make our way to the entrance door.

'I wonder what we'll be doing tonight?' I say.

'Probably sharin' tips on how to feed through a straw.'

Wow!

I can't make a joke like that, can't belittle my mum with that type of off-the-cuff remark. No bother to Lou though; I'm beginning to think he enjoys the outsider role, having

81

that freedom to speak his mind. Maybe it's the Yankee blood in his veins.

'Check you two out,' Harriet says as we walk through the door. 'You look like Dumb and Dumber on that thing.'

I puff a laugh.

'Go fuck yourself, Harriet,' Lou says.

I shrug her a meek apology. She smirks, shakes her head.

'Charming as always, Lou,' she says, walking away from us.

'Know what, Bobby?' Lou says.

'What?'

'I like Harriet, there's no shit about her.'

'Yeah, me too,' I say.

'And ...' He shoulder-nudges me.

'What?'

'I think she may have the hots for you.'

'Don't talk crap,' I belt at him, as if insulted. He's definitely stirring shit.

'I know these things, Bobby, trust me. She does.'

If his love radar was so sharp, he'd have known this conversation is wasted on me.

'Rubbish,' I say.

I don't want girls having the hots for me. I don't ever want to have that *it's-not-you-it's-me* conversation, which in this case *is* true. Lou doesn't need to know any of that though. And I don't need the volley of his inklings.

My problem.

My problem entirely.

Sleep

My brain's screaming: *Please sleep, I beg you!* Sometimes I flick on my computer, plug in my earphones so as not to wake Danny. Danny being woken without reason is another headache altogether. I've an ear plugged in and the other exposed in case Mum needs me. It's never anything forbidden I look at online. I fire Lou's name into Google, and Harriet's. Try Facebook, Instagram. Find nothing to excite me.

Occasionally I play dead, listening to the darkness: a peace that only occurs in the calm of night. The thoughts that swirl through the mind at that time tickle and torture in equal measure. It's exhausting.

It's Mum who keeps me awake, I know it is. She glides between the walls and floats beneath the floorboards. Her spirit is ever present. I hear every grunt and groan, every whimper. Suddenly I'm up, eyes wide, ears pricked, ready to spring into action.

The snoring is the worst, not because she sounds like an overweight builder after a skinful of booze. See, the actual snoring I can deal with: bizarrely, that's the comforting part. It's when it stops abruptly that I am riddled with panic. I can easily nod off to the rhythm of Mum's snoring: my bedtime story, my hot milk. So I'm constantly checking on her, making sure she's comfortable, that she's not going anywhere.

Too often I find myself watching Mum sleep, following the laborious piston action of her stomach. And I pray. Well, not as such, but I do think if there's a God up there, why does he allocate certain people this existence? The chosen few. Where does he bugger off to when disease raps? How does he decide who lives to a ripe old age and who doesn't? Why does he let people die slowly, devastated by pain? Why does this God rob my family's potential? This damn God is no friend of mine. And, as far as being my saviour, don't make me vomit! Maybe that's why you never hear his name uttered at any of the Poztive meetings. I guess we all feel abandoned by him. Might not even be a *him*.

I stand over her bed pretending she's normal, that our little family is normal. I blank out the fact that her speech is regressing; becoming progressively more slurred by the day, with words that sound like gargled water. I visualise her walking without my help, or without those bloody sticks. And when we're harping on about the future, I know it's all bullshit, all pretence. Lou's discussion with Roddy plays in my head: his pessimism and dour outlook rebooted my brain. You see, Mum's getting gradually worse while we all jam our heads in the sand and stay mute. Mine jammed the deepest. I do all the intimate stuff; I stroke her bones, I know how her muscles work and I see the intense sadness and humiliation in her eyes because her seventeen-year-old child has to wipe her arse and wash her most private areas. And all I want to do is tell her that she should feel no shame, but for some reason I choose not to. I do the tasks impassively, as if she were a mannequin, a non-human. And that fucking shame is all mine.

The urge to slide into bed beside her and snuggle up tight is always a powerful one. To role reverse all the cuddling and cradling she gave us when we were toddlers. When I'm standing at Mum's bedside in the quiet of night, the desire to pull her into my arms is so overwhelming that it envelops my entire body, like being grief-wrapped in cling film. And I don't know how to navigate: I'm rudderless, directionless.

Now I think of my mother in that room, lying contorted, eyes planted on specific ceiling points. I can't imagine where her mind travels to. I hope it's to somewhere magical.

Dining Out

Danny decided the venue for our family celebration – *not* my birthday – because he needs to be familiar with places. If we'd gone to some starched-tablecloth job Danny's brain would have careered out of control. Mum wouldn't have wanted to be exposed to that either.

'I don't want to put people off their dessert, Bobby,' she says before we go.

'What you on about?'

'Would you like to be next to someone like me?'

'I only care about the people at my table, Mum.'

'People stare.'

'Let them stare.'

'People comment.'

'So let them comment.'

'I don't want to be that person, Bobby.'

'What person?'

'The person who affects others' ability to enjoy themselves, who stops laughter, who silences the world around
them.'

'Let them be silent. Prejudice deserves to be silenced,' I
say, allowing my voice to demonstrate a level of anger that
makes Mum raise a brow.

She pauses, subtly nods her head. I can tell she's supressing
a smile.

'Is this the part where I should say how proud I am
of you?'

'Well ...'

'Think it is. However, you've yet to make me a small
fortune, so I'll put that phrase on the long finger until I see
some hard cash.'

And so we're all off on the bus to Danny's preferred eatery.

'I want a Happy Meal,' he says when we get there.

'They're for kids, Dan,' Mum says.

'I want the toy.'

Mum gives me a knowing look. She hasn't the gut for the
tussle.

'Just get him one if that's what he wants.'

'And you, madam,' I say. 'What can I get for you?'

'Can I see the menu, please?'

'I'm afraid we've run out, madam.'

'It's written on the wall, Mum,' Danny says. 'All the burgers
and stuff are up on wall.'

'Thanks, Dan,' Mum says. 'I'll have … I'll have … a Filet-O-Fish.'

'Excellent choice, and would madam like chips with that?'

'They're called fries in here, Bobby.'

'Fries would be great.'

'Drink for madam?'

'Any McWine?'

'I'm afraid we only have McWater, McTea, McCoffee and an array of McSugar drinks.'

'It's just Coke, Sprite and Fanta. They don't say the "Mc" bit before the drinks,' Danny says. 'It's like you've never been here in your life before.'

'Right,' I say. 'Be back in a minute.'

'Get ketchup, Bobby. Loads of it. Tons of it.'

Danny's delighted with the little magnifying glass and activity map his Happy Meal provides. He holds up a chicken nugget in front of the glass. Then looks at magnified ketchup, magnified napkins, magnified fingernails and just about anything else that's on our table. Mum nibbles away without committing herself to actual biting, chewing and swallowing. She shuffles uncomfortably in her seat, trying to hide facial contortions. I know the signs: pins and needles, numbness, sore muscles, gravel throat. I've seen it all before.

In a flash, everything changes.

'Mum, can I get a McFlurry after this?' Danny asks.

Mum's sitting with us, but she isn't *with us*. She isn't here.

'Sure you can, buddy,' I say.

'This place is ace. Do you think so, Bobby?'

'Yeah, it's great.'

'You think so, Mum?' Danny asks.

But she is somewhere else, somewhere darker. I keep her snugly in my vision.

'She loves it, Dan,' I say.

'We should come here with Bel. She'd love it too,' he says.

'No doubt.'

Mum pecks at the bun, like a crow in the snow. Suddenly I don't want my double cheeseburger; every morsel feels like a brick is being dropped into my stomach.

'Finished!' Danny says through a mouthful of chips. 'Can I get my dessert now, Mum?'

She looks at him, lips dry, says nothing.

'Why don't you go and ask for it, Dan?' I say.

'What, wait in the queue?'

'Yeah.'

'On my own?'

'We'll be here watching. You'll be fine.'

'Can I, Mum?'

Mum gives Danny an affirmative grin. I reach into my pocket, pull out what I have and hand Danny some money.

'It's fine, go. We'll be here,' I say.

'Cool.' Danny slides out of the seat, full of life.

I reach across the table and hold Mum's hand. Cold. Her eyes don't deviate from her tray.

'Mum?'

'My legs, Bobby.'

'What is it?'

'I couldn't control it.'

'Control what?'

'I couldn't feel anything.'

'Mum, you're scaring me. What is it?'

'I'd no idea it was happening, son. I'm so sorry.'

'Know what was happening?'

'Everything below.'

'Mum, I don't understand.'

'Look under the table.'

Not exactly a puddle, just a few drops on the floor, but her jeans are sopping. Her thighs sodden. I disgrace myself because I allow anger and annoyance to momentarily brush over me. While under that table I close my eyes, grit my teeth and hope that it will all disappear, just for a few hours at least. Why us? Why our family? Why not any of those sitting around us? Those who stare? Why do they get to enjoy normal things? Why the fuck does it have to be *my* mum? *Our* mum?

I return my head and look at my mother through glazed eyes.

'I couldn't feel it happening, Bobby. I'd no control.'

'It's OK, Mum. It's fine.'

'I'm so humiliated.'

'Mum,' I say, squeezing her hand and furtively looking to

see if anyone has noticed the scene. I hate myself for doing this. 'We'll get you cleaned up in the toilet.'

'In fucking McDonald's? I'm done with this, all of it.'

'Please don't cry, Mum, please. You'll set me off.'

All I want to do is hold her tight.

'I'm sorry, Bobby.'

'You've done nothing to be sorry for.'

'I can't get up. I can't move.'

'I'll help you, don't worry. I'll always help you. So will Dan. We're your sons. We'll do anything for you. Please don't worry.'

'I'm so scared.'

And Mum's tears become heavier. The sound alerts sneaky scans. I badly want to launch a McSomething in their direction. Her tears jolt me too; I'm not used to seeing this level of emotional frailty in her. She needs us to be strong, to be her granite.

'Hey, come on. I'm here for you, Mum.'

Danny bounds back to the table, dessert held aloft, smiling wildly. However, one glimpse at our faces and the McFlurry slumps, his beaming face dims.

'What happened?' he says. 'Mum? Bobby? What happened?'

'It's nothing, Dan. Mum just spilled some water on herself.'

Danny holds out his dessert as an offering.

'You can have my McFlurry, Mum. If you want.'

'Thanks, sweetheart, but you have it.' She can hardly get the words out.

'Don't cry, Mum,' Danny says.

'She's just sad about all that water, mate,' I say.

'I hate it when I spill water or juice or milk. It makes me want to pee myself,' he says.

Mum and I snort out a throaty laugh, both glad this one-man battering ram of diffusion is here. God, we're so glad he's here.

'We should do the drive-thru next time,' Danny says.

'We don't have a car,' I say.

And that's that.

Another day in our lives: anger » frustration » peace » laughter.

Balance restored.

Stars at Night

That night I toss and turn, shove the covers down to my waist, pull them up again. Roll left side, right side, on to my stomach. Finally settle, arms behind head, staring at my ceiling. I know every crack and stain on it by now. Still has the remnants of glow-in-the-dark stars from when I was a kid. Their glow power was always a bit shit.

The sound of the vrooming Vespa reverberates around my head, engine kick-starting my thoughts.

It's noisy, Lou, I say to him.

That's its tune, he says. *It's a beautiful symphony.*

And I imagine us riding through the streets, me perched on the back, giddy and unnerved; him at the helm, commanding and calming. I picture hugging him like he's an oak tree as he throttles us away. Far away.

I get to run my hands through his hair when he removes

his helmet. Flick a wayward strand from his eyes, tuck a clump behind his ear. He doesn't protest. He relents.

Thanks, Bobby, he says.

I'm good with hair. I do Mum's all the time, I say.

Did he wink?

I should have Mum on my mind; I should be considering her needs, worrying about what seems more inevitable than ever, but I can't. I can't stop seeing the both of us on that Vespa. Vintage.

I roll over, again. Those old glow-in-the-dark stars blink drowsy sparkles down at me. And there he is again. Brash, uncouth. Sitting on this slightly menacing Vespa, but I'm drawn to it, to him.

Hop on, he says.

Sure?

More than anything.

Eyes open or closed, I see us whizzing past. The poetry is tangible.

#3 ... *complete*

vibrations
drum my hamstrings
inside
butterflies sting
  going nowhere
on full throttle
  going nowhere
somewhere

never to return
    here

Music

And I think it could be a beautiful symphony. I really do.

Mum's Present

I follow the yellow flow of my piss as it splashes against the tin urinal and think about Mum's busted bladder. She has zero control; betrayal can just happen any time. Since last week's McDonald's trip, the times I take her to the toilet have practically doubled; fear does that.

The toilet door thrusts open as I'm shaking off the residue.

'Shit, I've been holdin' this throughout that whole goddam meetin',' Lou says as he unbuckles his belt. I put mine away; he pulls his out. I make my way to the taps. 'Oh, sweet Jesus,' Lou exhales, almost bouncing on his heels. 'That feels like heaven.' His pissing stance is how I expected it to be.

I wash my hands, twice.

'You OK, dude?' he says over his shoulder.

'Yeah, fine,' I say. 'Why?'

'You seem a little … distant. Fuck, I dunno. Down maybe. You seem a little down.'

He noticed!

I flick off the excess water, dry what remains on my arse. Lou theatrically shakes it and fastens himself. I look away. He approaches and puts his hand on my shoulder … same one that recently held his cock. Thanks for that! It takes effort not to flinch.

'You sure you're OK?' he says.

'Just Mum, Lou. She's just in a bad place at the moment,' I say.

'I hear you, Bobby.'

'Thinks she's starting to get affected up here now.' I point to my temple.

'It's a psychological battle. It affects everyone.'

'Yeah.'

'Illness is a damn wreckin' ball, Bobby. We're all beaten down by it.'

'Does the same thing happen to your mum?' I ask.

Lou removes his hand from my shoulder, skips past me to the sinks. The rushing water is loud.

'Look, Bobby, it's this wax and wane shit that fucks with our minds. You just need to stay positive for your mom, do exactly as you've always done, don't change routines, don't change the way you treat her. Show consistency. Rely on good friends,' he says, opening his arms. 'Keep your balls up.'

I laugh at this, definitely a Louism as opposed to an Americanism.

'Is that how it is with your mum, Lou?'

He begins to button his denim jacket up to his neck. Deals with his imperfections in the mirror then checks the time on his phone.

'Shit!' he says.

'Is it, Lou?' I ask again. 'The same with your mum?' I don't want to seem as if I'm interrogating him. I guess I'm looking to make more of a connection. Solidify the chemistry. Do we even have any chemistry?

'Look, Bobby, when a person's confidence is shot to shit, someone else needs to be a solid. In this case that's you. You get me?'

Not really.

'Yeah … I think so.'

'I'm here any time you need to blow off some steam, dude.'

'Thanks, Lou.'

'I'm late, but I can give you a quick ride home.'

'Cheers.'

*

Whenever Mum wants to listen to her *when-I-was-younger* music, I prop her up and we listen together. Actually, I'm ordered to 'appreciate' as opposed to listen. I've now garnered a healthy *appreciation* for an array of bands: Carter the Unstoppable Sex Machine, Cud, The Wedding Present, The Smiths, Gene and Ned's Atomic Dustbin. The list, and education, never stops. I can just imagine Mum flouncing around to these groups back in the day when she was a different person, rejoicing in an alternative universe: no kids, just herself, her friends, great songs and the thrill of youth; life's blank canvas to splatter. Exactly the place where I'm at now, I suppose.

This music transports her to a much happier and gratified world. A place she's regretted leaving ever since. Not my fault. Not hers. Life!

While listening to Portishead, Mum drops a little bombshell, not an earth-shattering cluster bomb, more like one of those child–parent awkward *I-want-a-giant-hole-to-swallow-me-up* conversations.

'This takes me back, Bobby,' Mum says, eyes closed. Remembering those days when she answered only to Anne. When nobody referred to her as 'Mum'.

'Bet it does.' Portishead isn't doing it for me; whatever floats your boat and all that.

'This album … God, I loved this album,' she murmurs. No point expressing my honest opinion of the music. I want her bubble to float beyond height.

'I'd say it brings back loads of memories, Mum.'

'Oh, it does, Bobby. It really does.' She utters something to herself that I can't make out.

'What was that?'

'I said, if you only knew the half of it.'

We lie on her bed listening to the songs in silence. Mum's eyes clam shut; mine spy small cobwebs that have assembled in the top of the lampshade. I think I need to change the sheets too. More jobs to the list. Portishead continues to massage Mum's senses and assault mine.

'We used to get as stoned as fuck to this album back then,' she says with a girly giggle, before adding, 'completely zonked out our fucking faces.' More giggling.

I keep my eyes fixed on an ailing cobweb.

I don't blink.

I don't face her.

I kind of freeze, not because I'm offended or anything like that – and definitely not due to any moral stance I have either – I freeze because of the image in my head: seeing the younger and healthier version of your mother monged out her nut as the colourless tones of Portishead echo in the background is ... immensely unsettling. No, I take that back. It's not *unsettling*, it's completely disturbing. An image too potent for any son to bear. Just glad it isn't The Sundays she was getting stoned to. Maybe it was. Maybe it was every band she listened to. Maybe Mum was this wild hedonistic stoner in her day. I don't ask. No desire to know. Let her skeletons remain where they are.

Before she got sick she was a proper mum: principled, virtuous and discouraging of all society's ills. All she wanted was to protect her boys. But the illness has gradually made her give zero fucks about that. It's down to Danny and me to navigate life with our own compass now.

'Be honest with me, Bobby?' she says.

'About what?'

'Just be honest.'

'Of course I will.'

There's a pause as long as a song.

'Am I a decent mother?'

'What?'

'Was I a decent mother to you and Danny?'

'What do mean *was*? You *are* and always will be.'

'That's all I wanted to be.'

'You're a brilliant mother,' I say. 'You're amazing.'

'Even like this?'

'You've given me more than you'll ever know, Mum.'

'I love you so much, Bobby. You and Danny.'

'It's the same for us.'

'I know it is. I know it is.'

'But I have a tiny confession,' I say.

'You can tell me anything.'

'Don't hate me.'

'Can't guarantee it.'

'I'm not feeling the Portishead thing. I actually think they're bland and a bit rubbish.'

'That's cos you're a tasteless idiot with very few brain cells.'

'While you're all taste and intelligence, I suppose?'

'And you call yourself a poet?'

NO, I DON'T.

GOD, SHE HAS READ SOME, HASN'T SHE? SHE
DID A PARENTAL SNOOP THROUGH MY STUFF
IN THE DAYS WHEN HER BODY COULD SHIFT.
BET SHE HAS.

As the final Portishead tune plays, Mum slides her bony
fingers into mine. Icy cold. The rings she once wore have long
since gone. Her thumb gently rubs the back of my hand until
the song finishes.

'You've nice hands, Bobby,' she says.

'So have you,' I lie.

'Promise you won't waste them by strangling people.'

'I've no intention of following your profession.'

'Do something with your brain, son. You've a good one in
there. You're clever. Kind.'

'That's the plan, just waiting for the cells to mutate.'

'Manual labour leads to a manual life,' she says. 'And a
manual life leads to an unhappy life. I always had big dreams
for you, Bobby.'

'I have big dreams for myself too, but don't stop your
dreaming. It all helps.'

Mum lifts my hand to her mouth and kisses it. One short
and two long ones. Needs her lip balm. I mentally fix it to the
chores list.

'There's no way I'll stop dreaming of you,' she says.

'Thanks, Mum.'

'Guaranteed.'

We lie in silence for a moment longer.

'Can you put The Jesus and Mary Chain on for me, son?' she asks.

'Which one? The depressing one?'

Which one? Stupid question. They all have an air of gloom about them.

'*Darklands*,' she says.

'I was right, the depressing one.' I get up from the bed, search for what she wants.

'Sorry for not liking Ed Sheeran or one of them boy bands you're into.'

'But I don't like either of –'

'Sorry for liking *good* music,' she says.

When the opening guitar chords of *Darklands* kick in, Mum's left foot tries to tap along with the rhythm. Once again she's back in that place. She doesn't notice me, the lump, lying beside her. *Darklands* is all about dying or wanting to die. Painful. I need to cleanse the mood.

It's Mum's birthday soon. I want to do something memorable for her, cook her a nice meal – just the three of us eating together like a proper family. I could also ask Bel. Maybe I could also get Mum a professional massage? She wouldn't go for that though.

'Mum.' I nudge her.

'What?' she says, as though I've interrupted something enormous.

'You know your birthday's coming up soon?'

'I can still say my name, you know, Bobby.'

'Don't make me test you.'

'Who are you anyway, and why are you lying next to me?'

'Listen ...'

'Don't forget your mother still has a sense of humour floating around in here.'

I laugh. Feels good.

'So, what would you like for your birthday then?' I ask.

'Birthday, birthday ... let me think ... let me think,' she says, gazing wistfully up at one of the cobwebs.

I'm about to hit her with my massage and meal idea, but she gets there before me with her own brand of humour. Humour helps her forget, like sprinkles of gold dust. These moments are unbeatable, however gold dust never floats for long, does it? When Mum shares fragments of her past it's as though I am drowning in golden delights. When she jokes, I joke. When she scoffs, so do I. When she laughs, it spreads like a virus. When she writhes around in pain I want nothing more than to suck it out of her and have it as my own.

'What about a nice –' I begin to say.

'Walking holiday in northern Spain?' she says.

'Sorry, no can do.'

'Skiing in the Alps?'

'Sold out.'

'Trekking in Nepal?'

'Too far away.'

'El Camino?'

'Is that a dress?'

'I know what you can get me,' she says.

'What?'

Now a pause so long I could've driven an articulated lorry right down the length of it.

'Promise you won't go all teenage angsty on me?'

She lets go of my hand.

Suddenly the nerves jangle.

'OK, no angst,' I say.

'Turn the music down first.'

I slide myself off the bed and lower the volume.

'So, what would you like then?' I sit at the bed's edge to create a protective barrier between us. 'I'm ready,' I say.

Mum has a solemn look about her. She's wearing her *I'm-on-a-mission* face. She tries to push herself upright. I help. As I sling my arms around her waist I become physically locked into whatever sordid plan she's concocting; she has me in her clutches. Mum is right about one thing: she hasn't lost any of her mental faculties. I place my arms behind her lower back, hoosh her up.

She takes my hand again, only this time with some severe thumb-rubbing included. She looks intense. Talk about shitting bricks!

'What is it, Mum?' I say, breaking my promise not to go all teenage angsty. She frowns. 'What is it you want to say?'

'Bobby.'

'Mum.'

'I'm going to talk. You're going to listen, OK?'

'OK.'

'No interruptions.'

'Lips zipped.'

'If I slur, give me a sec?'

'Right.'

She inhales a gulp of air into her lungs, concentrating hard.

'You know how much I love you, Bobby. You and Danny are the most precious things I've ever had in my life. Bar none. Nothing else even comes close. I know caring for me has been tough going on you, don't pretend otherwise. It's something no child should ever have to do – you've no idea what having you around means to me. I'm beyond proud, Bobby. And I do understand how much effort Danny is as well.' My turn to swig the air, trying to disguise the bulge inflating my throat.

'I'm not going to get any better,' she says. I'm about to add some futile phrase of encouragement, but Mum's hand rises to halt me. 'We both know this, so let's not kid ourselves, OK? Things *are* going to get worse, Bobby. Things are going to get much worse, but that's not the scariest thing. The scariest thing is leaving you and Danny behind, seeing you two suffer because of –'

'Mum, don't …'

'No, let me finish.'

'OK.' I focus on our entangled hands.

'You shouldn't see me suffer, Bobby. I don't want to be in severe pain day after day, night after night, waiting for the inevitable to happen. And you having to do the most unimaginable things.'

'It doesn't bother me.'

'Well, it bloody bothers me,' she spits. 'Bobby, look, son, when a person loses their ability to communicate there's just no point in –'

'Why you talking like this, Mum?' I say. 'We're doing fine.'

'We're just ticking along, but I feel the gaps between the ticks, Bobby. You don't.'

'I know it comes in waves, but lots of times we have a laugh,' I say.

'I'm spending more and more time in this room.'

'That's because you need to lie down. You're exhausted by it.'

'It's not living, Bobby. It's existing, existing inside a bag of bones. I'm turning into a shell.'

'Can we not talk about something else?'

'I don't want my mind, my imagination, to be a prisoner to a lifeless body. I don't.'

'What about books and films and music?' I offer.

'What's the point if I can't discuss those things? Without a voice, what's the point?' I don't know if these are genuine questions or not. I don't know what to say. 'Once the voice goes, this won't be too far behind.' She taps her head.

I'm locked in her eyes.

'But I know you won't let that happen, will you?' Mum pauses, her stare harder, serious intent behind it. 'Will you, Bobby? You won't let that happen?'

'What's this all got to do with your birthday?' I say, trying to steer the conversation on to a more pleasant path. *Just tell me what you want for your birthday and let me get on with the planning, for God's sake,* I want to scream.

'I'm getting to it, Bobby.'

'I'm listening.'

'What I want for my birthday is to be taken back,' she says.

'Taken back?' I say, perplexed.

'That's right, taken back,' Mum says, as if I should know what she's going on about.

'Taken back to where?'

'To my youth.'

'Your youth?'

'To a time when I was blissfully loved-up with life and everything in it. To a time when I didn't hate this world.'

'Erm … Right.'

'I want to experience those feelings again, Bobby.'

'I'm not really getting this, Mum. What feelings?'

'The feelings I had when I watched my favourite films or listened to my favourite bands.'

'But you do listen to your favourite bands.'

'I can't feel them the way I used to. I can't move around to the songs, can I?'

'But you can watch your favourite films whenever you want.'

'Not the same, Bobby. Something's missing,' she says.

'What then?' I say. 'What's missing?'

Then, between a break in one of the songs, she drops that bombshell.

KABOOM!

'I want to get stoned once more. Just once.' Mum looks at me with these little lost-kitten peepers. My mouth gapes. Maybe if I'd been a stoner myself I'd have understood, but I'm not. I don't have a clue about that stuff. When people at school brag about their weekend stoner escapades, I smile and nod like everyone else, each wading in our own sea of bullshit.

I'm not sure if my mouth remains open or not. I've an inability to speak.

'I want to watch *Grease* or *The Breakfast Club* or *Pretty in Pink* as stoned as I used to get back in the day.' *Back in the day?* Really? 'Maybe I'll watch all three.'

'God, I was thinking that I'd cook a nice dinner and maybe organise someone to come in and give you a massage,' I say.

'*This* is what I want, Bobby.' Mum's voice takes on a tone of seriousness, as does her face. 'And you know why?'

This is more profound than Mum existing in a lifeless body.

'Course I know why,' I say, but I'm not sure that I do.

'So, can I have my birthday wish then?'

'Why not.'

'One problem though,' she adds.

'What?'

'*You* need to get the stuff.'

You might have thought that would knock me for six, but I was expecting her to say something like this. I awaited its arrival.

'The films, no bother, I can download them,' I say. 'But the other stuff ...'

'Hash. Grass.'

'Yes, well, whatever. I can't exactly charge over to the local shop, can I?'

'Come on, you must know someone at school.'

'I'm like an angel, Mum. I'm whiter than white.'

'What about Bel? She's a bit shady, isn't she?'

'Bel?'

'Yes, she's got that look about her. Mothers can spot it a mile off.'

'What look?'

'The dark-side look.'

'I've never seen it.'

'Just ask Bel.'

'And what if she can't help?'

'You're clever, you'll think of something.'

'God, I can't believe we're even having this conversation. Most teenagers fight with their parents over curfew time or money. Not me, I get to be *my* mum's resident drug dealer.'

'It's only a bit of hash, Bobby. Come on, do it for me, please?'

'And what if I get caught?'

'Me and Danny will come visit you every two weeks.'

'Seriously, Mum, what if I get caught?'

'I'll take all the blame. They can hardly shove me in jail, can they? And, anyway, by the time it goes to court I'll –'

'OK, OK, I'll do it!'

'Thanks, Bobby. This means a lot to me, you know.'

'Bet it does.'

'It might even take some of the pain away.'

'Suppose.'

'Sure, I'm riddled with drugs anyway. What harm's one more going to do?'

'So, that's your birthday then? Stuck alone in here, watching films and getting stoned out your tree?'

'Who said anything about being alone?'

'What do you mean?'

'We're going to celebrate together,' she says.

'Who is?'

'You and me. Together.'

'What about Danny?' I say.

'We'll just take him to McDonald's,' she says.

'Really?'

'That's a joke, Bobby. I've checked his school calendar – he's an overnight coming up soon.'

'That's right, I forgot about that,' I say. 'Looks like this is happening then.'

'Can't wait,' Mum says.

Things you do for family.

Sweet and Sour

On our first Junk Food Friday shebang, Bel almost chokes on a sweet and sour chicken ball when I tell her about my upgrade from being Mum's humble caring son to her proud drug pusher. Probably shouldn't have told her while she was in full munch mode. I don't even know the Heimlich manoeuvre – mortal sin, given my domestic duties.

'Bobby, seriously? Please tell me you're shitting me.'

'I'm not shitting you. That's what she said.'

'Pass me that Coke over.'

I watch her suck the Coke bottle until the plastic deforms in her hand. She wipes her mouth dry.

'Honestly?' she says.

'Honestly.'

'No shit?'

'Not even a hint of shit.' I bite into the soggy fried egg

that's flopped on my noodles. 'She definitely wants to get stoned.'

'How cool is your mum?' Bel says, before lashing another chicken ball into her gob.

'Do you think you'll be able to get it for me?' I ask.

'Do I look like Pablo fucking Escobar to you, Bobby?' she says, licking her sweet and sour fingers.

'It's for Mum,' I plead.

'No, no, no. Don't you do that.' Bel jabs her fork towards me. 'Don't you dare do that.'

'Do what?'

'Pull that one out.'

'What?' I raise my hands up.

'Play the emotional blackmail card.'

'Bel …'

'You're not playing that card, Bobby. I'm not allowing it, so put it away.'

'I'm only asking …'

'I mean it,' she says, actually stabbing at my arm with the fork.

'Ouch! That's sore,' I yelp.

'Is it away yet?' She threatens more stabbing.

'It's away! It's away!'

'Good.' She wolfs down the last of her fried rice.

'God, Bel, I was only asking. You didn't need to attack me.'

'You knew what you were doing.'

'Well, can you at least advise me on how to get some then?'

'Ask someone at school. Ask Jimmy Dick Toes, he's well into that stuff. Or Spud Murphy.'

'No chance. It's an automatic expulsion if you even get caught asking. You know that.'

Bel slumps back on the sofa, rubs her stomach.

'There's only one thing for it then,' she says.

'What's that?'

'You'll have to ask that scooter guy.'

'What scooter guy?'

'The guy who gave you a lift to your therapy session.'

'You mean Lou?'

'That his name?'

'And it's a young carers' group not a therapy session.'

'Whatever! Same shit, different name.'

'You reckon he'd have some?'

'You kidding me, Bobby?'

'What?'

'Around here a scooter's not a mode of transport, it's a special delivery service, if you know what I mean?'

'It's a vintage Vespa, by the way.'

'Still does deliveries though.'

'You think Lou delivers … stuff?' I say, thinking back to that *seeing-a-man* conversation we had.

'God, you're so naive, Bobby Seed. It's very cute though.'

'You serious, Bel?'

She glares, smiles ruefully.

'Maybe.'

'You think Lou will be able to snare some stuff for me?'

'I don't know, worth asking. He can only say no, can't he?'

'Suppose so.'

'And do me a favour?'

'What?'

'Don't use the words "snare some stuff for me" again, cos you sound like a dick.'

She has a point.

'Way I see it, Bobby, you're not laden down with options, so Mr Scooter might be your only one.'

'Bel, it's a vintage Vespa.'

I push away what's left of the noodles and look intently at her.

'Will you come with me when I ask?' I say.

'Don't –'

'No, it's not emotional blackmail, Bel. Honest it's not. Please?'

'Fucking hell, Bobby.'

'It'll just make life easier if you could, like, be my support.' Her eyes close. 'Come on, I'll make it up to you.' I instantly regret saying that.

'Yeah, by doing what?'

'Don't know, I'll think of something.'

'It better be good.'

'So, does that mean you'll be my wingman then?'

'Don't ever call me a wing-anything again. But, yes, I'll support you.'

'Brilliant.'

'If I'm free.'

I leap towards Bel and give her a massive hug.

'Love you! Love you! Love you!' I say, and then, again, regret saying it. So this is what being caught in the moment feels like.

'Are you going to finish those noodles?' she asks.

Mum Cradles Her Boys

Two nights after Junk Food Friday, Mum wakes at six in the morning, screaming. It's not your typical seen-a-spider-climbing-up-the-wall scream; this is a deep, guttural howl that oozes panic. The kind of sound that fires you out of bed no matter how deep your sleep is. Danny appears in my room all flustered.

'What's that? Bobby, what was that?'

'Calm down, Danny. Stay here and I'll go check.'

'What's happening?'

'Dan, go back to bed.'

'Is it the burglars?'

'No, Danny. It's nothing, go back to bed, buddy. I'll make sure Mum's OK.' Throughout our exchange Mum's cries continue to stab our ears. It clearly isn't the 'nothing' I said it was.

'I don't want to go to bed in case they get me,' Danny whispers.

'Who's going to get you?'

'The burglars.'

'There are *no* burglars, Dan.'

'They'll tie us up and steal Mum's jewellery.'

'What are you –'

'I've seen it on *Crimewatch*.'

'Well, stay there then,' I say, pointing to a spot on the landing outside Mum's door. 'OK?'

Danny tuts.

'OK, Dan?'

'Roger that.'

'And what have I told you about watching bloody *Crimewatch*?'

When I enter her room, Mum's lying on her back. Light from the landing creeps in and fondles her face. Her cheeks glisten with fresh tears. She's barely moving, almost still, her hands contorted near her chest.

'Mum, you all right?'

I move closer.

'Mum,' I utter. 'Mum, what happened?'

Her body begins to vibrate. I can't tell if she's silently crying or her muscles are in some aggressive spasm. Her ribcage sobs through her T-shirt.

'Mum, it's Bobby. Talk to me.'

She remains mute.

Danny joins me.

'Bobby, I'm scared. I don't like standing out there.'

'Danny, I told you to wait on the landing,' I snarl at him. 'Do that or go to bed.'

'But what if they get me?'

'For fuck's sake, Danny!' I snap. 'Can you not just do as I say for once in your life?'

His head disappears.

I'm usually calm under pressure; I don't lose the rag easily. It's natural for Danny to worry for his mum, wanting her to be safe. And all he does in life is exactly as I order him to do. I know he'll be sitting on the landing, head in his hands, terrified that, at any moment, a squad of balaclava-wearing goons will beat the shit out of him. But Danny's feelings have to be put aside.

'Mum, can I do anything?'

Tears surge and loiter at the corner of her mouth; her lips slowly part, allowing them somewhere to go.

'Mum, please talk to me.'

With her eyes rooted to a fixed spot on the wall, I see her chest expand with an intake of breath.

'Happening, Bobby,' she says.

Her speech clearly slurred.

'Happening? What's happening?' I say.

'Started, son. Started for real.'

She sounds drunk.

'Are you in any pain, Mum? Shall I get you your painkillers?'

'No painkillers.'

'Mum, you're beginning to scare the shit out of me. Can you please tell me what's going on?' I hate being so forceful but she needs a jolt.

'I didn't mean to scare.'

'Tell me what's going on,' I say. 'Look at me.'

She doesn't.

'Mum?'

'My legs,' she says. 'My arms.'

'Are they sore?'

'I tried to lift. Can't lift.'

'Are they too heavy?'

'No.'

'So …'

'I can't feel them, nothing's there.'

'Is it bad pins and needles?' I stupidly say.

Mum's eyes flare up at me.

'Not pins and needles, Bobby. Not this time. I can't move anything. They're dead.'

'Maybe you've just damaged something in your sleep.' I don't know what else to offer.

'I've not been sleeping, been lying here all night.'

'Do you want me to give your legs a massage or something?' I ask.

'Won't make a difference.'

'It might get the blood circulating and the muscles working again.'

'Won't make one iota of difference.'

'Maybe a bath?'

'No.'

'This is just a relapse, Mum. These are going to happen more and more.'

She lets out a loud screech, half pain, half inner agony. I kneel down at her bed, arms resting on the mattress. The praying position.

'Bobby, we knew this day was coming. The brain will be next and ...' Her eyes dart off to some distant place. 'Oh, God.' She releases a gasping wail.

'Maybe I should call the hospital,' I suggest. 'Should I do that? Can I do that?'

'No point,' she says, sniffing hard. 'Doctor comes tomorrow anyway.'

'Tell me, what can I do now?' I ask.

Mum tries to reach her hand out and straighten her fingers. 'Lie beside me, that's what I want.'

I link my fingers with hers, careful not to clench too hard. A kind of mother–son harmony. I want to say something totally naff, like, *You won't have to go through this alone. I promise I'll be by your side every step of the way.*

'Lie down, that's what I want more than anything,' she says.

'I can do that.'

'Where's Danny? I heard his voice.'

'On the landing, I think.'

'I want Danny to lie as well.'

As I suspect, Danny's head is in his hands when I go to get him. I hunker down and wrap him in my arms.

'You all right, mate?' I say.

'You swore at me,' he says.

'I know, I'm sorry.'

'You told me to fuck off.'

'I didn't say that, Dan.'

'Did.'

'I said "for fuck's sake".'

'Same thing.'

There's no point arguing when he's convinced about something.

'Well, I'm really sorry about that. I shouldn't have said it.'

'You're right, you shouldn't have.'

'I was just worried about Mum, that's all.'

'So was I,' he hisses. 'It's not all yours, Bobby. I worry too.'

'I know you do. I know you do, mate.'

'I count as well. It's not about you because you're older.'

'You're dead right. I'm sorry. It won't happen again,' I tell him. 'Do you want to come see Mum?'

'Does she want to see me?'

'What do you mean? Of course she wants to see you. She always wants to see you.'

'Really?'

'You're her favourite.' Danny takes his head away from his arms, his eyes slightly red. 'And you're my favourite too.' I kiss him, to which he flinches.

'No poof moves,' he says. I pretend this hasn't registered.

'Come on.' I get back to my feet and indicate for us to go into Mum's room.

Danny rolls his body on to the bed, next to hers; I snake mine in behind her. Mum spoons Danny while I spoon Mum. The mother of all sandwiches.

'Do you want me to put some music on?' I ask, reasoning that this would be an excellent moment for one of her Smiths or Nine Inch Nails records. I mean, what could be better than cradling your children towards dawn while listening to 'I Won't Share You' by The Smiths?

'I just want to listen to my boys sleeping,' she whispers.

After a few reassuring kisses from Mum, Danny conks out. 'I'm enjoying listening to his breathing. I don't get to hear it now. So sweet. Takes me back.'

As I spoon Mum, I jab my legs into the back of hers. Tiny sharp knee digs into her functionless legs. An experiment of sorts. I want to inflict pain upon them, just enough to make her react, to sting her a bit in order to see if the limb thing is real or nothing more than a psychosomatic head muddle. I press harder. Not so much as a jolt. Perhaps she just *thought* she couldn't feel them. Maybe Mum's mind is so intense that it infiltrates and controls what her body is telling her. Or something like that.

I'm glad when she nods off; it means no more sobbing into Danny's neck or worrying, wide-eyed, about what will be.

It would be so easy to be wrapped around them forever, shield them from the outside world. Who else do they have?

As I listen to their tandem puffing patterns, all I want to do is chuckle. It's a fleeting moment but it surges through my bones. I'm with the two people who matter most to me on earth, one a failing body and the other a clumsy mind, and all I want to do is heave laughter from the pit of my stomach. I don't.

I must've slept because I have one of those visceral dreams again about Mum dying: this time she's lying at the bottom of a swimming pool. Nose clipped, hands cuffed to walking sticks.

#4 ... complete

here we lie:
the blundering brain
the strongest wean
knotted around
the fading frame

Cold Margherita

I decide to wait after one of the Poztive meetings. Corner him. Beg him to come to one of our Junk Food Friday nights. How else am I going to get my hands on some quality Class B? Sitting in that session, I can hardly concentrate on what Roddy's prattling on about or what he wants us to do: discuss issues related to the United Nations Convention on the Rights of the Child. Hands go up around me and voices bellow things like:

The right to an education.

The right to health.

The right to an opinion.

The right to a family life.

The right to get pissed in the park.

I sit there thinking: *The right for Lou to come to my Junk Food Friday event.*

My nerves jangle at the notion of asking Lou for 'dinner'.

'I can't give you a ride home tonight, Bobby,' he informs me at the end of the session.

'That's OK.'

'Gotta see a man about some puppies.'

'What?'

'Don't matter,' he says, as if I'm not part of the gang. Think this is what's called being blown off.

My guts are in bits as I watch him walk towards the exit door. Why do I let him walk?

'Bye, Bobby,' Erin says, as she makes her way out. 'See you next time.'

'Catch you later,' Tom says, following suit.

'Aw, not going with your boyfriend tonight, Bobby?' Harriet says.

Why would she say that? Is it seeping out of me? I know what I am, who I am. I'm not a virus.

'Slumming it on the bus, Harriet,' I say, with one eye on Lou's movements.

'Perfectly efficient, perfectly comfortable. The right to a good public transport system is what I say,' Cal adds.

Harriet and I look at each other, then Cal.

I have to go, move, shift.

I catch up with him just before he slides his helmet on.

'Hey, Lou.'

'Yeah?'

'I was thinking …'

'Be careful, that shit can hurt.'

'Eh?'

'So, you were thinkin'?'

'Yeah, I was thinking. Would you like to … erm … would you like to … thing is … we … my mate and I …'

'Jesus Christ! Spit it out, Bobby. I'm growin' a beard here.'

'Just wondering if you want to come over to mine on Friday night?'

'*Mine*, as in your house?'

'Yes, me and a mate are getting a takeaway and just, like, chilling and stuff.'

God, I hate how I sound around him.

'A mate?'

'Bel. She's a girl. I mean, she's a mate, but she's also a girl. She's a friend. Not my girlfriend though. Just a mate. A female mate.'

I want the concrete to crumble beneath me. Left side of my brain is screaming: STOP BEING A KNOB. BE YOURSELF, BOBBY.

'Friday night?' Lou says.

'Yes.'

'Takeaway?'

'Yes.'

'You do know takeaway is worse than horse shit, Bobby?'

'You don't have to eat it.'

'You're right, I don't,' he says, patting me on the shoulder.

'I mean, if you prefer toast and jam – sorry, *jello* – I can sort that out no problem.'

'I'll stick to the horse shit, Bobby.'

'So, you up for it then?'

'Sure. Sounds average. What time?'

'Say, seven?'

'Cool.'

'Great, it's a date then,' I say.

Another concrete-crumbling moment.

Lou gives me a raised brow.

Does he wink?

We exchange numbers.

'See you Friday, I guess,' Lou says.

'Friday,' I say.

I watch him rev off into the night. I jog, hoping to catch up with the others.

*

I settle myself on the edge of Mum's bed, trying to conceal my worry. Eyes can't lie though. Covers are up to her neck, just a sorrowful head popping out the top. I swipe a few hairs away from her eyes. I badly want her to shift her arse into gear, to get up, face the day, fight the bloody world. *Stop lying down, stop convincing yourself that you're bedridden, that every ounce of your body is numb and unresponsive. You're consigning yourself to all this: these four walls, questionable music and starched sheets. Come on, woman, it's supposed to be me and Danny who cave under this inescapable fear, not you.* Oh, shut up, Bobby. You don't live in her body, do you? You don't feel yours withering inside, do you? No, you simply observe and make crass judgements from the edge of a fucking bed. Allow her a little defeatism, for God's sake.

And that's the thing I sometimes fail to see: the physical struggle versus the mental torture. I guess that's how her thoughts spin: I'll never be able to jump inside Mum's psyche, Mrs Sneddon'll never get into mine and I'll never occupy Lou's. That's how it goes.

'Who's coming again?' Mum asks.

'It's a just a friend from the Poztive group,' I tell her.

'A friend?' she says.

'Just some guy. His mum isn't well. He looks after her.'

'Oh, right.'

'Me, Bel and the guy –'

'Who doesn't have a name.'

'He's called Lou, Mum.'

'Well, I'm glad you're making friends, Bobby.'

'Just a takeaway and a bit of music. Maybe watch a film. Want to come down and meet him for a bit? Bel's already here. You could eat with us?'

'Can't, I'm going out dancing with the girls,' she says, fierce grin painting her face. I'm reassured when Mum cracks her rubbish jokes, elated when her speech is coherent. 'Some other time.'

'Mum?'

'Bobby?'

'The guy from Poztive, *he's* the guy.'

'What?'

'Lou, *he's* the guy.'

'Speak English, Bobby.'

'Lou's the guy who might be able to get some gear for your birthday.'

Mum twists her face as though I've said something horrific. She manages to extend an arm over the covers.

'Gear? What gear? What you on about?'

I lean towards her and whisper, 'You know, *the gear*. The hash or grass you asked me to get for you.'

She looks at me with utter bemusement.

'Bobby, I've honestly no idea what you're talking about.'

'For your birthday.'

'Whose birthday?'

'You asked me a couple of weeks ago, remember?' I plead. 'It's what you want for your birthday, Mum.'

I see the wheels turning as she scuffles with her memory. And there it is: in that little exchange, any reassurance or elation I might've felt is blown to pieces, my soul shredded.

'I didn't ask you for that,' she says. 'I assure you, Bobby, I didn't ask for that.'

I want to shake it out of her, to shake all the pennies rattling around in her memory bank. Scream into her face. Suck the answer out of her ears. Wrench it out of her mouth. I want to howl. Because, at the very beginning, at the diagnosis stage, the doctors warned us that this could happen. *At first, there might be absent-minded moments, which could deteriorate into more serious episodes of short-term memory loss.*

We're a hop, skip and jump away from Mum being locked up in a wasteland. Welcome to Fuckedland.

'You're right, sorry,' I say, wanting to diffuse the situation, avoid terrorising her. Too late, it's happened. It's alive. I know it and she knows it. 'I was joking! It was a joke,' I say.

'It's not too late to hand you back, is it?' she says.

'I'd better get down to Bel and Danny.'

'Have a good night with your deaf friend.'

'He's not deaf.'

'Not yet, but he'll wish he was after a night with you and Bel.' She smiles.

'What can I say, Mother? Comedy gold.'

I wash my face before ambling downstairs. Plop a couple of drops in my eyes. It's almost seven. What's the point in even asking Lou now?

'Hey, I'm pure starving,' Bel says.

'Me too,' Danny says. 'I could eat a nun's arse.'

They snigger.

'We should order,' Bel says.

'I want pizza,' Danny says.

'Pizza and then up to your room, Dan. OK? You can play Xbox,' I say.

'Don't want to stay down here with you bores anyway,' he replies.

'Hey … excuse me, Danny,' Bel says.

'No, you're decent, Bel.'

'Better be.'

'Right, I'm warning you two – when Lou comes, don't just sit there staring at him like a couple of mental patients, OK?'

'Oh, shut up, Bobby,' Bel says. 'You'd give an Aspirin a sore head.'

Danny repeats Bel's words and almost wets himself on the sofa. It's like being a primary school teacher sometimes.

'I'm serious,' I tell him. 'Just act normal. In fact, scratch that. Don't!'

'Keep your skirt on, Bobby. You'd think the priest was coming the way you're strutting about,' Bel says.

'Just don't want to make a show of us, that's all,' I say.

'A show of us? Listen to yourself. He's only someone who goes to that daft self-help group of yours.'

'Thanks, Bel. You have about as much compassion as an acid attack.'

'Just telling you to cool the jets, that's all.'

'Yeah, well, we don't get many visitors here, do we?'

'I think he'd better hurry up,' Bel says, looking at her phone.

'We should just order without him,' Danny adds.

'How rude is that, Dan, eh?' I say.

'Why don't we order *for* him then,' Bel suggests.

'Good idea. Isn't it, Bobby?' Dan says.

'We can't do that,' I say.

'Yes, we can,' he says.

'It's no big deal,' Bel says. 'Just order him a Margherita. If he doesn't like pizza he's obviously been born without taste buds.'

'Or he's gay.'

'Danny!' I shout. 'What have I told you about that?'

I know I should be monitoring Danny's internet use, be more vigilant with him. I can't be letting him go around spouting this shit. Can't have a Trumpian bigot on my hands now. Maybe I need to have a word with his teachers. Or have a Sibling Night, just the two of us. I'll add 'stop my little brother from having offensive views' to my list of chores.

We order.

Danny and Bel maul their food like they're competing for the title of World's Most Repulsive Eater. I leave four slices of mine. Lou's pizza lies chilling in its box. Bel glares at it like a serial killer sat in a van. Danny takes himself up to his room, burping loudly en route. Nice one, Dan.

'I don't think your drug dealer's coming, Bobby,' Bel says.

'Ever thought of becoming a detective, Bel?'

'Don't take it out on me because your scooter boyfriend hasn't turned up.'

'I'm not.'

'Not my fault.'

'Did I say it was?'

'No, but I can tell you're thinking it. I know you, Bobby Seed. You've got one of those weird-working brains.'

'I think you've overdosed on pizza.'

'Listen, if Mr Scooter's a no-show I'm having his Margherita. Just saying.' I shake my head. 'No use going to waste.' I tut. 'What? Think of the Africans, Bobby.'

'Whatever, Bel. Charge in.'

'Why don't you just give him a call? Ask what his deal is?'

I take out my phone, thumb through to Lou's number. Stare at it, try to memorise it. Who memorises numbers these days?

'Maybe I should send him a text instead?' I say.

'No.'

'Why?'

'Because he might come back with a question, and before you know it you've each sent twelve texts to each other and you're still none the wiser why he's blanked you,' Bel says. 'Call him.'

'Right.'

'Say, *Hey, Mr Scooter, why did you stand me up?*'

'Can you stop with the date shit, Bel?' I snap.

I mean, is a guy not allowed to be friends with another guy without this shit being slung at it?

'Touchy.'

'And it's a vintage fucking Vespa he rides, not a scooter.'

'Whatever. God!'

'How many times?'

I'm heating up. I sense steam building inside me, but it isn't what Bel said, it's all to do with the conversation I had with Mum. I see the future – a kaleidoscope of horrific images – zipping through my mind. My brain's like an ailing heartbeat: clobbering, thrashing, pounding. But I guess it is also about Lou not turning up.

Then my phone buzzes and blinks.

Hey dude, apologies for my absence. Mom was in a bad way earlier. Totally fucked up day. U no how it is. Nother time. Thats a Lou promise. Be Poztive. Stay Poztive … whatever it is. It's full of shit!!!! HaHa.

I thrust my phone into Bel's face.

She holds on to my wrist and reads.

'See, he's a carer for his mum. It's not easy for him to get away, Bel.'

'OK, calm down to a riot, Bobby,' she says.

But I'm not calm, am I?

#5 … incomplete

lou is margherita red
bobby is future blue
bel ate all the pizza
whoop de fucking doo

Dan Does His Homework

A few days later the doctor and nurse come after we get back from school. The nurse spends time bathing and massaging Mum. I think they hate the playlist I've made for those moments. No doubt she's into some sterile shit and hasn't a clue who Slowdive, Sonic Youth or The Smashing Pumpkins are. Truth, I'm a sterile shit fan too. Whisper it.

I know by the doctor's face things look bleak. Need to shield Danny from it, make sure his uniform's folded properly and set aside, allow him some pre-homework telly time to munch Rice Krispies (evening course) and watch *Horrid Henry*. How he loves that show. Always good to hear his laughter wafting through the house.

I know what to expect. Google told me, as have the doctors, the nurses and the countless documentaries I've watched about it. The internet's full of bad news pages.

Like an evil magnet, the internet grabs hold of your jugular and distorts your sense of rationale. It's nigh on impossible not to gorge on WorstCaseScenario.com.

I catch the doctor at the bottom of the stairs, out of Danny's earshot. She's actually very nice; always caring and kind. My only issue is that while she understands Mum's body, no dispute over that, she hasn't the foggiest about what goes on between her ears. That's where my tepidness comes from.

'So, what do you think?' I ask.

'It's hard to say. On the surface she seems fine, but clearly she's not. Some memory loss is definitely beginning to show up. Thing is, she might be back to normal tomorrow, that's how unpredictable this can be. It's the nature of relapse and recovery.'

BUT IT'S YOUR JOB TO KNOW!

'But when will ...'

'With this illness, Bobby, we just don't know with any degree of certainty. As you know, your mum's condition is lifelong. She's not terminal, but she is deteriorating. I see this in cases time and again.' PLEASE DO NOT REDUCE MY MOTHER TO A *CASE*. 'Your mum is reaching the second-ary progressive stage.' Or, as I call it, the BBBBB stage – brain, body, bones, bladder buggered stage.

'You're sure?'

'We've suspected this for a good while. I think your mum has been expecting it too.'

I say nothing. Doctors, what the fuck do they know?

'You've probably noticed that your mum has lost some bowel function.'

'I have.'

'And her balance has been … troublesome.'

'Worse than that. She can hardly get out of bed now.'

'And she's exhausted more than ever.'

PLEASE, SHUT UP. I GET IT!

'She is,' I say.

'How's her speech been?' the doctor asks.

'Sometimes you'd never notice, but other times you do,' I say. Reality is, she's like a blathering drunk.

'That's common.'

I've done my research. I know Mum's body is fuddled, a matter of time before her whole system regresses. We've discussed the implications over several listens of Nirvana and Teenage Fanclub albums. The whats, ifs, whens and whys have been aired. Full-time hospice care terrifies her, and me, yet it might be the only viable option. However, if it all goes belly up before I hit eighteen, then the social workers will be sniffing around us. She's scared for me and Dan, I think.

'Her birthday's coming up. Do you think she'll be OK by then?' I ask the doctor. 'What I mean is, will she be OK to celebrate it? Like, celebrate it properly?'

'Well, I don't think she'll be doing any dancing, if that's what you mean.' The doctor smiles.

Wait a minute!

WAIT A FUCKING MINUTE!

Did the doctor just crack a joke? Did she just rip the piss out of Mum's situation? Did I hear that right? My expression warns her: I'm not going to be complicit in any unprofessional piss-ripping activities here. Only Mum (and me) can piss-rip her situation. Everyone else: door closed.

The doctor's face alters: sincere, caring. 'I can't say, Bobby. Really I can't. They'll probably give her some further tests to assess things.' She now looks desperate, etched with worry and concern. Or is it pity?

'Will she be OK up here?' I say, pointing to my temple. 'Will her senses remain intact?'

'As I said, each case is different, so I can't say one way or the other.'

There it is again, Mum reduced to a case.

'Is she sleeping?' I ask.

'I gave her a couple of tablets. She really needs sleep. It's unhelpful if she's constantly exhausted and lying awake all night.'

'Agreed.'

Two minutes later I'm opening the front door and waving the doctor off.

'Have a good night, Bobby, and try not to worry too much,' the doctor says, hotfooting it to her shiny car.

I want to follow her. I need to escape the house, get some air into my lungs, allow the wind to ransack me. I imagine the sound of a vintage Vespa, close my eyes for a second and

143

listen to its clattering engine fizz around my insides. I inhale the exhaust fumes and smell that freedom. And I'm away. We're away.

I wave and slam the door.

'Danny, finish watching that TV!' I shout into the living room.

'Two minutes.'

'No, not two minutes. Now.'

'One minute.'

'You've homework to do,' I say, walking into his space.

'Twenty seconds.'

'I'm not waiting any longer.'

'Ten seconds.'

'Fine. I'll tell your teachers you couldn't be arsed.'

'No. No, I'm coming.' He practically knocks me over in his eagerness to get his homework done. Strange. Must have gained a healthy fear of his teachers.

I settle him at the kitchen table in the company of school books. Head down, brain active.

'Do the best you can, Danny. Try and impress your teachers.'

'Can you help me, Bobby?'

'Look, you're going to have to learn to do your own homework. You need to get the finger out.'

'But I can't do this maths stuff, it's really hard,' he says.

'How many times have I've shown you? I've lost count. Do you want people thinking you're ...' And that's where I stop myself from saying the word 'stupid'. Anyway, thankfully he's stopped listening to me banging on about his homework. I mean, who gives a shit about homework? Really, who gives a toss? I'm glad Danny's head is still in Horrid Henry's world. I'm irrationally annoyed because I can't call him stupid, thick, dim, brainless or an eejit when I want to. That's how it is between us: I get irritated at Dan for the slightest thing, then feel guilty for getting irritated, so I compensate by indulging him.

I reach into my pocket, pull out a coin.

'Here, Dan, do you want fifty pence to get yourself a packet of crisps in the tuck shop tomorrow?' I say.

His face beams.

'Really?'

I flick him the gleaming coin, which he catches one-handed.

He examines it.

'Fifty pence, brilliant.'

Feeds it to his pocket.

'That's to buy crisps, not chocolate and *not* a sugar drink, OK?'

'Gotcha. Thanks, Bobby.'

'I mean it. No fizzy drink.'

'Roger that.'

'Right, get that homework done now.'

'Double Roger that.'

I open the fridge to see what's available. Slide the two

drawers at the bottom towards me. Listen to the huffs and puffs Danny makes over his maths. I remove some bright orange cheese, start cutting its crusted edges away.

'Bobby?'

'What is it, buddy?'

'I don't think Mum is in an OK place.'

'Why do you say that?'

'Her eyes are different. I see them – she thinks I can't but I can.'

'Her eyes are tired, mate.'

'It's like her eyes have lost weight.'

'Just lack of sleep, Dan.'

'But she hardly ever comes downstairs any more or asks how our day has been.'

'The stairs knacker her. They're too much sometimes.'

I see him withdrawing into himself and tutting.

And tutting more.

'She doesn't even crack jokes the way she used to.'

'She's not a bloody comedian, Dan!'

I don't mean to snap … actually I do.

'Keep your jeggings on! I'm just saying.'

'What, Dan? What are you just saying?'

'I don't think she has a cold like you said.'

I did say that. Guilty!

'Did I say that?'

'Yes, you told me that she had a cold, but I know it's much worse.'

'Like what?' I fire at him, and continue hacking at the diseased cheese, hoping he'll stop.

'It's not a cold, is it?'

I glare at my cheese-gripping hand.

'Is it, Bobby?'

'No, it's not a cold.' I can't look at him.

Now, here's a conundrum: should I lie, tell him everything's one big jolly lollipop, manipulate his misunderstanding of Mum's illness, take full advantage of Danny's sense of the world, or should I tell the truth?

'So tell me,' he says. 'I'm part of this family too. If *you* know, then so should I.'

I go to him. Sit down. A gesture that makes his eyebrows droop with worry.

'What, Bobby? What is it?'

'Look, mate, Mum needs a bit more help these days. Her illness is affecting her more than it used to.'

'Like how more?'

'Well, she'll need someone to work her muscles, Danny.'

'Like footballers?'

'A bit, I suppose.'

'Maybe we could put her in a bath.'

'What? Why?'

'With ice. Cristiano Ronaldo does that and it helps him play like a demon.'

'Mum needs to exercise her legs, to get moving. She needs us to help her with walks and stuff.'

'She's not a blinking dog, Bobby.'

'No, I know, she's –'

'So don't treat her like a dog!' Danny screams. 'She doesn't bark.'

'Dan, it's her muscles, they aren't working so well.'

'Why don't her muscles work, Bobby? I don't understand how your muscles can stop working.'

'It's just part of what's happening to her.'

'Is that why she wobbles?'

He's on the cusp.

I know the signs.

'Partly, Dan. Partly.'

'Bobby, tell me, is she going to be OK tomorrow and the next day and the next day and the –'

'Stop, Dan!'

'Answer then.'

'Yes, she's going to be OK tomorrow. You shouldn't be thinking things like that.'

'You promising?'

'Look, Danny, Mum's going to have days when she's feeling really unwell and days when she'll be upset because she's unable to do things she used to do.'

'What things?'

'Like going to the park and the shops.'

'And McDonald's?'

'And McDonald's.'

'And coffee at Costa?'

'Look, she might be in a really good mood tomorrow,' I say.

'So that's a promise then?'

'No, Danny, I'm not promising anything ...'

'I told you, I'm not stupid, I see things. I know when the shit stuff is happening, like the other night.'

'No one is saying you're stupid, Dan. No one's ever said that. I don't even know why you're saying that.'

'People at your school think I'm stupid.'

'My school? What's that got to do with it?'

'They think I'm stupid. That's why they wouldn't let me go there.'

'Not true, Danny. And don't go around saying stuff like that, OK?'

'That's why I was sent to my school.'

'It's a bit more convoluted than that.'

'I know what *convoluted* means, Bobby, so there's no use using big words.'

'Well, it *is* convoluted.'

'I don't want to go to your shitty school anyway.'

'What you talking about then?'

'I'm talking about why you won't tell me that Mum isn't going to die.'

'God, would you give up, Danny!' I spit. 'Mum's not well, she's fucking ill.' I find myself welling up, which I never do in front of him; it isn't something I want Danny to witness. 'She's sick and in a lot of pain sometimes.'

'Is that why she cries a lot?'

'Partly.'

'So it isn't me who makes her cry then?'

I'm not sure if I should scud him with his maths book or squeeze some love and security into him. I freeze, stare his way and compose myself. I speak calmly.

'No, it isn't you, Dan. She's having a rough time and it's important we're there for her, that we don't cause too much trouble around the house. You and me both.'

Danny's eyes are glued to the kitchen table.

'I well and truly Roger that.'

'You wouldn't like to see her in pain, would you?'

'Never. Not Mum.'

I try to redirect our conversation, more for my benefit.

'How's school going?' I ask.

'It's going shitey knickers.'

'Can't be that bad.'

'It is.'

'I thought school was going well?'

'It's flaps!'

'Danny! Who's teaching you these words?'

'I know loads of cool words.'

'Yes, but who told you that one?'

'Bel.'

'Bel?'

'Yes.'

'When?'

'When you went to that group thing one night.'

'Well, it's not a good word. I'll be having it out with Bel. I don't want you saying it again, OK?'

Danny nods. And yet again I morph into his parent. Suppose I'd better get used to it.

I resume cheese-slicing duties and put bread under the grill.

'Cheese toastie good for you?'

'Bobby?'

'Yeah.'

'Will you look after me if Mum dies before we do?'

Feels like a stiletto slashing my spleen. I want to yank him from his chair, hold him tight against my chest, reassure him, stroke his hair. I look at him. Pause. I don't know how to react; I tell him what he might want to hear.

'Jesus, Danny, of course I'll look after you. Course I will.'

'You'd better,' he says, shoving his nose back into the maths book.

'I'll always look after you, Dan. Always.'

He doesn't look up from his homework.

'Can I have ketchup on my toastie?'

'Sure.'

Alphabet Chat

It's quite possible Mum doesn't want it now, since she doesn't remember asking me in the first place. Yet her memory could be restored any time: tonight, tomorrow, next day. And when it does, I want to be ready with her present – if Lou can sort me out. However, if she doesn't recall a thing, well, I guess me and Bel will be having a *Joint* Food Friday sesh. A win-win situation.

I hover around outside the hall plucking up the courage to go inside. I know tonight's meeting is going to be different somehow. I play over what I'm planning to say and how I should say it. And, after that, I do it again. Bel and me have done some serious practice, although practice never really prepares you for the real thing, does it? Practice doesn't account for severe dry tongue, a croaky throat and the other person's interjections. In this instance, practice will certainly not make perfect.

I'm standing out of sight, watching them all roll in. Roddy arrives first, driving some pure dive of a car. This gunslinger gets out, twirling the car keys around his finger and whistling some ditty. He opens the boot and removes a large suitcase. New clothes for the poor young carers? He slams the boot shut, locks the doors manually – that's how old this car is – all the while maintaining his twirling and whistling. Safe to say, Roddy is riding on some high cloud.

Lou follows shortly after. He takes his helmet off, fixes his hair in the little mirror on his bike. He then unstraddles, stands for a split second before yanking his jeans up, and I mean really yanking them up. Runs his hands through his hair another time and adjusts his shoulders: a prizefighter at a weigh-in. This is followed by further jeans-yanking. God, imagine if he sees me, standing here pure gawking at him. What excuse could I provide? Imagine if the others see me. Lou heads inside, sort of semi-running, bounding even. Strange eagerness, I think, given his apathy towards anything to do with Poztive.

Harriet has her hood up – it isn't hood weather – and walks purposefully, a human *Do Not Disturb* sign. I guess her hood is to do with street cred. Or to shield her from embarrassment in case anyone in her school nobbles her.

The rest follow as though they're straight out of a Lowry painting.

Which leaves just me. They won't start without me, will they? They won't make any plans? I give it a couple of minutes to allow the nerves to settle.

No crescent-shaped seating this time. People are lounging on the floor. On beanbags. I pause to take in the scene. Very hippy, dippy, trippy. When I see Roddy I do a double take. He's standing rigid, microphone in hand. Behind him a screen, and on it are words: words of song titles. The penny drops. Oh, no. Please say it isn't so. Can we not do the sticking-pins-in-eyes game instead? Where in Roddy's mind did he get the idea that bringing a karaoke machine to our Poztive meeting would excite anyone? At what point in his day did he think, *I know, I'll force a group of reticent young carers to sing in front of each other, that'll be a wicked idea.*

I arrive just as the music kicks in. I recognise the song instantly. 'Bat Out of Hell' isn't a bad tune, but I hate it with a passion.

With his non-mic hand, Roddy waves me forward, indicating that I should plank it on a beanbag. As I walk towards the rest of the group, Harriet turns and fakes her own hanging, complete with dangling tongue like a dog in a drought. Lou catches my attention too, his eyes wide as if to say: *Get this guy, dude – what the fuck!* The others are in a state of hypnotic, cultish mortification. I sit, well, sort of collapse next to Harriet, who gives me a look that captures her sense of exasperation perfectly. Her face suggests that she'd much rather be at home reading *Chat* magazine to her mother, anything not to have to bear this torture.

'All right?' I say.

'Don't even ask,' Harriet murmurs.

'We're doing karaoke now?' I whisper.

'No *we* about it,' she says.

Roddy's eyes are closed and he's well into the guts of the song. The sound quality is awful, but nowhere near as bad as his singing.

'I don't even know what he's chanting,' Harriet adds. 'Is that even a song?'

'Don't know what it is,' I lie, but I could've sung the whole song myself without the lyrics being beamed on to a screen.

'It's crap, whatever it is,' she says.

'Tell me about it.'

'*Like a bat out of hell ... Like a bat out of heeeellll.*' Roddy holds that final note much longer than the machine music requires, finishing with an enormous crescendo and sweeping swipe of an arm.

You can practically hear the toes curling inside everyone's knackered trainers. This definitely isn't the first time he's performed this, no way. This is born out of hours, maybe even years, of rehearsal in a bedroom somewhere.

There's no applause. No whooping. No congratulations. Just lots of staring at the floor, shuffling feet and miscellaneous beanbag noises. Erin looks as if she wants to burst out crying. I know how she feels. Lou seems paralysed by this parallel universe he's somehow found himself in.

Breathing heavily, Roddy lowers the mic.

'Who's next?' he bleats.

There's no way any of us are about to volunteer our singing

services. No stampede to rush and tackle the mic out of his hand. We could be sitting here until the Queen dies and no one would volunteer. Roddy points the mic towards each of us in turn. What ensues is a kind of karaoke stare-off.

'No way I'm getting up to sing,' Harriet finally pipes up.

'Just exercising the right to say no,' Cal says.

'Me too,' Erin says. 'Sorry.'

'No danger, don't even ask,' Tom adds.

'Not even if you paid me, dude,' Lou states.

'Kill me now,' Clare says.

I don't give Roddy the courtesy of a verbal rebuttal: a simple finger wag is enough.

'So ... OK then ... that means ... well ... OK, that's fine ... I accept your decisions, I am cool with that ... I mean, you're adults, right? Young adults. You can opt out of activities, yeah? You can say no, that's your right, right? I mean ... I mean, it's not Stalinist Russia we're living in here, is it?' Roddy stutters out.

I genuinely feel sorry for him. The way he's being demeaned by the group is wrong. All he's doing is trying to cut us some slack, trying to help us escape our domestic strife. Trying to put a smile on our miserable mugs. He only belted out a song. Not as if he ran his own child-burning cult. No crime has been committed. Well, maybe against light entertainment.

It's clear he wants to let loose a torrent of abuse, roar at us for being selfish and ungrateful little bastards. And who'd blame him? But that's the thing with the type of teenagers we are: people are warned to tread carefully, to show compassion. In other words, don't do anything to knock our emotions off-kilter. While I sympathise, Roddy should know the score. He's been where we are. I'm half thinking of grabbing that mic and telling him to hit the 'All You Need Is Love' button. Only a fleeting thought though.

'But look, guys, when we go off on our residential in a couple of weeks there will be many activities that you'll be expected to take part in,' Roddy states.

'But we're not at the residential, Rod,' Lou says. 'We're sittin' on some nasty-ass beanbags.'

'I'm aware of that, Lou, but the message I'm getting here is that people are reluctant to drop their guard and participate in something that will take them out of their comfort zone.'

'I guess that's about the size of it,' Lou says.

'I'm so bad at singing,' Erin says. 'Really sorry.'

'I'm a terrible singer too,' Roddy says.

'Yeah, we know,' Lou says.

Everyone laughs.

'That's the point,' says Roddy. 'Who cares? It's about having fun, enjoying yourselves. Fun! Remember that feeling, guys? That feeling of being young, of letting your hair down, remember it? Of not caring what people think about you, of not giving a shit about what perception you're giving off? No? Well, you should be living that time right now. These are the times when great memories are created, guys. I'm talking about *you*, you the individual, not the stuff that goes on at home, that's out of our control, but this –' Roddy points to his head and heart '– this right here, this is something that you and you alone have real control and power over. Never let anyone take that power away from you, guys. And don't ever let anyone tell you that you can't or shouldn't do something because it makes *them* feel awkward or embarrassed. Do it because it makes *you* feel good.' Roddy's panting and a little sweaty with the strength of feeling he's put into his speech. Although that could be the remnants of 'Bat Out of Hell'.

After those rousing words, if he isn't able to get the masses to rise as one and break into a rendition of 'Single Ladies' or 'Uptown Funk' then I'm afraid Roddy is flogging not only a dead horse but an entire stable full of them. We sit in a shameful silence.

'Right, speech over,' Roddy bellows, clapping his hands. 'Someone help me put this stuff away, and get yourselves into pairs. Shove those nasty beanbags to the side and grab a chair. Face your partner. Girls you can create a group of three.' We dance to his tune, do exactly what he asks.

Lou makes a beeline towards me. Sits his chair in front of mine. I rub my sweaty hands on my thighs.

'Hey, sorry for the no-show on Friday, dude.'

'Friday?' I act like I don't know what he's talking about. 'Friday? Oh, yes, Friday. Not a problem, Lou.'

'Some other time, yeah?'

'Totally some other time.'

'Cool,' he says, but doesn't move away, obviously wants to make sure we're paired together. I'm trying to be ultra-smooth but my insides are like a simmering volcano.

'That Roddy shit was super intense,' Lou says.

'Intense is the word,' I say. We sit facing each other. I cross my legs. Lou's are spread apart. I focus on his eyes.

'Gonna be one of these shit improv games,' Lou says.

'Looks like it.'

'It's our punishment.'

'Yeah, maybe one of us should have sung,' I say.

'Fuck, no, I'd much rather be doin' this.'

'Right,' Roddy bellows over the cynical chat. 'Listen up, this exercise is all about thinking fast and using your intelligence to drive and advance conversation.'

'Told you,' Lou says.

Does he wink?

Roddy continues, 'What you're required to do is a simple exchange of dialogue –'

'What's the *but*?' Harriet interrupts.

'The *but*,' Roddy says, 'is that the first word each person speaks must begin with the next letter of the alphabet.'

This is greeted with a chorus of 'Eh?'s and 'Don't get it's.

'You all know the alphabet, don't you?' Roddy asks. Silence. 'Good, that's a relief.'

'And?' Tom says.

'So person one here –' Roddy taps me on the dome '– starts with letter A. For example, "*Are* you coming out tonight?" And person two –' he rests his hand on Lou's head: Lou flinches '– answers using letter B. For example, "*Better* not, as I've a ton of homework to do."'

People begin nodding their heads. Not Lou though.

'Do you get it, Lou?' Roddy asks.

'I get it. I get it. Just don't touch the head, dude,' Lou spits.

'Oh, pardon me for messing that hair of yours,' Roddy says, looking around at some of the others. 'We've a hairdryer in the back, if it helps.' There's some muffled laughter. Not from Lou, who looks bullish.

'Just respect personal space, dude. That's it, no big deal.'

Everyone's eyes are on the two of them. I'm rigid, trying to move only my eyes.

'Well, I apologise for the invasion,' Roddy says.

'That's what they all say afterwards,' Lou says. God, I want to gasp, to open my mouth wide. I feel the need to be melodramatic.

Roddy glares at Lou.

Lou glares in return.

'Well, as I said,' Roddy starts, ending the glare-off, 'this exercise helps with quick thinking. It also aids communication skills, and above all it's a fun thing to do. Fun, remember that, Lou? Let's embrace some fun tonight.'

Lou nods sarcastically.

'Fun it is,' he says.

'OK, you can start when you're ready.' Roddy walks away from us. I remove my heart from the blender.

Tom and Cal dive straight in. The girls wave Roddy over for further clarification. Lou and me stare at each other. I shift up in my chair. Lou's still got the dregs of annoyance in his eyes; his chest bobs and weaves through his denim. A bull on the comedown.

'You OK?' I ask him.

'Yeah, fine.'

'Don't let Roddy get to you.'

'It all just gets to you sometimes, don't it?' I can't tell if he's talking about Roddy, his mum or something else. Not a good time to press, I think.

A flash of clarity arrives. Light-bulb moment. I could use this game to ask Lou what I'd been wanting to all along, help me beat the nerves. 'Ready?' I say.

'Can't wait,' he says.

'OK, I'll begin, if that's OK with you?'

'Shoot.'

I pause for thinking time.

'*Are* you able to do something for me, Lou?' I say.

His eyes tighten, not understanding if the game's started or if I've veered off course. I give him a look of encouragement. He shuffles himself up in his chair.

'*Being* honest with you, dude, depends what that something might be.' A little smile drifts across his face, suggesting

161

that he's well up for the game now. He's mastered letter B. How hard can this be?

'*Can* you get your hands on some stuff for me?' I lean in closer. 'Gear?'

Lou guffaws.

This isn't what Bel and me had practised; in fact, it's so far away from what we'd practised.

Lou scratches the back of his head. My left knee shakes up and down.

'*Do* I look like the type of guy you can pin labels on, Bobby?'

'*Everyone* can be labelled, Lou.'

'*Fuck* that shit.'

'*Grass* or hash, come on, I know you can get me something,' I say, through a wry smile. Lou grins too, which then becomes a snigger. He rubs his thighs, fixes his hair. Is he sussing me out? I think he is. His cheeks inflate.

'*Hash* I can maybe get,' he says.

'*In* a few days?'

'*Jesus* Christ, dude. Give me some time to process this shit.'

The K is tough. I have to think hard. Lou seems to enjoy my struggle. I have something, but I'm a bit wary of saying it, split between embarrassment and fear.

'Come on, dude, I wanna get outta this place tonight.'

I swallow saliva and blurt it out:

'*Kisses* are coming your way if you can,' I say. Lou's smile vanishes. 'No, no, metaphorical kisses, I mean.'

162

'*Let* me ask my man and I'll get back to you.'

'*Maybe* you can give me his or her number when we get out of here?'

'*Not* going to happen.'

'*Or* maybe not.'

'*Probably* not.'

'*Quite* a relief, you helping me out,' I say, puffing my own cheeks out.

'*Right*, let's talk how much you want and how much you wanna pay,' Lou says.

'*Seriously*, I know next to nothing about these things, but I am thinking maybe enough for three or four joints.'

'*That* can be arranged my friend, thinkin' five per joint.'

'*Unless* you do mates rates, that is. Do you do discounts for friends?' I ask cheekily.

'*Very* big balls you've got there, Bobby.'

I giggle. '*Would* you roll them for me as well? I wouldn't know how to. Please?'

Lou shakes his head at my brazenness. Or my very big balls. He's struggling with the letter X. The torment of searching for an appropriate word is scratched all over his face. Until, that is, Roddy interrupts with a loud, 'You can skip the letter X if you want.' Lou's smile reappears.

'*Yes*, Bobby. I can get you some joints, which *I* will roll for you. And I'm willin' to go four-fifty a joint. Friend's price. Anything else?'

I shake my head.

'*Zilch*,' I say and lean forward with my hand extended.

Lou's hand is cold and dry.

'That seemed to work,' Roddy says. 'Now, would any pairing like to show the rest of the group the conversation you created?'

Lou and me stare at each other knowingly.

I really didn't want to ask Lou in the first place. However, desperate times and all that. I want him to see me as this sorted, confident high-achiever type, not some crazed loser, which is maybe how I come across. Pot, kettle, black if he did.

Whatever.

Is what it is.

Am what I am.

Skinheads

I want to rush to Mum's room and tell her that I've sourced some gear. All systems go and all that. But I don't do anything. I'm flopped on my bed enjoying the silence of the house and the flickerings of my thoughts. I replay the conversation exercise with Lou and chuckle at its bizarreness. It was like we had this telepathy going on. Bel texts to tell me she's almost at our front door.

When I do go into Mum's room I'm startled. She's sitting upright in bed, smiling. In no obvious pain. She knows who I am.

'You're up,' I say.

'Honestly, Bobby, you should join the police. They're missing your genius.'

'No, I mean, it's good you're up. You feeling OK?'

'I feel fine. I've had lots of sleep.'

'You in pain?'

'Only now that I'm seeing you.'

'Brilliant news!' And it is.

I don't say anything about the gear. I don't want to know if she remembers.

'Bel will be here in a minute. Want to come down and see her?'

'Maybe she can cut this mop of mine,' Mum says, rummaging through her stringy hair.

'What about me? Am I sacked?'

'No, but I do think Bel has a genuine future in that industry. We should help her.'

'Mum, don't be cruel.'

'Guilty.'

'You want her to do it or not?'

'OK.'

'Right, I'll text her, tell her to get into role.' I send a quick message. Then hear her arrive downstairs.

Mum tries to swing her legs off the bed. She winces, but hides it.

'I need a pee, son,' she says.

I carry her to the toilet, place my hands on her shoulders: she requires balancing even when seated. I whistle The Smiths song 'The Boy with the Thorn in His Side'. In mid-flow, she turns her head, beams up at me. I see her teeth, still holding their pearl colour. Everything about her glows. She looks youthful, like a girl actually, her eyes momentarily without torment. And, from my viewpoint, you wouldn't have known; you'd have thought nothing was wrong. She was just a woman full of life, full of beauty. My mum, full of health. And I know what she's thinking, what she wants to say. It doesn't matter, there's no need for her to tell me. I know. I love her as well. In buckled body or fine frame, I love her in return. She approves the irony of my whistling choice.

When she's done, we wash up, I help her downstairs.

'Hi, Anne, welcome to Bel's Beauty Emporium,' Bel says, standing in the kitchen, instruments in hand. I help Mum into a chair.

'I like what you've done with the place, Bel,' Mum's voice slurs.

Bel looks at me.

I widen my eyes.

Bel wraps a towel around Mum's shoulders.

'Just the usual, Anne?'

'Actually, I might have a change,' Mum says.

'Change is good.'

'Yeah, Mum, change is good.'

'Give me a skinhead then,' Mum orders.

'Sounds good to me,' Bel says, getting ready to snip her scissors into action for a trim. 'One female skinhead coming right up.'

But I see that Mum isn't kidding.

'That's exactly what I want,' she says. 'I'm serious.'

Bel searches for my support.

'I think she is serious, you know,' I say.

'You serious, Anne?'

'As cancer.'

'So … do we even have clippers, Bobby?' Bel asks.

'Eh … I think we have some upstairs,' I say.

'Go get them, son.'

From behind Mum's back, Bel mouths a '*What the fuck?*', clearly reading my mind.

'Why don't we hold off on the haircut for now?' I suggest.

'It's going to be my birthday soon and I want a skinhead. Always wanted one.'

'You do have the right-shaped head for it actually,' Bel says.

My turn to mouth a '*What the fuck?*' to Bel.

'But your birthday's already been sorted, Mum. I got that stuff you asked for.'

I don't mean to tell her, it just blurts out.

'Yeah, he got it, Anne.'

'Remember you asked me?' I say.

'Course I remember, Bobby.'

'Great!' I say, nodding positively. I want to crush her with hugs, and it's got shit all to do with the gear.

'Was it expensive?' Mum asks.

'It's on me. I cut a deal,' I say.

'Listen to you,' Bel says.

'Sounds like a Wall Street banker,' Mum says.

'More like Wally Street wan–'

'OK, OK,' I say.

'You're a good boy, Bobby,' Mum says.

'When do you get it?' Bel asks.

'Picking it up any day now. Leave it to me.'

Bel points to herself and mouths, '*I want some.*' I tease her with a slow headshake and a '*No chance.*'

'Right,' says Bel. 'Are we doing this skinhead or not?'

'Skinhead? Honestly, Mum?'

She lifts her head, shows both of us those pearly teeth.

'You two really are a couple of eejits, aren't you? Of course I don't want a skinhead. I'm ill, not whacko.'

'Thank God for that,' Bel says.

'Yeah, for a moment I was thinking you'd totally lost it,' I tell her.

In that instance her expression changes. She has that look. It's defiance. Rebellion. Whatever it is, it isn't my mum. Her fingers stroke her hair.

'Actually, Bel,' she says. 'Take it all off.'

'What? All of it?' Bel asks.

'Everything,' Mum says.

Blowback

On the bus to Lou's house I'm on edge. I feel like someone's rammed all my organs into a NutriBullet and is about to force-feed them back to me. The bumping bus fails to ease matters, and it's roasting too. Off to collect my contraband, a criminal on his maiden mission. The new shirt I'm wearing is giving me gyp: should I fasten it all the way up or open the top button? Basically, to show or not to show. I attempt both and check out what looks best in my phone's screen. I text Bel, who's holding fort while I do the mule run.

Just give me a squeal if u need anything. All OK?

Who is this?

Bel, I'm serious.

STOP annoying me!

Wot you doin'?

Just watching some YouTube.

Right.

All good here. Don't get murdered.

My mouth is dry, eyes sting with tiredness.

I check the messages.

Lou had written: *Hey dude, got my hands on dem apples you asked 4. U can pick up from my place if easier.*

I'd written: *You got GEAR?????*

Lou had written: *Apples, Bobby. Fuks wrong with you? APPLES!*

I don't want to judge, but I'm surprised that Lou's doing the deal at his house. I thought we'd do it after a Poztive meeting or in a park.

The vintage Vespa is chained up outside his front door. I have no idea of the protocol. I grasp money in one hand, knock with the other.

'Bobby,' he says as he opens the door.

'Hi, Lou,' I say.

'Looking sharp, dude.' He scans my clothes.

'Just chucked it on. I was in a rush.'

'Life's one goddam rush, if you ask me.'

'Yeah.'

'Well, don't just stand there, come in. Come in.'

He steps aside and I enter.

Place doesn't smell uncared for.

I follow him into the living room. Nice. No disability bed under a window or anything like that. I wish I could keep our gaff as tidy. But Lou doesn't have a Danny to look after, and our Danny is basically Stig of the Dump.

'No one here?' I ask.

'Just us,' he says.

'What about …'

'Oh, and Mom. She's upstairs. Sleepin'. She's on some pretty rad meds, so she'll be out cold for the night. You wanna drink or somethin'?'

'No, I'm good.'

It's awkward just standing there without knowing what to say or how to act. Lou makes his way to a cupboard under the telly and whips out a small phalanx of white pencils. Joints.

'This is what I'm talkin' about, Bobby.' He smiles at me. 'The black gold, my friend. The black gold.'

'Cool.'

He holds one joint aloft like he's holding the Olympic torch, as if it's a symbol of great cultural significance.

'These are yours,' he says, showing me a battalion of immaculately rolled joints. 'And this one here is our little treat.'

I was ready for a quick exchange but it looks like Lou's having none of it. He wants to initiate me into the murky world of illegal highs; he won't release the joints unless I puff one he's pre-rolled. Or, as he puts it, 'Only fools flash cash before testing the quality of the hash, dude.'

The Olympic torch is in front of my face. Hypnotic. Never having smoked anything banned in my life, I'm scared shitless. Too terrified to protest. Before I know the score the joint's lit and Lou's sucking the life out of it, the tip poker-red as he drags goodness into his lungs. After holding the smoke in his bloated cheeks for a few seconds, he blows a cloud over my head. I blink, twitch my nose. The smell is intense. I am rigid with fear.

'That shit's the bomb.' Lou holds it out to me in a gesture of kindness and kinship. My turn.

Oh, God!

I guess this is what you'd call peer pressure. It's a strong pulling power. I know I have to hop on a bus home later with all these commuting strangers staring at me – the stoner. I swot the offer away.

'Erm ... erm ... I've ... erm ... never ... really ...'

'That's cool, Bobby. I get it, man. You've got virgin lips, no problem. We all have to start somewhere.'

'No, I want to. I do. I mean, I just don't want to have a whitey, that's all,' I say, trying to sound as though I know all the jargon. 'Will your mum not smell it?'

'She's out cold, don't worry about her.'

'What about your dad?'

'The old man is on business. He does his thing, I do mine.'

'Sisters? Brothers?'

'Just me, dude. Just you and me.'

I run my tongue around my mouth.

'Thing is, Lou, I've never been much of a smoker. I don't fancy the pain of it hitting the back of my throat.'

'No problem, I can sort that. I'll just give you a little blow-back,' Lou says.

Come again?

A what?

I almost vomit up my own heart. For a split second there I thought ... I thought. I can't say what goes through my mind in the gap of that split second.

'Er ... a ... a ... what?' I say.

'A blowback,' he says again. 'It's when you take a puff, hold it in your mouth, then blow it into someone else's mouth.'

'Oh, I see.'

'Think of it as a kind of karmic transference, dude.'

'Karmic ...'

'If nothin' else it will soften the inhalin' process for you.'

'Oh, right!' I say, as if I'm some old-timer, totally entrenched in the joint-smoking fraternity. 'Blowback! Yeah, a blowback could work,' I say.

'OK.' He raises his chin. 'Ready?'

NO!

'Yes. Ready.'

Lou draws the joint to his lips, sucks like a plughole draining water. This boy has impressive lung capacity. He advances, looks me directly in the eye, lifts his free hand to my face and cups it around my jaw, which opens fully. His mouth comes closer to mine. I squeeze my toes. Tighten my hands. Tense my thighs. Our mouths meet. Well, when I say *meet*, what I mean is that there can't be more than three millimetres between us. I feel the heat of his lips. I close my eyes and wait for the surge of smoke to flow from Lou's mouth to mine. It arrives. Boy, does it arrive.

'Inhale it all in, dude,' he whispers.

I do as instructed.

'Come on, don't let it go to waste, Bobby.'

My eyes are still closed but the heat emanating from Lou's lips is making them flicker.

'Want another?' he asks.

'Go on then,' I say, seemingly unable to open my eyes.

And the process begins again.

When I brave sight once more, Lou's slumped on his couch. The sheer embodiment of wasted youth. At first I feel nothing except a readjustment to the light.

'That is one fuckin' profound hit, dude,' Lou says.

Then it happens, the dam bursts directly from my toes and rises all the way up to my head. Like a tornado swirling towards me, affecting all balance and ability to focus.

'Shit, Lou,' I mutter. 'I need to sit down for a minute.'

'Park it, dude. Park it.'

I practically slouch myself right on top of him. He doesn't care. What a state I've become: two blowbacks and I'm gubbed. A deflated balloon. A melted candle. Perhaps all this getting mangled lark isn't my bag after all. Having said that, being stoned for the first time is a rapids ride: a confusing blend of exhilaration *and* distress. I honestly don't know whether I should be in fits of giggles or in deep conversation about existentialism, or just zonked out my noodle, staring at the wall.

Lou has decided on the latter course of action. I skim his living room: typical sort of thing. Couch, two armchairs, coffee table, a few standing plants, a shelf with some books on it and a flat-screen television blinking away in the corner. Very unlike my place, where you'd think squatters had set up home.

Seems like weeks we've been sitting here. Can't recall any conversation we've had. I think we communicate in a series of grunts until it's time for me to jump ship, which is an ordeal in itself. I slide down Lou's couch. That, I remember.

On the bobbling bus ride home – every bit as traumatic as I'd first thought – something rankles. Not a big issue but, still, I can't get it out of my mind. I don't know … Maybe it's the remnants of the hash? So, take my house, for instance: inside there are mountains of clothes piled everywhere and prescriptions of varying kinds line up in the kitchen alongside manky plates and glasses. I do get around to cleaning the mess as often as I can. Basically, what I'm saying is that there's evidence that a sick person is living in my house. But take Lou's place: it's remarkably different, which is no big deal in the grand scheme of things, right? Perhaps it would only take someone in my position to notice the unnatural state of order: the pristine living room, the gleaming kitchen, no empty packs of prescription drugs on view. There's nothing to suggest Lou's home is where illness and disability reside. I find it hard to imagine that he's holding the place together, that he's responsible for the impeccable state of the place, especially given that I left him a sagging mess on the couch.

Either Lou is a clean freak or someone must come in: it's the only explanation.

Stubborn Stones

I am dead late.

When I get back, my resident home help, Bel, is waiting, arms folded and face scorched. I'm half expecting her toe to be tapping. I know it's all for theatre. Bel would much rather be here than at her own place, being provocateur as opposed to the provoked. I'm predicting her to say that she's crashing here. Her dad doesn't give a shit.

'All right?' I say.

'You're cutting it fine,' she says.

I try to stop myself from laughing, I really do. I grit my molars, tense my face, clench my bum together. No use: I explode right in front of her.

'OMG, I can't believe this,' she says.

'What?'

'You're stoned out your box, Bobby Seed.'

'Please don't say OMG. You know I hate that, Bel.'

'I thought you were only going to pick the stuff up?'

'I was.'

'Looks like you swallowed it.'

My body hurls me into ruptured fits of laughter.

'You better sit down,' Bel says.

I try to plant myself on the couch, but collapse on to it instead. It isn't the smoke, it's the hilarity ... of nothing.

'Jesus, Bobby. Get a pure grip.'

I sit up, semi-composed.

'I'm fine. I'm fine.'

'You look wired to the stars. How much did you smoke?'

'Just a few puffs.'

'A few puffs? God, you're such a lightweight.'

My laughter turns into a light trickle of chuckles. Thing is, I'm not that affected by the joint; it's all but worn off, I think. I guess I'm happy(ish) about having been a free-spirited teenager for a few hours. Being Bobby, without thinking about who's eaten what or how to juggle cleaning duties with schoolwork. Sitting on a bus, going to a mate's house, smoking a joint and talking shit seems utterly invigorating. Normal.

'How's Mum been?' I ask.

'Fine, gave her some soup in bed, put the telly on for her, all good.'

'Did she seem better?'

'Just the same.'

'How's her new hairdo?'

'She's loving it.'

'You think?'

'She looks amazing with it, better than Sinéad O'Connor.'

'And Danny?'

'Xbox champion's in his room.'

'He do his homework?'

'What do you think?'

'He can be a little bastard at times.'

'It's tough for him, Bobby.'

'Tough for us all, Bel.'

'I know it is,' she says.

'I mean …' I say, but the words won't come out. It's as if I've swallowed a stone. A stubborn bastard of a stone that won't budge, just sitting blocking up my throat. And I strive to gulp that stone down.

'Hey, Bobby.' Bel comes and sits beside me. 'Why are you crying?'

I shake my head.

She pulls me tight towards her. Bel is strong. I can feel the top of her boob near my head, but I don't mind. I'm happy to rest and be taken care of. And, honestly, I'm not stoned. I'm not. I'm sad.

'Don't, Bobby. Don't,' she says, stroking my hair. 'Everything's going to be OK.'

'It's not, Bel. It's not.'

'Don't say that.'

'It's true.'

'You can't say that, Bobby. You can't. You've got to be strong for Danny, for your mum.'

'And who's strong for me?'

'I'm here for you, Bobby. I'll always be here for you. Do you think I'll ever let you go?' I don't look up. But I know Bel's body is wobbling like mine.

'Thanks, Bel. I love you too.'

Obviously, I don't mean *that* kind of love. Bel knows that, right? She knows it, doesn't she?

'I know you do, Bobby.'

'I just want to be normal, be like everyone else. Be boring.'

'You'll never be like anyone else, Bobby Seed. I mean, just look at who your mum is.'

'Yeah,' I sniff.

'She's going to be OK. She is, you'll see.'

'You've seen her, Bel. You've seen how bad she's getting.'

'That's just relapse, isn't it? That's what you've told me.'

'It's worse, more sinister.'

'What?' Bel releases me. We face each other. 'Sinister how?'

I puff out my cheeks, look up to the gods. What for, I do not know.

'She's now got something called secondary progressive MS.'

'Which means?'

'She's fucked, is basically what it means.'

'Don't, Bobby. Tell me what it means?'

'Worse case?'

'Yes.'

'She'll probably lose her sight, she'll have lesions on her brain –'

'What's that?'

'Like tumours.'

'Fuck!'

Bel falls forward and puts her hands on her head. She turns to me.

'Aw, Bobby, I'm …'

'I know, Bel. I know.'

'Does Dan know?'

'No, and he's not going to at this stage, OK?'

'OK,' she says.

Just Passing

I wake with a hash hangover: feels like someone's playing basketball with my head. Utter skull-pummelling stuff. Maybe it's post-crying brain. I peek in on Mum. All I see are her tiny hair prickles poking out of the covers. The compulsion to rub them is great. I exit.

Danny's lying with two hands above his head as if he's been shot.

Bang!

I hear the sound from outside.

When I go downstairs Bel's already bolted, spare covers neatly folded on the arm of the couch. She could've at least made us breakfast. I rummage the medicine cupboard for paracetamol. Yes, we have an entire cupboard.

Bang!

Stutter!

Spit!

I look out the window.

Shit.

Spit!

Here?

Now?

At this time?

Lou's vintage Vespa sounds as though it needs a paracetamol too. He removes his helmet as he saunters up our path. My action is frantic. I'm flushed. I run to open the door before he reaches it. 'Lou, what are you …'

'Hey, Bobby. I was out meetin' some dude about some shit and thought I'd check to see if you got home OK.'

'Yeah, I mean, yeah. I got home fine … but …'

'I was pretty out of it last night myself, so I was a bit worried, you know?'

'Strong apples, eh?' I say.

He laughs.

I ooze cool. Or maybe not.

'You want to come in?' I ask.

'No, I better boost. Get back home, duties and shit like that, you know?'

'Only too well.'

'Just wanna to make sure you were OK,' he says. 'That's all.'

'I'm fine, honestly.'

In the conversation gap Lou tilts his head up at the house, to Mum's bedroom window.

'Your mom, she doin' well?'

'You really interested?'

'Sure, why not?' he says, without taking his eyes away from the window. His head falls. 'She's the reason you do what you do, why you're stuck in here most nights. So, yeah, I'm interested.' There's lightness in his tone, which I've rarely heard before. 'She doin' OK, Bobby?'

'Good days. Bad days.'

'I hear you.'

'Doesn't get easier,' I say.

Lou reaches out, rests a hand on my shoulder. Is it my eyes? Are they still emotional red? I'm pretty sure I haven't given anything away.

'If you ever need any help, Bobby, just holler.'

'Thanks, Lou, will do.'

Him help me? Doesn't he have enough worries of his own? Ferrying me to and from Poztive meetings is ample help. Maybe that's the type of thing he means. Or keeping me stocked up in ... apples.

'It's cold, Lou. Sure you don't want –'

'I'm good, I'm good. Need to split,' he says.

'Well, thanks for popping round.'

When he's midway down the path he turns.

'I mean it, dude. Anything you need.'

'Cheers, Lou.'

I'm pretty sure he winks.

I close the door and breathe again.

#6 ... complete

dude, do you feel my voice?
do you hear me holler?
will you help me, dear dude,
rise up and flutter?

The Great Outdoors

'Why can't they have Xbox camps or something funner?' Danny says.

'An outdoor pursuits camp *will* be fun,' I say.

'I'm not Bear Grylls, Bobby,' he whines. 'And I don't want to pursue anyone either.'

It's hard not to agree.

'You'll love it,' I say.

'Bet I won't.'

'Bet you will.'

'Bet you a punch in the face I don't.'

'Just put the rest of the stuff in the bag. The bus'll be here soon.'

Danny fires the clothes I've neatly folded into the holdall. Tuts after every item chucked in.

'Remember to call me when you get there, OK?' I say.

'Unless I get murdered in a field.'

'By who? A cow?'

'Cows kill people, Bobby, don't you know that?'

'Erm …'

'Cows are evil.'

'Thanks, Dan. I'll bear that in mind next time I see you guzzling milk.'

He zips the bag and hurls it on to the floor, sits on the bed; his face forms into a magnificent sulk. Topped off with huffs and sagging shoulders.

'What is it now?'

'I'll miss Mum's birthday as well,' he says.

'We can have a little celebration when you get back,' I say, joining him on the bed. 'It's no big deal – really, it's not.'

'Says you.'

'Look, when you get to Mum's age birthdays are a pain in the arse, the saddest day of the year. Trust me, Dan, there'll be no celebration.'

'What are you going to do this weekend?'

'Schoolwork – I've loads.'

'Think I'd rather do schoolwork too.'

'Now, Danny, we both know that's not true.'

'It's not *not* true. Just don't want to be rolling on the ground. I hate muck.'

'Come on, it's nearly time.' I stand up.

'I can't climb trees, everyone will laugh at me.'

'Phone me every day. Twice a day if you want.'

'God, that would make my days worse.'

'Aw, cheers, mate.'

Danny launches himself off the bed, rattles me full pelt in the belly. His superhero hug, apparently.

'Going to miss you, Bobby,' he says.

'It's only two nights.'

'Still going to miss you.'

'I'll miss you too.'

'Better.'

'Now go kiss Mum and tell her you'll see her soon.'

'OK.'

'Tell her you'll be fine and not to worry. Tell her you're becoming a man now.'

'Will do.'

'And tell her to enjoy her birthday.'

'Roger that.'

Bed and Breakfast Club

'You lot have Richard Linklater, but in my day we had John Hughes,' Mum said a few days back. 'His movies were life-changing.'

If this birthday night is to be a success then some John Hughes films better be on the menu. Bel downloaded them for me. She also put *Grease* on the USB in case Mum got a second wind.

I'm sceptical as to whether Mum's up for a celebration. The last time she was downstairs was when Bel butchered her hair. Her tongue still throws fire though, which is always a good sign. But I think (I know) staring at four walls from the vantage point of her bed is soul sinking.

When I produce the joints, her eyes fizz, her mouth gapes. Huge grin, haven't seen it on her for ages; I'd almost forgotten what she looked like with it. Bobby done good, methinks!

It takes four feather pillows to completely prop her up.

'Where did you get it, Bobby?' she asks, without taking her eyes off the contents of my hand. I'd already told her where, but she doesn't need to know that right now.

'Mum, come on, you know I can't reveal my sources,' I say. 'Just tell me you didn't get it from some hardened criminal who now sees you as his bitch.'

'Mum, relax, it's fine,' I say.

I shuffle beside her so we're in the same position.

'So, how do you want to do this?' I sound nervous and inexperienced. 'Will we spark up before the film? Or …'

Mum sniggers.

It's good to hear laughter. I enjoy it.

'What's so funny?' I ask after a bit.

'You, with all your clichéd stoner language. "Spark up" – hilarious.'

'Well, help me out. It's not as though I've done this before,' I say.

'Maybe put on *The Breakfast Club* then light the bloody thing and hold it to my lips.' Mum takes a deep breath, replacing what she's lost. 'How's that for starters?'

'Sounds good.'

'Just prop me up a little further, will you?'

I place my arms around her waist and heave her up in the bed: heaviest rag doll you could ever imagine. Given that her entire lower half has literally no function, I know I'll have to go through the same routine about a dozen times throughout *The Breakfast Club*. It's her birthday after all. I click on the film, dim the lights.

I suck hard on the butt to ignite the thing fully, spluttering when the smoke wafts into my lungs. Mum finds this funny. Almost instantly I sense my body and mind sweeping away somewhere. Four drags later and this novice stoner is totally zoobified.

I can't take my eyes off the film. Don't ask me if it's any good or not. Who knows? Just a series of unrelated images.

'Are you going to pass that thing, Bobby?' Mum says.

I hear her but involuntarily tune out.

'Bobby! BOBBY!'

'Sorry, what?' I mumble.

'Are you going to put that up to my lips now?'

'Oh, right. Sorry, I wasn't …'

'Don't be hogging it all for yourself.'

I need to puff it back to life again, another two drags. I bring it towards Mum's mouth. She tongues her lips then puckers. I pop it into the little gap provided; she sucks until the tip glows, holds the smoke in for a few seconds before exhaling, just as Lou did. Experience! She doesn't thank me, nor comment on the quality; her eyes remain glued to the film, saying nothing, clearly relishing the return to her past.

'More,' she says.

I repeat the process four times. There's zero conversation between us, not about the film, not about life. I doubt my ability to chat anyway. The only communication we have is when I offer her water and wait until she latches on to the straw, and even that is inaudible rumbles. It doesn't seem awkward, nor does it bother us too much. To be fair, we're engrossed in *The Breakfast Club*.

She slides down the bed at a pace akin to coastal erosion, but I can't muster the energy to humph her back up. I don't think she wants me to though; her slouched position isn't impinging her view.

'I love this song,' she says during a musical montage sequence. It's not directed at me. A tear runs down the side of her face.

'You OK, Mum?'

'This song.'

'Mum?'

'This song brings back so many memories, Bobby.'

'You're crying?'

'Tears of remembrance.'

'Right,' I say.

It feels like an intrusion to ask who, or what, Mum's tears are really for. With a single swipe of my thumb, I wipe the moisture from her cheek. I say nothing.

'Want me to spark the next one up?' I ask.

Her belly springs up and down.

'Go on,' she says.

I do.

It's probably been about ten minutes, but it seems as if I've been staring at Mum's duvet pattern for about four hours:

these never-ending lines of orange cars travelling in the same direction. I imagine hopping inside one and riding off into the unknown, escaping my existence. Bliss! The film means nothing to me. All I can think about is getting the hell out of the hell I'm in. I swear I see myself in one of those cars – in Mum's duvet – driving off into the sunset. One problem though: the car keeps returning to the starting point again and again and again. Going nowhere fast, which scares me shitless. It's like, what's the point in even trying to go anywhere, to better myself? What's the point in having dreams and aspirations when you can't share them? When you feel guilty by having them.

In that moment I vow never to get sucked into this smoking dope lark. I need a mind that's alive and vibrant. This stuff dulls the senses, distorts time and brings out the melancholic in me.

'What did you think?' Mum asks when the film's credits begin rolling.

'Yeah, really good,' I offer. 'Although don't ask me to explain anything that happened in the last forty-five minutes.'

'Me neither,' Mum giggles.

'At least you've seen it before.'

'Long time ago.'

'Maybe I'll watch the next film without smoking anything,' I say.

'Can I have a drink, Bobby?'

I put the straw into Mum's mouth. She sucks. Earlier I

considered buying a special birthday bottle of wine as well, but now the thought of mixing alcohol with everything else is unthinkable. We'd be a mangled mess.

'Thanks, son.'

After I wipe her mouth dry, she mumbles, 'Can you hunch me up a bit before the next film?' She sounds different. Can't tell if she's slurring because of the smoking or something more disturbing.

'Course I will,' I say.

I feel the dampness as soon as my hand reaches Mum's lower back. I subtly lift the duvet and peak under. A map of piss confronts me. Not pungent enough to make me recoil – white piss, water piss – but enough for her to notice my changed expression.

'What is it, Bobby?' she says.

'Nothing, it's …'

'Bobby, tell me. What is it?'

'Not anything major, just a tiny accident.'

'What accident?'

'A little bit of pee, that's all.'

Mum's head sinks into the pillow; she appears to slide down the bed, like her body has a slow puncture.

'Don't worry,' I say, dragging myself off, 'I'll have it sorted in a jiffy.' I don't wait for an answer. My rapid dismount turns everything into one terrifying roller coaster. With the aid of a few supporting walls I make it safely to the landing. Think this is officially called 'being baked out your tights'.

I always make sure that the airing cupboard is well stocked with clean, crisp sheets. I've been doing three to four changes per week lately.

'What do you want next? That *Pretty in Pink* film or *Grease*?' I shout over my shoulder. No answer. 'I vote for *Grease*,' I shout louder. Still no answer. I grab a bundle of clean sheets, tuck them under my armpit. 'Bel gave me *Deadpool* a few weeks ago. It's supposed to be really funny,' I say on entering the room again.

Mum's locked in a daze, her face damp. The whites of her eyes are now a deep pink colour; her whole face appears puffy, as if she's taken an allergic reaction to whatever was in the joints. Frightens me.

'Mum? Mum, what is it, what's happened?'

Silence.

'Mum, you're scaring me. What's going on?'

Her lips move. She says something but I can't make out what because of the tears, drugs and sniffing.

'Mum, I can't understand you.'

More tears then a howl. I'm genuinely scared.

'Should I call someone?' I say. 'Mum, talk to me.'

She gulps saliva.

'I don't want to live like this any more, Bobby,' is what she says.

It isn't what she says that's the worst part; no, the worst part is that I don't have an answer for her. I've no words of comfort, no soothing clichés. Zilch. I stand there like a stoned lemon, staring at my petrified mother with fuck all to offer. So I do what I know best and start doing the physical part of caring. I remove the wet sheet and mattress protector; I roll Mum over, yank both bits of bedding out from under her. I can't bring myself to put on the fresh sheets though; I can't pretend I haven't heard what she's said. I have school, some friends and Poztive to offload my shit on to. Who does she have?

Before changing Mum's nightclothes, I climb on the bed, lie beside her. I don't say anything. We exchange no words. I pull her close, carefully manipulating her figure so we can fit into a proper embrace. Her body's listless. Legs limp. I slither my frame into hers and clench her tightly. Kiss her head.

'Happy birthday, Mum,' I whisper.

'Thanks, son.'

'No need to thank me, it was a pleasure.'

'Sorry for crying.'

'Don't be …'

'For getting emotional then.'

'I'd be disappointed if you hadn't,' I say.

Mum smiles, yet I detect no happiness or joy. 'We don't need to watch the other film if you're not up to it. I mean, if you're too tired or something.'

'Sorry for peeing,' she says.

I flick away her apology, and a rogue tear.

'Mum, it's fine.'

It isn't the complete loss of bodily function that renders this a defining moment. Now it's all about the disconnect between her mind and body, the ever-expanding gulf that exists between them. Her bones an anchor, her intellect a prisoner. I get it. I do.

'No, it's not fine, Bobby. It's not fine and will never be fine.'

'These things happen,' I say.

Mum laughs, almost mocks me.

'You actually think it's about this?' she says, indicating the incident area. 'It's got nothing to do with this.'

'What then?' I ask. Question number stupid. Of course I know what it's about.

She shifts in the bed, her eyes narrow. With her menacing punk hair and defiant expression, she's a threat.

'Do you have any idea what it's like to forget your own name, where you are, why you're where you are? Have you any idea what it's like to be trapped in your own forgetfulness? Seeing all the action unfold around you and you can't contribute? Wondering who the hell people are? Have you any idea what it's like to exist without living, Bobby?'

'Mum, you know I …'

'That's how it is for me, that's how I live now. Not every day, but it's going to get worse. And by worse I mean I won't recognise you or Danny, and that terrifies me more than anything else. It does. The very notion of it makes me gasp for air, and sometimes when I gasp for the air I can't feel it entering my lungs. I can't feel it. I think that gasp will be my final one. Can you hear what I'm saying, Bobby?'

I nip my nails into my lower arm, dig really hard, trying to inflict something physical that'll knock the fuck out of the emotional pain that Mum's transmitting.

'I hear you, Mum.'

'This is me now, Bobby,' she says. 'This is who I am. This is the best you'll ever see.'

'You're still my mum, our mum.'

'I want to stay that mum, the one you remember.'

'You will be.'

'It's not about who I *was* any longer, Bobby.'

I squeeze into her, caress her cheek. Her head. If only I could reach in and disconnect the MS from her brain.

'We can leave the other film for another time,' I say. 'Watch it tomorrow maybe.'

'Did you hear what I said, son?'

'I heard.'

'Not just then. When you came back into the room after getting the sheets?'

'Just then? Just now?'

'Yes, did you hear what I said when you opened the door?'

Course I heard what she said. I don't want to admit it, do I? Block-out Bobby.

'I didn't, Mum. No,' I lie.

She twists herself, stares at me for what seems like a life-time. Some white has returned to her eyes again, pastel colour splashes her cheeks. The effect of the hash has worn off and her brain is evidently rotating in the correct direction once more. Mine too.

'Listen,' she says.

'What?'

'I said I didn't want to live like this any more, Bobby.'

'Mum, don't ...'

'*That's* what I said.'

'I know. I heard. I did.'

'It's true. I don't want to live like this any more,' she punches at me. 'I don't. And I want you to help me.'

'This is crazy talk, Mum.'

'Please help me, Bobby.'

I return focus to my lower arm.

'You have to help me.'

And with one request, it's bye-bye to the old Bobby.

Sleep Watcher

More than once I've discovered Danny in Mum's room while she's asleep, perched at the end of the bed, gazing, transfixed by her peacefulness. No tears, talk or movement. Other times he'll be closer, tenderly stroking her head or fiddling with the covers.

I've never disturbed him; these are Danny's moments. Seeing my little brother's courage and independence fills me with pride. I guess I should be more open about what's going on with her, about what the consequences will be, but I've always thought that I should protect him by not revealing every grubby detail.

Secretly watching him secretly watching her is a kind of beautiful, heartbreaking connection we've all shared.

I know Mum's breathing patterns as she sleeps; I know the sounds that radiate from her; I know every flicker her eyes make, every detail. And whenever Danny's been there I know she hasn't really been asleep: she's pretending. This is Danny's time, you see; Mum doesn't want to intrude upon it any more than I do, nor does she want him exposed to her deterioration. Even at her weakest, she's thinking about sheltering her son, as any mother would.

#7 ... incomplete

mum is brilliance
mum is compassion
mum is laughter
mum was fire

      mum is sincerity
      mum is warmth
      mum is love
      mum was safety

            mum is me
            mum is him
            mum is we
            mum was life

Mother

Mum will always be ... Mum.
Our mum.
No termination.

The Weight of a Thousand Feathers

The night Danny returns from his school trip, all he wants is scrambled eggs with toast and jam. Two eggs, bit of milk, pinch of salt, a squeeze of ketchup and a mash-up. That's the way he takes it. I've missed him. I'm stirring the ingredients. Danny's doing that annoying knife and fork thumping on the table. I want to yank them from his hands and sling them against the wall. *That'll teach you.*

'Stop that, Dan.'

'What?'

'That hammering on the table. I've a sore head.'

'*I've a sore head,*' Danny imitates me.

It's as if I'm in the middle of the road braced for the impact. I close my eyes and await the collision. Double-decker runs right over the top of me, shatters every bone in my body, utter skull-crusher. I continue to whisk.

I can't control the bounce of my shoulders. I tense up my stomach to stem the flow, but mostly so I don't howl. Over and over I replay the conversation with Mum, can't think of much else. Over and over I end up in a heap. When I do cry out I sound wounded, like I've stabbed myself with a fork or put my hand on a naked flame. Danny jumps.

'Bobby, what happened?'

'Nothing, mate. Just …'

He's on to me, wants to see the damage. Examines my hands. Nothing. He lifts his head. Our eyes meet.

'Bobby, you're crying?'

Can't blame onions.

'Bobby, why are you crying?'

'I don't know, mate.'

LIES. LIES. LIES.

'Did something happen?'

'No, I'm just a bit down, bit sad.'

'Was it because I banged my knife and fork?'

'No.'

'I didn't mean to bang so hard.'

'It's fine, Dan. It's not that.' He's scared. I can't look at him any longer. I cover my eyes with my arm, flex my face. My entire body shakes with grief. Can't control it. This must be how Mum feels, times infinity.

'Bobby, don't. Please, don't.' Danny gets on to his knees, hooks his arms around my thigh. For some reason I continue to whisk. My head is scrambled.

'Are you sad for Mum?' he asks.

'Yes, and for you too.'

'Don't be sad for me,' he says, gripping harder. 'We should keep all our sad times for Mum, and all our happy times for her too.'

'You're right, Dan, we should.' I sleeve my face.

'Is Mum sad too?'

'Yeah, Mum's sad too.'

'Maybe it's because I was away doing outward pursuits?'

'No, Dan. She was happy you were doing that. She's sad for other things.'

'But has something changed in her, Bobby? Something worse?' He asks from his position around my leg. I don't want to drag him off.

'Yeah, she's becoming worse.'

'But she's going to get better, isn't she?'

'I don't think she's going to get better, Dan.'

His grip hardens; he burrows his head into me.

Those dreams about finding Mum dead have stopped. I've never told anyone about them. Everything is locked in, key thrown away. Just me and my thoughts. I hunker down to join him. We sit on the kitchen floor.

'Why will she not get better?' he says.

'Looks like the illness has shifted to her head, her brain.'

'Which means?'

'She'll start forgetting things more and more. She might not be able to move too well either.'

'Sounds bad, Bobby.'

'It is bad. It is.'

'What will we do?'

'Just be there for her, make sure she has everything she needs, make her comfortable,' I say. 'I'm not sure really.'

Danny brings his head up to meet my wreckage. He's calm. He parts my hair.

'Bobby?'

'Yeah?'

'Is our mum going to die?'

I can't answer him. I can't. I swallow hard and cover my face. For some reason I'm ashamed of the state I'm in. I'm supposed to be the granite in this house. I feel like wet paper. Danny embraces me, rocks me like a newborn. I sob.

'I'd like us to go to the park again like we used to. Remember?' he says.

'I remember. It's all in here, Dan,' I say, tapping my head.

'Me too,' he says, tapping his.

Danny has never stopped hoping Mum will just get up one morning and make a full recovery, that we'll be a normal, proper family again. Sure, who wouldn't hope for that? I've been asked to destroy this possibility. But while Mum is ill, while she exists only in body, motionless in a bed, we'll never be a normal family again.

When I think of what Mum has asked me to do my torso buckles under the burden of responsibility. I see it all in a stream of haunting images; they launch sustained attacks on me, won't let me be. Images filled with Mum's lifeless figure, the peacefulness of her face, her unseeing eyes, the stillness of her stomach, her body submerged in a massive feathered pillow. I doubt these images will ever fuck the fuck off and allow me to be *me* again. That pillow is a load I know I'll never be able to push away. I feel the weight of its thousand feathers pressing, pressing, pressing me down.

Mum's request alters me, like actually alters my appearance: I age inside and out. Bags appear under my eyes. My appetite wanes. School becomes irrelevant and insignificant.

I start seeing things with more clarity than ever before. The mere thought of it knocks me sideways, consuming my every waking thought. And yet, it makes sense. Sense so perverse that it tramples down the dirt of everything in its wake. Mum's had days, weeks and months to drool over it, to consider that whole pros-and-cons thing. She's a dogged woman who understands her own mind better than anyone; she knows I *am* her only hope, that I am the only one who can free her. She's lucid enough to know, for now, that I am the keyholder ... the keyholder to everyone's freedom.

I know the logic of what she's saying, but the idea of it is so agonising to even comprehend – there's a hope that she's forgotten she's said anything, like with the hash.

Slopes

It wasn't the uncontrollable bladder or the distorted speech or the limbs as heavy as tree trunks that made me grasp the gravity of Mum's illness. My realisation that MS was dominating her body came when I noticed she couldn't tie her shoelaces. At first I put it down to simple clumsiness or one of those momentary memory lapses, when you forget how to spell a three-letter word or something. I laughed at it. But then it happened again. And again. She suggested a major bout of pins and needles to ease my distress, but I knew differently. We howled whenever I had to do them up for her.

'That's you all done,' I'd say, slapping her instep.

'Right, that's me ready to take on the world.'

'Now, don't be jumping in any puddles.'

I quite enjoyed our little ritual, but it became embarrassing for both of us. Before she changed to wearing sandals and pumps, I tied Mum's laces in total silence. I felt emotionally useless to her and vulnerable in my new role as her chief dresser.

Then her symptoms became more noticeable. I remember once as she was watching some music documentary on BBC Four her left leg started shaking. And I mean uncontrollably shaking. Her thigh muscle rippled like water after a stone's been dropped.

'Mum, look,' I said. 'Look at your leg.'

'It's nothing, Bobby.'

'But, look!'

'Sshh, I'm watching this.' She slapped her thigh like you'd swat at an unwelcome wasp.

I knew something was wrong. The tiniest domestic chore would leave her shattered, as if she'd vacuumed the world. We're talking about making toast here, nothing strenuous. But we could handle it then.

After school I'd either find her zonked in bed or flaked out on the couch. That's when I got the finger out and started doing most chores: making dinner, food shopping. Her desire to wheel around Asda practically disappeared. I washed our clothes, her dirty underwear. I didn't mind. Really, I didn't. Danny was a problem though; he was younger and didn't appreciate that Mum needed rest. He threw mega tantrums, craving her affection. Eventually Mum got her arse in gear and visited a doctor, who, being the medical wizard he was, told her she had some type of aggressive virus and that she'd be as right as rain in no time. He packed her off with a course of pills. Everyone's a winner! Even with only four years of school biology behind me, I knew this doctor didn't know his arse from his stethoscope.

Mum had some strange Lazarus moments at the beginning of her illness: occasionally I'd discover her in the garden, head to toe in dirt and sweat, like she'd hoed a rainforest. Thing is, she hated gardening. It all came crashing down on top of us one night when she returned from the garden clearly terrified. Her leg had buckled. It wouldn't support her weight and she kept stumbling and falling down. I carried her upstairs like a fireman that night; it shocked our core. A pivotal moment, because she understood these little episodes were connected to something more sinister ... bugger all to do with clumsiness.

She cried that night.

It was the first time I'd seen her cry. Parents aren't supposed to cry, not in front of their kids. The crying was one of the hardest things to get used to. We had to accept it, because when Mum received the diagnosis she wept buckets, a daily soundscape ranging from sweet soft sobs to explosive bouts of wailing. Danny's head was constantly in his jumper or buried under his pillow, poor soul. This MS was a WMD that didn't discriminate: everyone was going to feel its wrath.

I wanted to hide my head at times as well, but couldn't. Too busy making sure Danny was surviving. I embraced him, held him whenever he felt like lashing out. I read and reread stories, made sure he ate properly. I was the one who tried to explain in the simplest terms all about Mum's illness, spoon-fed him information on a need-to-know basis. With Danny it was all about amputating his panic and worry. I didn't want him to go directly to Google, with its smorgasbord of scare-mongering shit; it could've seriously triggered a meltdown.

Around this time there was no place for my indulgent thoughts: *Who'll embrace me? Who'll hold me tight? Who'll eliminate my fears?* I guess the answer to these questions was Danny. He became my blanket, as I was his.

And that's how the slippery slope began. Minor problems in light of what we now know. But I never imagined how fast and in what direction things would accelerate. Here lies a woman who's not so much slipped down the slope as been propelled from it.

But where to?

#8 ... complete

you didn't stir
I snuck into your room
you must have heard me

you must have heard me
I bent down
put my lips to your ear

whispered:
I can see your chest hum
hear your heart weary

you must have heard me
weeping

no?

Jaggy Head Kiss

After Danny scoffs his scrambled eggs I bring him up to Mum, hoping she's awake to see him. She's on her side, serene.

'That hair makes her look mad,' Danny says. 'Like a black thistle.'

'What, madder than before?' I say.

'Think I should get mine done like hers, Bobby?'

'Don't even think about it.' I ruffle his hair.

'Shall I give her a kiss?' he asks.

'Always give her a kiss.'

Danny approaches and places his lips on the side of Mum's head.

'It's jaggy on my lips.'

'I've been there,' I say. 'Listen, you go put all the dirty washing in the basket and I'll fix her covers.'

'Roger that.'

I study her. I miss brushing her hair, putting on my hairdresser voice. Having our banter. Skinhead? What woman in midlife gets a bloody skinhead? End-of-life crisis women, that's who.

Mum peels open her eyes.

'Did I just hear our Danny?' she croaks.

'He got back a while ago, Mum.'

'Did he have fun?'

'Seemed to,' I say. 'You OK? Need anything?'

'No. Too tired to eat.'

'I'll go, let you get some sleep.'

She closes her eyes. I decide to wait until I hear her breathing, see her body rise and fall. Danny's humming filters through from his room. Mum's eyes flick open.

'It's just Danny, Mum. I'll get him to stop.'

'It's fine, I like listening to him.'

'OK,' I say and make to leave.

'Bobby!'

'What?'

'Have you told him?'

'About what?'

'About what I asked you to do?'

She's not letting this go. I know her: she's got a bone and no way she's loosening her jaw. It's far too juicy.

'Remember, Bobby, truth opens doors.'

'I know.'

'So it's important to tell him, don't let it drag on too long before you do.'

Why is this my job? Why can't Mum tell Danny herself? Because she won't be able to spout it all out without cracking? What makes her think it'll simply roll from my tongue? I almost do a full-on teenage foot stamp.

'Mum, please!' I hiss. 'He's in his room, he'll hear.'

'OK,' she says. 'Keep your man bra on.'

'Funny.' My face is serious. I turn on my heels.

'Bobby.'

'What?' I shoot at her.

'I'm really hungry. Could you get me some soup?'

'Tomato or lentil?'

'Chicken.'

'Thought so,' I say as I close the door.

*

'You've some soup on your chin. Let me clean it,' I say.

'My lips are going, Bobby.'

'No, it's just a dribble.'

'I'm a baby.'

I run the wet wipe across her chin, clean the chicken soup away.

'There.'

'Bobby, I need you to end this for me.'

'Nearly finished.'

'You know what I'm talking about.'

'Mum …'

'Help me,' she says. I fully expect to see tears, but she's clear-eyed and steadfast. 'Please? You have to.'

I grapple with it every hour, some hours better than others. Mum wants to make a criminal out of me and motherless sons out of us. Danny deserves his mum. Who am I to take that from him?

'Don't talk, Mum. Concentrate on eating the soup.'

'I know this is something no mother should ever ask her child to do.'

'Mum …'

'I'm aware what I'm asking, Bobby. I am. I know you'll have to carry this around for life.'

'Every waking hour,' I say.

'I'm turning into a feeding receptacle, son. I can't have the indignity of that before, well, before the inevitable happens. Danny couldn't handle that either.'

Danny would hate me, I know he would. And if anyone found out – Christ, if anyone found out – I'd be deemed evil, mad and selfish. A disaffected youth. Mum wouldn't be there to verify my truth. They'd twist everything, spin me into a nutter. What other options do we have though? It's not as if we have the funds to whisk her off to the Dignitas clinic in the Swiss Alps. All we have is each other.

Is my only option to stand by and watch Mum's unimaginable suffering? Disregard her only wish? Spend the next fuck knows how many months/years witnessing her intolerable pain, hoping that today will be the day nature finally acts?

I chew over my own pros and cons list and conclude that, as big brother, chief rock and ship-steadier, I can't allow Danny to live with a mother who is nothing more than a feeding receptacle, unable to respond to the most basic of human emotions. Unable to touch us. Unable to guide us. Unable to rejoice. A mother who is simply, well, unable to be a mother. I can't live with that possibility.

Mum's request has to be carried out. It just has to be. Call me the dutiful son. Call me whatever … I don't care.

The Residential

It's been a week since Mum's sledgehammer, and I'm more than happy to be going on the residential. If nothing else, to escape the constant stinging in my head, the need to disguise my anxiety whenever I check her. Thinking about what she's asked me to do is exhausting.

I chuck random items into my sports bag. I'm calling it a sports bag but it hasn't seen a sniff of a sweaty trainer or the hint of a football park or gym since Mum bought me it.

'You sure you're happy for me to be here all weekend?' Bel says.

'Just as long as you don't rifle through my knicker drawer,' I say.

'Can't promise.'

'Sure. What else would you rather be doing this weekend?'

'Well, it's a toss between watching dad fart his way through Sunday or … let me think … nothing.'

'Mum'll appreciate it, Bel,' I say. 'You don't need to do anything. They're sending in a cavalry of healthcare workers while I'm away.'

'No sweat. I'll just make sure Danny doesn't download too much porn,' she says, flicking through my wardrobe and taking out a woolly jumper.

'Don't even think about packing that. It's not bloody Siberia I'm going to.'

'Thinking about night-time?'

'I'll snuggle into some of the others who are going, won't I?'

'Oh, very modern. Very progressive. Make sure you film it,' she says, rehanging my jumper. 'What about this?'

I agree to the hoodie she's holding. She folds it and tucks it in the bag. 'What's the plan for the weekend then?' I ask.

'Oh, don't you worry about me, Bobby Seed. While you're trudging through sheep crap and sleeping in a damp-infested shit hole I'll be getting down and dirty with Junk Food Friday on my lonesome. Saturday I'll Netflix it and Sunday I'll probably write an essay for school.'

'Oh, please stop, Bel,' I say, theatrically holding my chest. 'My heart's about to pop a chamber.'

'I'm thinking pizza and *Pretty in Pink*.'

'Bel, you've seen that film, like, twenty times by now.'

'What can I say? You're such a cultural influence on me, Bobby.'

'It's my dedication to your education.'

'You've made me fall in love with John Hughes's films.'

'I'm honoured …'

'Except maybe *Home Alone* and –'

'But I think we need to give Mum the credit for the whole John Hughes enlightenment. I didn't have a clue who he was until she told me.'

'Naturally she should take all the plaudits.' Bel holds up an imaginary glass and points it towards Mum's room. 'A toast to Anne Seed.'

'I'll drink to that.' I echo her toasting mime.

'You know, you should really give *The Breakfast Club* another try when you're not mangled,' she says. 'It's brilliant.'

'Yeah, maybe I will,' I say, but I doubt it.

'I'll pencil it in for one of our Friday nights then.' She holds up two shirts. Red-and-black checked and a greenish tartan one. 'Which of these?'

I consider her question, try to picture myself in a situation where shirt compliments will be flying around.

'I'd say the checky one.'

After a militaryesque fold, Bel gently places it in the bag.

'Right, that's it. Just your make-up, nail varnish and condoms and you're good to go.'

I take Bel's hand and don my most earnest face.

'Bel, I just want to say thanks for the help these past few weeks. I couldn't have done it without you.'

'Yes, you could. Even you aren't that thick.'

'Actually, I was just being polite,' I say, dropping her hand. 'Who else is going to make you feel good about yourself?'

'And who else puts as much care into folding shirts as I do?' she says. 'I was born for this kind of shit – just take a look at them folds. It's like I'm a teen mum of twins.'

Bel takes a pace back from where I'm standing and clutches her left boob with both hands. Her face contorts.

'I can't believe it, my baby's going on his first overnight,' she says in a fake comedy voice.

'Oh, shut up,' I snort through laughter.

Bel gives out a little gasp and moves her hands to her cheeks. Something about her expression suddenly feels too real though, and the laughter drains from me. I see Mum in her mannerisms.

'My baby's going off on his first holiday.'

My ears fail to hear the comedy. It's lost. I can't maintain my fake smile. I wish she'd stop now; what I'd give to hear one coherent beat of Mum's own voice again, one of her caustic putdowns, anything. This vile cover version is an affront.

'Oh, be quiet now, will you,' I say.

'My little boy's now a man …'

'Seriously, Bel, shut it.' I hear the shudder of my own voice.

She stretches out her arms and edges towards me again.

'Oh my! My little man's heading off, all alone, into the big bad world …' she pretends to cry.

This is what my brain transmits: not only is Bel attempting to imitate Mum's voice, she's openly mocking her. That's how I'm hearing it. Whatever she's doing, it stopped being funny a long time ago. My face is clear about that.

'Come here, my boy, and give Mummy a massive hug.'

Her arms are about to embrace me. Touch me. The room narrows.

'Shut the fuck up, Bel!'

I know I shouldn't have roared directly into her face. I know I shouldn't have lost the rag. I shouldn't have shoved her on to the bed. And I'm sorry she whacked her head off the headboard. I know all that.

It wasn't hard. Honestly, it wasn't. I wish I hadn't done any of it, but I have and I can't take it back. It wasn't hard though.

I grab my bag and shoot out like a cannonball. I don't know how much hurt I've caused or if her head has marks. Have I left bruising? Not the foggiest.

I'm sick with shame. I hate myself for how I reacted. Tough to explain exactly what happened: as if this whirlwind came out of nowhere and enveloped me. Swept me up. Gave me no option other than to lash out.

It was only a push, a violent push though. Some carer!

*

Roddy drives us in this dirty white clapped-out minivan. I stare out of the window and watch the urban world transform into the rural. I play out the whole Bel incident again. And again. And again. Devours my entire brain mass. Thing is, we've had loads of arguments in the past, really serious ones too, ones where we've been trying to see who could stab the deepest, who could sling the thickest mud. Real touching-the-bone stuff. But never before have I felt such a swell of anger, nor lashed out like that.

While excited voices clamour around me I mobilise my thoughts. I should be bang in the middle of the fun, orchestrating or just laughing along, but here I am, sitting irritated and isolated, the remnants of my anger sucking away the positive atmosphere instead. Talk about guilt. I twiddle my phone in my hand, leaving sweaty prints all over it. Nobody questions my mood; pretty sure they think the worry on my face is to do with Mum. I clean the wet print marks from the screen. Without thinking too much about it, I set my fingers to work.

Bel. SO SO SORRY. Cnt express how bad I feel. Please dnt hate me …

As much as I stare at my phone, willing a pinged response, nothing comes. I turn it on and off. Change settings. Alter the volume. Nothing. It's the waiting, the silence that kills me the most. It screams that I've ballsed up my friendship with Bel. I keep seeing her flying on to the bed. It's a throttling image that I can't shake off. I see her eyes laced with fear and confusion; I see the tears crawl down her face after her skull batters the headboard. Those eyes! Shame doesn't even come close.

The racket around me gets louder.

'Hey, dude,' Lou says, plonking himself down beside me.

'Hi, Lou,' I say.

'How did those joints work out for you?'

'Erm ... yeah ... erm ... good,' I say, attempting to jolt myself back into life. 'Really good.'

'Likey likey then?' He raises his eyebrow.

'Yeah, a lot,' I lie.

'Well, there's more of that shit to be had.' And from his jacket he furtively pulls out a little bag of three pre-rolled joints.

Shit! That's all I need, my mind yelps.

'Jesus, Lou,' I whisper, looking around to see if anyone has seen him doing it. Then realise that I'm the one who is being conspicuous. 'If you get caught with that stuff, you're ...'

'What? Roddy's gonna whack me? What's the worst that can happen?'

'Don't know, sent home, I suppose.'

'Exactly. What a shit cloud that would be, eh?' he says. 'Dude, if I'm gonna be spendin' days surrounded by horse shit and pig piss then I'm gonna need somethin' to take the edge off.'

'I'm not sure it'll be that type of trip, Lou. Look around, do

226

we look like countryside rambler types to you?' (Lou glances over his shoulder.) 'Even Roddy doesn't have that look about him. No, I think we're going to be spending the time playing indoor games, being bored, moaning and telling each other all the time how desperate we are to get back home.'

'All the better to have a bit of extracurricular then,' he says, patting his jacket pocket. The denim.

Something inside stops me from screaming, NO! NO, I DON'T WANT TO BE PART OF THIS SORDID ESCAPADE, LOU. I'm mute. His ability to creep under my skin is impressive, overpowering almost. I'm about to say, 'Count me in,' or words to that effect, when my phone vibrates in my hand.

'I better take this, Lou,' I say.

'Say no more. I'm outta here.'

I don't recognise the number.

'Hello,' I say.

In the ensuing conversation I say the word 'yes' four times, 'no' three times, 'thanks' twice and 'goodbye' once.

The phone call has deflated me.

I gesture for Lou to come sit with me again, attempt to sideline any thoughts of Bel. Not easy, but doable with Lou there.

'Mum's nurse,' I say.

'Problems?'

'No, she just wanted to talk about some stuff, double-checking things.'

'So what's the deal with your mom?' Lou asks.

'No deal.'

'Your face. Looks like a deal to me.'

'Aw, it's nothing serious.'

'Don't look like it.'

Lou places a reassuring hand on my knee; the heat emanating from his palm burns right through to my skin. His fingers are explosive. I want to rewire my brain, close my eyes and enjoy the rest of the journey. Lou says nothing because Lou understands: he gets my pain; he suffers and exists in it too. If I can't be open with someone like him without feeling vulnerable and weak, then who can I be?

'She's declining pretty rapidly,' I tell him. 'She's practically bedridden, not much control over her bladder, her muscles are so painful that it seems as if her nerves are like mercury. I think her brain is crashing too.' I pause and take in some air. 'In fact, it is failing.'

'Shit, Bobby.' Lou puts pressure on to my knee. 'That's an immense load, dude.'

'With each day that passes it's as if a part of her is leaving us.'

Lou nods his head, removes his hand and grabs on to the seat in front of him. He's mulling. His hand then connects tightly with my shoulder.

'You don't have to go through this alone, Bobby,' he says.

His hand tightens. I don't look to acknowledge it, neither does he, but it's there and it's real.

'Thanks, Lou.'

'I mean it. Don't isolate yourself with this, OK?'

'Appreciate it, Lou.'

'I'm sorry,' he says. 'I really am.'

'Thanks.'

'It's a fuckin' drag.'

'It's a pain in the arse all right, but we're hoping it'll all get better,' I say, surprised by my choice of phrase; not for a second do I believe it to be a pain in the arse.

'Still! It's one rough ride you got there, Bobby.'

'We all do, right?' I say.

'You got it.' Lou's hand falls from my shoulder.

'I'm no different to anyone else.'

'No, but if there's anything I can do, just yell my way,' he says.

'Thanks, Lou. I'm pretty sure you have your own problems to deal with though.'

'Yeah, maybe.'

It's all about ME ME ME. God, what a selfish prick I am at times. Lou probably has a similar experience with his own mother: the same sense of hopelessness and constant fear of what the future holds. You don't ever hear him pouring it over the heads of others. I don't want to be a burden to him.

'Roddy! Roddy!' a voice from behind shouts.

'What?' Roddy shouts back.

'Put some tunes on.'

'Music?' Roddy shouts.

'Yeah, duh! Something good,' Harriet shouts.

'As long as it's not any of that grime stuff Harriet listens to,' Cal shouts.

'Any rap?' Lou shouts.

'Crap, more like,' shouts Harriet.

'I wouldn't be a fan of that,' Cal agrees.

'If any rap music goes on, stop the bus so I can get off,' Harriet says.

'Technically it's a van,' Cal says. 'But let's not quibble.'

I can't see much of Roddy's face, only his twinkling eyes in the rear-view mirror. They suggest an ear-to-ear grin, delighted that his troops are in fine fettle, each and every one of them animated and energised by freedom. I'm playing catch-up.

'Wait until you hear this – you'll love it,' Roddy shouts over his shoulder.

'It'd better kick ass,' Lou roars.

Roddy fumbles with the van's antiquated stereo system for a few seconds. When the music blares he vigorously hammers the steering wheel.

'What's this shit?' Harriet screams.

'Shit? What do you mean, *shit*?' Roddy shouts.

'Pure shit.' Harriet returns fire.

'Don't dare insult the genius that is AC/DC. I'm giving you the classics here,' Roddy bellows over the noise.

'What the fuck is AC/DC?' I hear Tom say.

'Put something on that we know, Roddy,' Harriet shouts.

'Philistines, the lot of you,' he says, laughing.

'Something that has unifying qualities,' Cal bawls.

Roddy switches AC/DC off, replaces it with something to quench the musical thirst of the masses.

When the new tune kicks in most people seem to instantly know it and instantly like it. Heads bob, fingers tap the backs of seats and feet shift in time with the rhythm. Harriet, Clare and Tom are familiar with the song, so they sing along. But me – well, I think the Arctic Monkeys are a bit passé. But then I like the songs from *Grease*, so what do I know?

'This song is ridiculous,' Cal says.

'Eh?' Tom says, scowling at him.

And I'm just about to join in the chanting when my phone pings. Bel's name winks at me. My intestines tighten and twist. I swear they do.

Dnt sweat it Seed. I 4give ur angry mental arse

> *Don't forgive me, Im a dick. SOZ!!!!!*

I no ur a dick … couldv told u that yonks ago

> *Im dead soz, Bel! Just got me thinking about mum*

Well im SOZ 2 for being miss proper insensitive

> *No need. Still my buddy then?*

Always

                                        Luv u doll!!

U 2. Hav shite weekend X

                              Try my best. C u when get bak

K

My relief is akin to a ten-tonne cow being removed from my neck. I'm guilty as charged, but can head to the Borders a reformed, rehabilitated gentleman. I'm weak, I'm flawed and I do irrational things. I'm so sorry, Bel.

I squeeze my phone into the front pocket of my jeans. A different song comes through the speakers. I turn to Lou.

'This song is cracking.'

Music's all about mood and atmosphere, after all.

'I agree, quality tune,' he says.

'Love it,' I say.

'It's cool.' He starts tapping his hand on the seat in front. I mirror him.

As do Tom and Cal. Our heads move to the beat.

'Are we nearly there yet, Dad?' Harriet shouts at Roddy.

'Another half hour,' Roddy shouts back.

'Turn it up a bit then,' she calls.

Roddy cranks the volume up. A collective whoop thunders

out from everyone. Seats get thumped, heads bang in harmony and voices belt out the verse. No danger making it as a chamber choir, but who cares? We have spirit and togetherness. It surges through the van.

'Fucking love this song,' Harriet cries.

'Who doesn't?' I shout.

When the chorus kicks in it's pure party bus all the way to the Borders.

We're so far from home, from our duties, from that day we refused to sing karaoke. Embarrassment? What embarrassment? What a difference.

Playing Charades

Rooms are sorted – the three girls are sharing, Roddy's flying solo, Tom and Cal are in their own brain clash and I'm with Lou in the attic.

Then off we plod for a walk around the grounds of the country estate, to 'breathe in some of Scotland's finest air,' as Roddy puts it.

Can't really call what we're doing 'walking'; instead we shuffle along like an uncooperative flock of sheep cowering from the biting drizzle. The vibrant mood of the van has vanished.

'Country estate' gives it an undeserving grandeur; the gaff is a decrepit kip, makes the Colosseum look positively futuristic. Inside and out the place is crumbling in front of our eyes; everything creaks and smells of damp cats. In our attic room only the brave would sit their arse on the toilet or place a naked foot in the shower. The furniture in the musty grand rooms downstairs is archaic, while the grounds we lumber around are sodden and unkempt. No one, apart from Roddy, obviously, has brought appropriate footwear. What happened to escaping our troubles in luxurious surroundings?

We all huddle together pretending to be in collective misery. Naturally Lou, not a word mincer, is the first to vocalise his thoughts.

'This place is a shit heap, Rod.'

'It's pure rotten,' Harriet says.

'I agree, it's somewhat tired,' Cal says.

'It's perfect,' Roddy says.

'Perfect?' Harriet adds.

'It's peaceful,' Roddy says.

'You kiddin' me? Jeffrey Dahmer would turn his nose up at this place,' Lou says.

'Jeffery who?' Harriet asks.

'Think he's America's answer to Fred West,' I say. 'Right, Lou?'

'You got it, Bobby,' Lou says.

'Who the fuck's Fred West?' Harriet asks.

'A serial killer,' I tell her.

'Wasn't there that doctor dude as well?' Lou adds.

'Oh, yeah, Harold Shipman,' Harriet says. 'Proper evil bonkers he was.'

'*Unlike* the others?' I say.

'Who *are* these people? I seriously don't have a clue,' Tom tells everyone. Clare and Erin are taking in the scenery.

Our huddle gets tighter. To be heard you have to shout over the laughter. Is this camaraderie in action?

'All these people are serial killers, Tom,' I say.

'Why are we all talking about serial killers?' Tom asks.

'Beats me,' I say.

'Because this place has the look of a serial killer's retirement home,' Lou says. 'Nobody knows who's gonna be knockin' on their door tonight.'

'Yeah, I'd bolt it shut if I were you,' I say.

'No chance. They'd go for one of them first.' Tom nods at the girls. 'Saying that, maybe they'd give Clare a wide berth.' Clare aims a kick and Tom jerks away. Sniggers. But she manages an impressive hook to his shoulder. Hefty laughter.

'Maybe there's a serial killer among us now,' Harriet states.

'Shit, secret's out,' Lou says. 'Was it in my eyes?'

'I didn't want to say, mate,' she says.

'I forgot my toolkit,' Lou adds. 'So you're all safe for the weekend … at least.'

Even Roddy guffaws.

'Can we stop this serial killer crap?' Clare says. 'I'm absolutely Baltic.'

'Me too,' Erin says.

'Positively sub-zero,' Cal says.

Roddy crashes his hands together. 'Right, everyone back

inside. Relax for an hour or so and then we'll call out for pizza and watch a movie. How does that sound?'

'Can you even get pizza around here?' Harriet asks.

'We're not in outer Siberia, Harriet,' Roddy says.

'Feels like it,' Tom says.

'Watchin' a movie? What happened to "breathin' in Scotland's finest air", Rod?' Lou says.

'Bugger that, I'm freezing.' Roddy starts running full pelt back to the house. As needy little children we follow our leader. We're delighted to be exactly where we are.

Freezing.

But free.

*

A few inches more and we'd have been rattling our heads off the v-shaped attic roof. A rickety three-drawer unit separates our single beds; we're afraid to use the drawers in case the thing crumbles under the weight of a few pairs of boxers. The wardrobe next to the door looks like the oldest dry-rot survivor known to man: a grimy relic standing to attention, stalking us as we sleep, waiting for an opportune moment to pounce.

'I ain't puttin' my stuff near that thing,' Lou says.

I wholeheartedly agree. We decide to live out of our bags.

The mattresses are springy and concaved. No need to battle it out for the best bed. Both shit. I lie on mine, stick my hands behind my head and watch Lou potter about. Mainly he opens and closes doors, scans the sloping ceiling for the tenth time, murmurs lots and tuts to himself. His grumpiness doesn't bother me – if anything I find it amusing. Lying there with my eyes on him feels good: good not to be at anyone's beck and call. Choreless.

'Think I'll take a shower before the evenin' entertainment begins,' Lou says. 'Then, before we head down ...' He produces one of the joints from his top pocket.

'Are you sure you want to do that, Lou?' I say.

'Don't pussy out on me, dude. Just a quick de-escalator.'

'No, I mean about the shower. It's vile.' I smile.

'I'll keep my socks on,' Lou says, unfastening his belt. He then begins unbuttoning his shirt. The house's tang attacks my mouth. I consider licking my lips, but I don't. I just can't, can I? My conscience screams: *Stay on his eyes! Stay on his eyes! Eye contact at ALL times! At ALL times!*

'Yeah, fresh shirt needed for me, I think.' I hop off my bed, under the pretence of rummaging through my bag, and crouch down with my back to Lou. I breathe once more.

'Wish me luck,' he says.

'Good luck,' I say from my hunkered position. 'You're not going to smoke that thing in the shower, Lou? Are you?' I say, slowly turning my head.

'Sometimes I worry about you, Bobby. I really do,' he says. 'OK, here goes.'

When the shower next door starts, my heart resumes its

normal rhythm. There's a bead of sweat on my brow. Aware that the clock's ticking, I quickly pull the shirt around my shoulders, fire a generous spray of deodorant under my pits and leap back on to the bed.

Between the water stopping and Lou's return can't be more than fifty seconds. He exits the bathroom wearing only his towel. I jump off the bed again, fiddling with my shoes this time.

'Fuck me sideways,' he moans. 'That was like bein' waterboarded in a pig's trough.'

'Not to be recommended then?' I say, still with my back to him, undoing and retying my laces.

'Unless you're the kind of person who'd enjoy a weekend in Jeffrey Dahmer's fridge, I wouldn't recommend it.'

My body shakes with giggles.

When I hear the sound of Lou's legs entering his jeans and the chime of his belt buckling, I stand to face him.

'Cool shirt, dude,' he says.

He's bare-chested.

On his eyes!

'Thought I'd spruce up before we went downstairs.'

Lou takes a step closer.

Eyes!

'I need to get me one of them checky shirts.' He places his hand on my breast pocket. *DON'T look at the eyes! DON'T!* 'Very nice indeed.'

'Glad you like it,' I say, casual and unconcerned. 'I'm

bursting for a piss.' It's the only thing that springs to mind; it gives me the opportunity to escape for a few minutes before re-entering a new man.

When I get back from my bogus pee, Lou's fully dressed and standing with his head popping out of one of the attic windows.

'Here,' he says, holding out the joint. 'Want some?'

'Not sure, to be honest.'

'Come on, two hits and you'll be good to go.' Lou obviously sees the stress on my face. 'Don't worry, I don't intend to blast the whole thing myself. I'm not that dumb.'

'Don't want to be mangled in front of the others,' I say.

'Tell me, Bobby, what can two drags do?'

'To me, a lot.'

'It'll make whatever Rod has planned for us more bearable, think of it that way.'

'Two puffs,' I say. 'And nothing more.'

'Two's plenty, my friend.' He offers me the joint.

I take it from his hand and bring it to my lips as if it's the most natural thing in the world, suck it deep into my lungs, praying I won't cough.

'Here, blow it out of the window.' Lou opens it a little further for me. 'Good smoke, right?'

'Yeah,' I say. But, honestly, I wouldn't have known the difference between the good, the shit or the ugly. 'So, are you missing home then?' I think the joint's giving me a certain freedom to ask what I want. Confidence to do what I'd normally not do.

'Jesus, we've only been here, like, ten minutes.'

'I know, but still.'

'What's to miss, dude?'

'Well, your mum or dad for a start. The routine. I don't know. It just feels a bit weird that we're here, in this place. Don't you think?' I say.

'Do I miss my dad?' Lou makes a noise. I can't decide whether it's a snide giggle or an affectionate snort.

'You and your dad don't get on well?'

'He lives in the States. We don't see each other. We don't talk. Nothin' to miss. Nothin' to *get on* about.'

'Sorry to hear that.'

'Why the fuck should you be sorry?'

'I don't know. Maybe because you sound bitter, or angry at him.'

'Me? Bitter? Fuck, no!' Lou stretches out his hand. 'Hey, you gonna pass that thing or not?'

'Oh, sorry.' I fire it into my mouth for a final naughty puff. 'Here.'

Lou takes three drags in rapid succession. He holds the smoke in his mouth, lets his cheeks inflate. I have a strong urge to pop one of his puffed-out cheeks, but before I can lift a finger he's blown the smoke out the window.

'And, anyway, he's the one who should be sorry.' Lou's voice is high-pitched and crackly.

'Who should?'

'My old man.'

'Sorry? Him? Why? If you don't mind me asking.'

'Don't matter.' Lou tips his head out the window; his hair sways in the wind. He momentarily closes his eyes. 'That's just the way it is.'

'I shouldn't have pried.'

He brings his head back in from the elements.

'You're OK, aren't you, Bobby?' Lou's stare is intense.

'Well …' I can't seem to get the words out. I think I might have blushed.

'I mean, you're decent. You care about shit, don't you? You're what girls would call a nice guy.' He does that inverted commas thing around the phrase 'nice guy'. 'Actually, you're much better than that – you'd be a "*really* nice guy" or a "*super* nice guy".'

'You as well,' I say.

'I ain't no nice guy. I'm an asshole. I know it and so do the others.' He nods his head towards downstairs. 'I'm not like you, Bobby.'

'Maybe that's what having a sick mother does for you,' I say. 'Can leave you angry and bitter.'

We share a knowing look. I shouldn't have prodded; a smirk comes over Lou's face.

'Havin' a sick mom has nothin' to do with it. No, havin' a sick mom just makes you obligin' and guilty. Essentially you become a slave to them, but a slave who loves their master nonetheless.'

'I don't feel like that.'

'I'm payin' you a fuckin' compliment, shit-brain. Don't let your mom take the credit for everything, OK?' he says, ruffling my hair with his open palm. 'Sometimes you've got to stand up and be counted. Be an individual.'

A compliment, what's that? I don't get compliments. I could stand at this window all night blowing smoke into the ether and listen to Lou's words until the birds chirp. I'd listen to him wax on about all the stuff I'm good at, how he sees me. Actually, how does he see me? Know what? I don't like the notion that I'm anyone's slave. Not true. And no one is my master either. No one.

'OK.' I push his hand away.

I've had a total of four puffs of the joint. I'd say Lou has had about eight or nine. His eyes drift and look longingly into the cold Borders night.

'When Mom got sick, the old man ran off back to the States. Couldn't handle it, could he?' Lou's focus is firmly on the goings-on outside the window. He doesn't so much as glance in my direction. 'I mean, what kind of asshole does that, Bobby? What sort of person abandons his responsibilities? What weak sack of shit would do that?'

I don't have answers to these questions. If indeed they are questions.

The joint is starting to embrace me warmly, flooding my brain with that weird time sensory distortion thing.

'Mom and me didn't need him anyway,' Lou says.

'Is that why you never talk about your mum when we're

in the group meetings?' I ask. 'Because it brings back memories of your dad?'

He scratches his neck, fingerstyles his damp hair.

'Maybe. Something like that. Who knows?'

'I've never really heard you talking about your mum.'

Lou gives me the same intense stare as before. Harder this time.

'Which is perfectly OK as well, you know,' I add hastily. 'I mean, not everyone's comfortable with that type of stuff. I mean, I don't really talk about my mum in the meetings either. Just … to you.'

'There's not much to talk about, Bobby. Know what I mean?' he says.

'Yeah … of course … I mean … I get it … I totally understand,' I say, *not* really knowing or understanding what he means.

'Course you do. Everyone "understands" everythin' here, don't they?' And out come the inverted commas again.

'What's wrong with your mum, Lou?' I'd never have asked such an intrusive question if it hadn't been for my intrusive-questions-filtering-system being demolished by the hash. 'What I mean is … what's her illness?'

'Fuck it! Who cares, Bobby, eh? We're here to forget that shit, aren't we?' he spits. 'That's what this weekend is all about: forgettin' shit. That's what Rod says, and I'm with him.'

Lou sucks the final embers out of the joint – so much for

not blasting the whole thing – then flicks the butt high into the night sky.

'You're right, we should forget things at home,' I reply, which I'm more than happy to do.

'Best we head down, in case Rod comes lookin' for us,' Lou says, making his way to the door.

'OK.'

He scoots before I can close the window.

As soon as I see the others, paranoia and fear kicks in. Roddy chucks some pizza menus on a table and asks us to choose. There's no way I can concentrate on pizza toppings, no way.

'Get me anything, as long as there's no pineapple on it,' I announce.

'Anything?' Roddy says.

'Anything.'

Whatever combination arrives won't bother me. I'm so painfully famished that I'd scoff a tramp's dog if it were plated up. I'm grateful the room we're in isn't too bright. I neither want to be seen nor heard.

Three threadbare velvet sofas and a large television square off the room. I flop myself in the corner of one of the sofas. Lou sits alongside Harriet and Tom. For the first half hour I've no idea who I'm sitting next to. Definitely Erin or Clare, the smell can't be anyone else: that unmistakable fresh make-up and perfume fusion screams woman. Reminds me of Bel, and further back, Mum.

I'm conscious that I'm not contributing anything to the goings-on. I sit in silence while waves of guilt envelop me. Could be the hash. I think of Mum's wish. I visualise it happening. Actually fucking visualise it: I'm on top, pinning her down with my knees and compressing her throat with my thumbs. I think of Lou and my invasive questions. My act of aggression towards Bel. That's what guilt does: it judges the word 'sorry' to be meaningless. I take out my phone.

Hi dollface. Place is a shitstorm! Ud luv it! Miss U. SOZ AGAIN!!!!!

Seems as if we've been waiting days for those pizzas to arrive. My pangs of hunger are torturous, I'm feeling strapped in by starvation, a bit like being stuck in the middle seat on a long-haul flight.

During the wait, Roddy suggests a game of charades. Of course he does! Boys versus the girls and Roddy. Needless to say, the boys' team is severely hampered by a couple of useless stoned space eejits. We're in no fit state to do our best *Modern Family*, *Breaking Bad* or *La La Land* mimes. My sole contribution is to clarify whether the person's mime is a film, song, television programme, book or play. Lou's input is to gawp keenly at whatever's in front of him. Totally absorbed. In that moment, this game of charades is more important to Lou than, say, the Middle East peace talks.

His gaping mouth and savage stare put Cal and Tom off their stride. I think he might have muttered '*Friends*' at one point, but I'm not one hundred per cent sure. How we get away with it I'll never know.

When the pizzas arrive it's like zoo time. I don't inspect any of the slices before I put them into my mouth. 'Put' makes it sound mannerly, more like shove, thrust, drive, hoover … Take your pick.

'Fuck's sake, talk about *Man v. Food*,' Harriet says, looking directly at me in disgust and referencing one of Tom's mimes.

'Right, guys, we have a choice of a couple of movies.' Roddy holds up two DVD cases.

'What are they?' Erin asks.

'This one's called *The Babadook*,' Roddy says. 'And this is *Whiplash*.'

'No, not heard of them,' Tom says. 'Are these arty-farty films, Roddy?'

'Is that that film about a drummer?' Clare asks.

'It is indeed,' Roddy says.

'Is this some kind of punishment, Roddy?' Harriet says. 'Who wants to watch some film about some twat battering the shit out of a set of drums?'

'What's that other one about?' Erin asks.

'*The Babadook*,' Roddy says, holding it aloft, 'is about an imaginary monster.'

'Sounds intriguing,' Cal says.

'No way. I'll be shitting it,' Harriet says.

I don't challenge the decision, even though I really want to see *Whiplash*. But it's done.

We're settling down to a good old-fashioned horror flick in our dark and isolated house, where I'm sleeping in the attic next to some stoned guy who might or might not have anger issues. What could possibly go wrong? Well, for one, somebody (a girl) could snuggle up to Lou on the sofa and we'd be three in the attic. I try not to think about that prospect.

If anyone was going to have the hots for Lou I'd have placed all my chips on Harriet. That could be my lazy assumption about girls who wear music T-shirts: how they lean towards those rough-edged guys, or those with that tortured-artist aura about them. You know, borderline arseholes. Not that Lou is an arsehole, far from it, but I can see how others might view him that way.

Fact is, I'm wrong about Harriet. How? Well, the film's barely begun when I spy her and Tom mauling each other's face on the opposite sofa. Huge part of me is relieved Tom is not Lou. Huge part is jealous because I too want to be desired like that. Not by Harriet because, just … you know.

I conjure an image of being next to Lou on the sofa, me edging closer to him, a sudden craving for our bodies to vie for breathing space. Why can't I? Why can't I just hoosh myself over to him a notch? I'm fed up with always being the guy who's never desired. Mr Everybody's Friend. Bel doesn't count because … well … because Bel's female.

Long story very short. Not long after the film kicks in

Harriet was in such a state of terror that Tom offered her an arm of protection. That protection developed into a cosy snuggle, before quickly morphing into an affectionate hug, which then turned into little pecks on Harriet's head; from there it wasn't long before they were getting down to some serious lip-on-lip tongue-twisting action. Fortunately, Roddy's conked out, as has everyone else. Except Lou and me. The wide-eyed boys.

'I'm goin' to bed, dude,' he says to me. 'Fucked if I'm sittin' here with a big gooseberry suit on. No way. Not my scene. Time to crash.'

'OK,' I say. 'I might just stay and watch the end of the film though.'

'Whatever, dude. I'm outta here.'

'Night then,' I say.

'Yeah, night … and that.'

He boosts, leaving a slew of young carers in his wake. Some horny, most knackered. And one (me) confused as hell as to whether I have deeper feelings for him. And, if so, why him? He's tough to read and makes me awkward when I'm around him.

Revelations

I don't bother waiting until the film is over. Shame because it isn't too bad. I give Lou enough time to fall asleep. Fifteen, twenty minutes? It turns out to be yet another one of my stoned time distortions, because when I return to the room he isn't tucked up in bed snoring his head off, is he? No, he isn't. Lou's sitting on the edge of the mattress, holding his face in his hands. Is he still melted? On the cusp of a whitey? Or recovering from one? I can't smell puke, just the general reek of the room. My phone pings.

U dnt miss me so shut it! Ha ha ha. Plus, stop saying SOZ. 4gtten already. Enjoy kip. Wish I was there … NOT!!

When Lou looks up, the glow of my phone illuminates his face. His eyes are spiderwebbed. His cheeks moist. His tears continue to run.

'Hey, Lou. Are you OK? What's happened? Is it Harriet snogging Tom?'

'It's not that, dude,' he spits out through tears and snot.

'What is it? Can I do anything?'

'It's something else,' he says, returning his head to his hands. His shoulders jig up and down. I pocket my phone and take a step closer. Not wanting to intrude too much, I let my hand hover over his back.

'Lou?'

'It's something else, Bobby. It's just something else.'

Naturally the desire to ask what that *something else* is gnaws, but I don't dare. I rest my fingers on his shoulder. Part support. Part affection. He doesn't recoil. I sit beside him. He looks at me. Crimson eyes. Chaotic hair. Face saturated in despair. I don't dare ask.

We look at each other.

I do what I do when Danny gets into a similar state: I hold him to my chest, curl one hand around his body, the other around his head. I clamp him tight and make him feel safe. Lou becomes an infant in my arms. It works: his baby-like bleats come to a steady halt. After a while I release him and he's able to talk calmly. I don't push, he offers.

'Sorry, dude,' he says.

'You've nothing to be sorry about, Lou,' I say.

'I'm such a pussy.'

'It's good to let stuff out from time to time. Sure. I do the same. What we have to deal with overwhelms us sometimes. We have to let those feelings spill over.'

'That's the thing, dude. I'm not sure I belong to who you lot are.'

'You do. You're one of us. Every group needs the rebel. You're vital,' I joke.

'No,' he says abruptly. 'I'm not.'

'OK.'

'Sorry, dude. Didn't meant to snap, it's just ...'

'No need to apologise. Seriously,' I say.

'It's just that chat we were havin' earlier ...'

'About your dad and that?'

'Yeah. Well, it got me thinkin' about Mom.'

I nod.

'That's why I was upset,' he continues, playing with a loose thread on his jeans.

'Right.'

'When you came in I was thinkin' about her.'

'I'm with you, Lou,' I say, wanting to show him that he's not alone, he doesn't have to isolate himself. 'So many times when I think about my mum I want to tear the world apart, rip the moon to shreds. Even breathing becomes tough sometimes. It feels as if I've been gut-punched. It's painful, I totally get it.'

I realise there's a sense of selfishness about opening up my own feelings to Lou. This isn't about my experiences and emotions, so why am I spilling? Maybe he's handing me the rope to do so.

'But you *don't* get it. That's the thing, Bobby. You, Cal, Tom, Clare. None of you get it.'

Lou covers his face and lets out a muffled groan. My arm reaches again for his shoulder.

'I shouldn't be here,' he says.

'You should.'

'No, I shouldn't.' Lou fires me some serious sad eyes. 'See, thing is, Bobby, I don't actually *care* for anyone.'

I'm not aware I'm doing it, but I recoil from him. Not in condemnation, more confusion. He has a hangdog look about him. 'I'm no carer, Bobby,' he says.

'What … ?' I need a beat to process what he's said. 'What do you mean, *you're no carer*? I don't –'

'I have no one to care for. It's that simple. I don't care for anyone.'

'But, your mum? What about your mum?'

'Not any more, dude.'

My response is to shuffle a bit, do some serious blinking and exaggerate my oxygen intake. Melodramatic nonsense. All the time I'm letting his words percolate: he-has-no-one-to-care-for?

My hand goes to him again. I clasp him gently. He has the tension of someone keeping a secret. He doesn't need to do that. *You don't need to do that with me, Lou. You can let it all out. If your mum is no longer alive, tell me how she died; talk about your last moments together. I'm here.*

His bulk springs up and down, convulsing with sobs, but

I'm there to absorb and catch if needed. His hair is oily with sweat, as if his head's been sobbing too. I slide some of it away from his eyes.

He releases himself from my hands; now tears have welled up in me and I'm struggling to keep them inside. I consider his loss, but also think of my own pending loss. And I know he knows this, he does. We hold each other in a stare: it feels natural, no words need to be exchanged. I think I know what he's asking, what he wants us to do. We share grief.

'Thanks, dude,' he says softly.

'No need to thank me, Lou,' I say.

'You're a good friend. A good person.'

'I'm so sorry about your mum. I'm truly sorry.'

He says nothing, just tilts his head ever so slightly and approaches me. Reality: we approach each other, our eyes fastened. It happens. We allow it. Consent granted. Our lips connect, and it transports me to somewhere safe. Somewhere magical.

'I can explain,' Lou says when we break.

'There's nothing to explain,' I tell him, dropping my hand from his neck.

'No, not about that. I can explain about what I said. I can explain everything.'

'I think I know, Lou,' I say.

'No, you don't.'

I've known all along, if I'm being totally honest. Unlike

the rest of us in Poztive, Lou's never been racked with exhaustion or looked haggard when he turns up to the sessions. I can't recall him having to bolt to relieve whoever was watching his mum. We never heard him share information about his experience. And his house is showroom tidy. That time at his place I knew something was off. There were no visible signs that Lou cared for anyone. But all along I suppressed these thoughts. I mean, you'd have to be pretty fucking damaged to even attempt a stunt like that. Anyway, I wasn't going to chin him about whether his mother's illness was kosher or not, was I? Any suspicions I had remained dormant. Until now.

'OK, here I am. Give it to me. I'm all ears,' I say.

'It was what we were talkin' about earlier.'

'When?'

'Before we went to have pizza. All that talk about Mom and Dad.'

'Right. Are you telling me that was all bullshit now?'

'No, none of it was bullshit, none of it.' Lou gets up from the bed and begins pacing the room. 'My old man *is* in the States, he *is* an asshole and Mom *did* have a terminal illness and I *was* her carer. All that is true, every last detail of it *is* true.' He punches out the emphasis, sits again.

'Lou, I want to understand, really I do, but you're not making it easy for me. You're not making much sense.'

He lowers his head.

'Mom was dead, Bobby. She was dead. Every day she was

dead. Lyin' there in her room … dead. No body or brain function, not so much as the flicker of a goddam eye or the movement of a goddam finger. Dead! All that was keepin' her alive was a machine and a bag of fluid. Her organs reacted well to that apparently.' Lou looks at me, raises his voice. 'That fuckin' machine, Bobby. That fuckin' machine, huffin' and puffin' all night long. Night after night after goddam night. It was like livin' with an asthmatic monster. Every day I wanted to throw that fuck piece out of the window.'

I hold his stare. Allow the long pause to penetrate his brain. He lets more tears fall. These tears are no smokescreen: they're manifesting his dishonour.

'What I don't understand is, why lie all this time?'

'I know. I'm so sorry, dude.'

I doubted this though.

'Why are you even in this group? I mean, why do you go to the meetings if, you know, you don't need to?'

His demeanour and gait remind me of an altar boy. Maybe he is genuinely sorry.

'I need the group, Bobby. I need you guys, even though I don't show it.'

'Need it how?'

'It's complicated.'

'Try me.'

His posture changes; he stares at the wall in front of him, taps fingers off his thigh.

'I go for the company. I go because I'm kinda makin'

friends there. I go to forget. But I also go to remember, which is crazy, I know.'

'That's not clearing this up, Lou.'

'I get to remember those days of carin' for Mom. You guys transport me back to that time and what I felt like durin' it. I've experienced those things you talk about too, don't forget that.'

'I don't doubt it, but how does it help you forget? That I don't get.'

'Doin' stuff that's not about lookin' after sick people. Comin' down here, for example. I could be sat at home all weekend with my head buzzin'. Poztive takes me away from that world. It helps.'

I have little to offer him, no words of comfort, no reassurance that I understand. He just needs to keep talking.

'Look, Bobby, I *was* carin', but not like you guys. I'd no meals to prepare or no ass to wipe. A team of nurses did everythin' in the daytime, then I took over. My job was to make sure Mom was gettin' the correct amount of fluids in her system, or that the machine didn't run out of steam in the middle of the night. Pretty simple.' Lou looks into the fibres of the carpet. 'You can imagine how much sleep I got. I looked like shit all the time.'

There was one obvious question to ask:

'How did she die, Lou?'

He's on his feet once more, pacing the room, fiddling with that hair of his. He doesn't look at me.

I can't keep my eyes off him.

'What you have to remember, Bobby, was that she *was* dead. The stroke destroyed her, everythin'. She wasn't my mom any longer. Just some lifeless woman in my house every day.' Suddenly he stops pacing, covers his face. 'Oh, God!'

I jump up. Steady him with my hands. He needs me, and I want him to need me.

'Lou, what happened is a natural thing after a big stroke, isn't it?'

'I guess.'

'Sick people pass. They pass.'

His head arches downwards.

'Yeah, she passed, dude. She passed,' he says.

Gone are the tears.

I take a baby step back from him.

'I feel there's a *but*, Lou,' I say.

He smirks.

'There is a *but*. A giant *but*,' he says.

'So ...' I stretch out my arms in order to welcome what he's about to tell me. He's on the bed again, gathering his thoughts.

'I helped her along.'

'What?'

'I helped her pass, Bobby.'

He twiddles with that dangling loose thread on his jeans. If I'd brought scissors I'd cut the thing off.

'Lou?' I say gently. 'Are you telling me what I think you're telling me?'

He nods his head.

'I am, Bobby. I am. You got it.'

'But how?'

'The machine.'

'What? You turned it off?'

'Not exactly.'

'Exactly what then?' I don't want to seem as though I'm interrogating him but I'm immersed. I require fine details. I need them. Mum won't suffer any tin machine keeping her alive – no way will she allow one in her house. Stuff will happen before it gets to that stage … if she has her way.

'How, Lou?' I ask.

'One night I'm lyin' there listenin' to it, as I normally did – it's like the wind, you know, you live with its constant noise in the background. You get so used to it that sometimes you don't notice it at all.'

'Is that what happened? You didn't hear it?'

'I was readin'. I heard it, but I didn't hear it stop, if that makes sense?'

'I can see that,' I say.

'I remember thinkin' that I hadn't heard it for a while. The book I was readin' was cool. That noise became part of the night, as if darkness was breathin' in the house. Like I said, Bobby, I stopped noticin' it after a time, and I guess that's what happened when I was readin' that book. I didn't zone in right away, so I didn't know how long it was actually off for.'

'What alerted you?'

'If it malfunctions an alarm sounds after a few seconds. I heard it ring but chose to tune out the noise, and then eventually I sat up.'

'Then what?'

'I let it ring for maybe another minute or so. I knew what I was doin'. I was totally with it, in complete control.'

'That was it then? That's how your mum … ?'

'Not exactly,' Lou says, looking at his hands. I get the feeling that what he sees is something else entirely: he's looking at two weapons of mass destruction located at the bottom of his arms. I alter my position.

'What do you mean, *not exactly?*' I say.

'I went into Mom's room. She looked so peaceful, Bobby. She looked beautiful. I knew she was smilin' inside. I knew she was willin' me to do it. She looked so fuckin' beautiful, you see. In that instant I knew exactly what I had to do.'

I try to disguise eagerness for sensitivity.

'What did you have to do, Lou?'

'I didn't put the emergency switch on,' he says.

'So you let the machine break down?'

'No.' Lou's eyes remind me of a boxer's in those seconds before combat commences. 'I let the machine die, Bobby. I let it die.'

'Who else knows?' I ask.

'Not a sinner.'

Suddenly I feel a chill in the air.

'I was sleepin' all the way through it, right?' he adds. 'That was my story. My mantra.'

'But you didn't technically kill her, Lou. The machine failed, not you. You're not to blame.'

Lou's eyebrows hit the roof. He stares at the cracked ceiling.

'Right, Lou?'

'Right ... and wrong,' he says. 'There's more to it than that, Bobby.'

More?

'You don't have to tell me everything. If you don't want to.'

'No, I want to.'

He sits forward, arse on the edge of the bed. Legs spread wide. Very manly. Very worried.

'I removed the breathin' tube she had in her mouth,' he says.

What follows is the longest pause in the history of conversation; I'm a prisoner to the pause, his words, his stare.

'And then I smothered her,' he says. My mouth gapes. 'I put her out of her misery.'

Put her out of her misery! Really? Is that the technical term for a psychopath? Is that what Mum wants me to do? Is that what Harold Shipman thought he was doing before he became intoxicated by it and was unable to stop? Someone who could clean away other people's problems, wipe out their suffering. I mean, he was a doctor – he must've had some sort of brain function. Or are people like that just downright nuts?

It's horses with broken legs and cats with cancer who get put out of their misery, not parents. Not mothers. Not anyone simply because they've asked for it. I'm no Shipman. I'm no serial killer. I'm just a son with a sick mum.

'That's what I did, Bobby, I smothered my mom,' he tells me again.

I swear a shiver shoots right up my spine. I'm thinking just how much easier I could've made this for him. Perhaps I should be holding his hand throughout. All I'd need to do is share my own load, enlighten him about life's parallels. Throw him a bone. Empathise. Something. But why don't I? Why do I back off? Of course I know why. I'm no fool. I want to listen, to hear the black tale, to understand his modus operandi. Pick his brain without him cottoning on. Ultimately, I don't share because I haven't done what Lou's done. His crime is not mine. By telling Lou it would only make it real, and if I make it real it means that it's going to happen. And the thought of that drenches me in a whole lot of guilt, even though I haven't done anything. Yet.

'What? You … I mean … how?' I say.

'A pillow.'

'Over her face?'

'Covered her face and held it down. Forced it on to her.'

'But you could've just left the machine off, you didn't need ...'

'I never trusted that thing, I needed to be sure she was gone.'

'Fucking hell, Lou.' I try not to sound astonished or judgemental, especially given my own circumstances. 'Does anyone know about this?'

'If they do, I don't give a shit. The way I see it, I helped Mom out of her burnin' hell. I helped her live again, you get me?'

I'm nervous.

'Course,' I mutter.

'I freed her from her very own Guantanamo fucking Bay. Now, you tell me, Bobby, who wouldn't do that for someone they loved?'

My head spins. I consider my own situation, play through some of the scenarios that circulate. So many things I don't have the nerve to ask.

'*You'd* do that for someone you loved, wouldn't you?' Lou says. '*You'd* do that?'

'I don't know ... I mean ... I'm ...' My tongue is dry.

The whites of his eyes are pink diamonds. He's dropped the coolness he arrived with, doesn't care that his hair is disobedient. His hands shift between thigh-rubbing and clenching. I want to anchor him in my arms.

I want to hear more.

'It was like a mountain bein' lifted from my shoulders, dude. Like I'd been luggin' this dead weight around with me, a weight that kept forcin' me down, like a fuckin' elephant slouched on your chest. Know what I mean?'

'Was there no hope at all?' I ask. For someone in my position this is beyond being a stupid question. 'I mean, was it confirmed that she wasn't ever going to get better? No chance of her getting well?'

Lou digests my question, his face stiff and emotionless. He kind of half smiles to himself. I don't know if it's amusement or scorn. Knowing Lou, it could've been either. It unnerves me.

'I mean ... what I mean is ... that ... sometimes hope is all we have,' I stutter. Lou doesn't respond. 'Hope is what we cling to, right, Lou?' His eyes click back to reality.

'Hope? Fuck hope, man. What we're talkin' about here is goddam ethics. Forcin' people to stay alive against their body's will. Forcin' the dead to stay alive. Forcin' everyone to grasp on to the only thing that remains: Goddam hope. What a bullshit concept that is. Believe me, it's all about fuckin' ethics, dude. Ethics that forced Mom to exist without livin'. That stripped her of her damn dignity. Condemned her on some jumped-up dictum created by a band of legal fuckheads and religious moralists.'

I rest my hand on his. He stops fidgeting.

'I've never seen it that way before,' I say, and it's true.

He sandwiches my hand between his.

'Yeah, well, not many people do, Bobby.'

'Can I ask you something?'

'Sure.'

'How'd you get away with it?'

Lou unleashes my hand. Seems put out by my question. Does the whole hands-through-hair routine.

'You really wanna know?'

'Well, yeah.'

'I put the breathin' apparatus back in her mouth and turned the machine back on after it had stopped workin'. I covered my tracks. The story was tight. Machine fucked up and I was too late to fix it. Shit like that happens all the time, doesn't it?'

I searched for something behind his eyes, a sign of the confident Lou. This was him bare and exposed. I sat there nodding my head like a little lapdog.

'Were you not sad, Lou?'

'Sad? I was distraught, Bobby. Genuinely distraught. I'd just lost my mom. It's not as if I was doin' goddam cartwheels all over the place. People sympathised with me.' I nod in agreement. 'Mom died because the machine broke down.' He starts rubbing his forehead. 'No, scratch that. Mom died because of that fuckin' illness, that disease. It butchered every bit of her. It was nothin' else. Nothin' else. That's what I have to keep remindin' myself in order to remain sane. I get what I did, I get it, but I also know why I did it. I did it because I needed to carry out an act of compassion. That act of compassion, Bobby, is the knowledge that keeps me sane.'

'I get it, Lou, I really do. But what now?'

'Meanin'?'

'Well, how do you survive? I presume your mum's disability payments have stopped.'

'Dad puts something in my account every month. You know, to keep food on my plate and a roof over my head.'

'I thought you and your dad don't speak?'

'We don't, but he needs to do somethin' to ease that damn conscience of his, doesn't he?'

'Suppose so,' I say, yet I had further niggles.

'I see you, dude. Your eyes are fightin' to stay up with your mind,' Lou says. 'You want to know everythin', right?'

'I ... eh ...'

'Go ahead, ask.'

'When did all this happen?'

'With Mom?'

'Yeah.'

'Seventeen months ago.'

'I was also kind of wondering how you get to attend all the meetings without anyone questioning you being there? Considering ... you know ... considering ...'

'Considerin' that I no longer care for anyone? Considerin' that Mom's no longer here?'

'Right.'

'It's easy,' he says. 'No one has ever asked me to leave. I

used to go to similar meetings when I was lookin' after Mom – different Rod, different carers, but same shit really.'

'So no one has ever questioned you?'

'No soul, no sinner.'

'That's weird.'

'So I figured I'd stay until they kick my ass out.'

'They must know,' I say.

'What?'

'That your mum is no longer here, that you don't look after her. They must know.'

'Course they fuckin' know, how could they not? They're not stupid. They connect with the authorities, they do their research. They know.'

'So why you still … ?'

'What, you think because Mom is dead that I don't need help? That you stop being a young carer just like that?' Lou clicks his fingers. 'No, dude, I need just as much help as you do.' He softens his voice. 'They don't ask me to beat it because I guess they think the same – they sympathise with me.'

'But you hate it, don't you? I mean, you always look as if you never want to be there.'

'Who does want to be there?' he says.

'Well …'

'See, it's not a question of *want*, Bobby. It's all about *need*. We all need to be there, for our sanity. I might not say it too often but I need folks around me as well. I need to pour shit out to folks who understand, folks who …'

'Who empathise?'

'On the button, dude. Empathy.'

'So you need us then?' I say.

Lou scans me; his features have brightened.

'Yeah, I need you bunch of assholes,' he says. I release a tiny nervous laugh. 'There, said it. Happy now?'

'No, I totally understand,' I say. 'I need you lot too.'

There's a silence, or an awkward pause. Hard to tell the difference. During the silence/pause it feels as if my skin's tickling all over, making me fidget uncomfortably.

'I guess that means we need each other then, doesn't it?' Lou says.

He edges closer to me. I'm not sure I want him to. I'm not sure I don't want him to either. He comes nearer. My bones bite. As he moves in, I spurt out, 'Did he get you that scooter?'

'Who?'

'Your dad.'

'Seventeenth birthday present.'

'I got iTunes vouchers for mine,' I chuckle.

'Let's not forget he's still a grade-A asshole though.'

'Roger that,' I say.

Lou laughs.

I puff through my nose. Grin.

He's in front of me, places his hands on my shoulders. I take the strain of his weight as his eyes hijack mine. I'm flustered.

'You know what the best part was, Bobby?' he says.

'About?'

'About letting Mom go?'

'Erm … ?'

'Know what the best part was?' he says again.

'What?'

'It made me happy knowin' she was in a better place. It brought life back into my world. I started to notice things again. To enjoy the things I'd blocked out.'

'Makes sense.'

'She was liberated.'

He inches nearer, or is it me who advances? Everything is fuzzy.

'I'm with you, Lou. Listen …'

'Know what that feels like?' he says.

'What?'

'Liberty, Bobby. Know what liberty feels like?'

I see so many possibilities, but guilt, duplicity and death enter my mind. So many thoughts and images pass through me. Freedom for Mum. Freedom for Danny and me. I smell pizza and cigarettes off Lou's breath.

'Not really, no.'

'I do, and I'm tellin' you that it's pretty fuckin' exhilarating. Better than any high you'll get from smokin' some goddam joint, that's for sure. It's like … it's like a perpetual high. An infinite high. *That*'s what liberty is, Bobby.'

The entirety of what he's saying strikes more than a chord: there's a whole rhapsody of response playing inside my brain.

It's all there in Lou's story, the similarities. It's all there. Makes sense. Everything tells me to share my burden. If nothing else, so I can be relieved of the moral torment that's been plaguing me.

His hands dig into my biceps like he's trying to reassure me of something. Like he knows what I'm about to tell him. Like he's some sort of mind-fucker who sees inside people's thoughts.

I don't tell him. This is Lou's big night. I can't trample all over it with my issues.

We zip our eyes together.

'I'm here for you, Lou,' is all I say.

'And I'm here for you, Bobby. I want you to know that.'

'I do.'

Totally zipped.

'Think I want us to lie down now,' he says.

*

Exhilarating. Petrifying. Reassuring.

It's everything.

It'll be glued to my memory until I'm boxed up and topped with flowers.

Lou sparks up another joint.

Right there and then, lying on the bed in that manky room, I declare my joint-smoking days well and truly behind me. Lou doesn't force me to partake. He doesn't force me to do any of it. Everything was my choice, straight out of my head, my heart. All mine.

'I know it's such a goddam cliché,' Lou says, blowing impressive smoke rings high into the cold air outside our window. 'But I just have to have a smoke afterwards.'

'Everything about you is a cliché, Lou,' I say.

He crashes a pillow against my head.

'Watch it, douchebag.'

It's either extremely late or annoyingly early. We've been up all night talking. Well, mainly talking. Lou fails to finish the joint; he nips it halfway down. It's like he's been given a general anaesthetic: his body flops as his words become inaudible. We're both exhausted.

Lou's head is on my shoulder. His breathing forms tiny droplets of saliva on my chest. I don't mind. The breath's a tad edgy, not a problem. His snoring vibrates off my torso. I love its rhythm. His belly gently brushes mine on every exhale: a weary wave stroking the sand. I close my eyes, allow my mind to wander, imagine a deserted coastline with two stragglers lolling around on it. And that's the thing: we literally could've been there, we could've been anywhere. All it takes is some assorted images behind these bolted eyes of mine.

And now I'm bang inside my very own cliché. I try to formulate a poem in my head, something memorable, something short. I need to capture this moment so I can hang my fingertips off it when Lou won't be around.

All day Saturday is like wading through smog, as if none of it had happened. Lou doesn't mention his mum and we don't attempt to reignite the flames of the previous night. The Saturday is an extension of a Poztive meeting: lots of activities followed by awkward conversation. We barely crack a breath to each other. Beyond weird. We're both withdrawn. Call it remorse. Call it embarrassment. I want those flames again, I do, but we keep to our separate beds. I don't sleep much.

#9 ... complete

the smell of your hair, slicked back and sorted,
pasted to my skin
we both took the weight
you laid bare as I unstripped my own burden
joyless, serious and full of delicate plotting,
then we gushed
but held firm until it led us to now:

pore on pore
a mild movement
a lip parted
a subtle snore
and it was that hair I rested my hand upon

part support

part affection
you didn't recoil
and neither did I

Shoot 'Em Up

On the way home I fluctuate between ecstasy and misery, still trying to wrestle with everything Lou told me ... and the other thing. I picture him with his mother, watching that machine pump artificial life into her. I see him ponderous and compassionate. I understand his pain and want to soothe it.

As I'm walking to my front door, the spring in my step buckles, dark clouds descend. I brace myself as I enter.

'Bel!' I say when I see her, my arms wide and inviting. 'I'm so sorry about –'

'Are you still going on about that, Seed?'

'Just mortified and –'

'Bobby, it's done, it's over. I've forgotten about it. Shit happens and all that.'

'Thanks, Bel.'

'But, to put it mildly, you're a dick.'

'Well …'

'And I've always known you're a dick, so what's new?'

'Exactly.'

My arms still await her embrace.

'And if you think you're getting a hug you can get lost.'

'How's Danny?'

'He's in his room, been there most of the weekend.'

'Really?'

'It's a wonder he has any hands left.'

'Bel, please. Too much.'

'Just saying.'

'And Mum?'

'Nurse just says the same thing: "I've given medicine, just keep an eye on her."'

'Right.'

'She's been sleeping mostly, but I did put some music on for her from time to time. Danny gave her dinner.'

'Soup?'

'Mainly.'

'Thanks for the music. She'd like that, cheers, Bel.'

'Think I'd need medicine too if I had to listen to some of that guff.'

'Ever thought of becoming a nurse, Bel?'

'Every fucking day, Seed. Every fucking day.'

A quick examination tells me that a lot of telly watching and not much else has happened over the weekend. I didn't expect Bel and Danny to spring clean the place, but still! Who wants to live in a kip?

'I know what you're thinking, Bobby,' she says. 'I'm going to sort the place out.'

'You don't have to, you can boost. People must be missing you.'

'You're joking, right?'

'Maybe.'

'Don't you know this has all been planned?' she says, rotating her arms. 'I purposely left the house looking as though it'd been burgled by junkies, then I can spend more time here cleaning up.'

'You mean more time away from your place?' I say.

'Anyway, I'm on my last episode of this new Netflix series, so I'll start after that.' She sinks into the sofa.

'Hey, I was thinking of asking one of the guys from the carers' group to join us one Friday,' I say to her. Bel pretends not to hear, focusing on a ladder in her tights. Oh, but she hears me all right.

'Bel?'

'What?'

'I was thinking of asking Lou to come on Friday. He's cool. You'd like him.'

'Since when have you started using words like "cool"?'

'He's nice. That better?'

'The Vespa guy?'

'Yeah.'

'He bailed on you before.'

'He's a decent guy, that's all I'm saying.'

'Decent schmeecent. Do what you want, I couldn't give two hoots. It's only a pizza for fuck's sake.'

'What about a movie as well?'

'Seen enough John Hughes films to do me a lifetime, Bobby. Happy to scrap the movie.'

She could say no, which I'd probably understand, but she doesn't. She agrees, with all the grace of a Nazi in a mosque.

'So, will I invite him?'

'Don't care, do what you want. Your call, Batman.'

'Right.'

'Can I watch this now?'

'Don't let me stop you. I'll go see the troops,' I say, nodding to upstairs.

Mum's asleep, but her mouth opens and closes as though she's asking for water – reminds me of a baby requesting its milk. She could be bang in the middle of an epic dream where she has the gift of good health: dancing, skipping, running. Making her chums convulse at her hilarious patter. Who'd want to be woken from that? I dab the drool off her face, pick up her glass and slide the straw in her mouth. She sucks like a newborn. I leave without waking her and head to my brother's room.

Danny's sitting at his computer, playing some shoot/kill/explode/obliterate game. He hears but doesn't acknowledge me. His hands move like the clappers, shooting/killing. Blood splats everywhere. Men – mainly men – writhe around in agony. It's very real. Very worrying. Definitely need to have some serious computer/internet/games chat.

'Hi, Dan,' I say. 'I'm home.'

He continues to thumb aggressively at his control.

'What you playing, mate?'

'Game,' he says.

'Looks brutal.'

'It's got guns.'

'Any good?'

'It's OK.'

I stand behind him, pretend I'm interested.

'There's a guy wounded over there. He one of yours?' I ask him.

'Yes.'

'Why don't you help him?'

'He's going to die. If I help him I might die too. That'd be stupid.'

'But he's in pain, Danny.'

'It's not real pain, Bobby.'

'Doesn't matter. Do you want him to suffer?'

'He's going to die anyway.'

'Then maybe you should do something to help end his suffering, that's all I'm saying.'

'Bobby, it's *my* game. Not *your* game. If I go back and kill him then I might get killed, and then it'll be your fault that I got killed, and then I'll be in a rotten mood with you. More than the one I'm in now.'

'You in a rotten mood with me?' I ask.

'Go away.'

'Dan, what is it?'

'Please go away, Bobby.' His pressing becomes rapid. Someone comes out from behind a parked car and shoots his character in the head. The control flies across the room. 'Now look what you made me do!'

It takes a lot not to react to his tantrum. I adopt my calm parental voice.

'Danny, what's going on?'

'Nothing. I got killed.'

'No. What happened this weekend?'

'Nothing.'

'Danny!'

My voice rises. My head tilts. A veritable teacher in the making.

'She wouldn't talk to me,' he says, flicking his chin upwards.

'Who? Bel?'

'No.'

'Who then?'

'Mum.'

'Mum wouldn't talk to you?'

'Yes.'

'What do you mean she wouldn't talk to you?'

'I tried.'

'Speak sense, Danny. How did Mum –'

'I tried to ask her things, but she wouldn't joke or anything.'

'Was she sleeping?'

'No, her eyes were open.'

'Could just be the medicine, Dan.'

'I even tried to do a lie-down cuddle, but she didn't cuddle back.'

'What did she do?'

'Just made grunts and noises.' Danny retrieves his control and examines it for collateral. 'She sounds like a baby, Bobby.'

I stand mute and redundant. I need to rub my forehead, but I don't want to show him my own distress.

'It's what's happening to her, Dan. Don't blame Mum,' I say.

'I'm not blaming her, I just want everyone to stop being tragic. I just wish that pain in the arse disease would piss the fuck off.'

'I wish it would too.'

'But it's not going to, is it?' he says. I glare at the computer. Everyone's lying dead on the screen. 'Is it, Bobby?'

'Don't think so, mate.'

'That's not what you're supposed to say.'

'I'm sorry, Dan. I don't want to lie to you.'

'So don't lie to me then.'

I sway on my feet, dry sweaty hands on jeans. Suddenly my heart's fizzing. I'm hesitant and nervous.

'Danny?'

'What?'

'If I could make the disease go away, I would,' I say. 'Honestly, I would. I'd do anything.'

'If I could kick the fuck out of it, I would,' he says.

'I'd help you.'

'I'd stamp on its head until it wasn't moving.'

'I'd break its legs.'

'I'd saw its toes off.'

We snigger at the fantasy of the actions. It's OK for Danny: he's sheltered by his fictional world while I'm shackled to the reality of Mum's request. The opportunity to be part of Lou's compassion squad grapples with me.

Danny's sitting there and I can hear myself playing out the conversation:

You and me, Dan. We could do it together.

You think it'll work, Bobby?

If we're calm and organised it will.

And Mum really wants this?

More than anything, mate. More than anything.

And she'll be one hundred per cent free from all the pain in the world?

Like a kite in the wind.

I play it over and over.

My body is heating up.

Blood slushes inside me.

I want to ask him to help.

You and me, Bobby?

You and me, Dan.

How?

I sit on his bed. Danny hates people sitting on his bed. I smile warmly at him.

'Maybe one day you and me *will* make that disease piss the fuck off,' I say.

'Yeah, one day,' he says.

And I'm about to open myself wide and tell him, to share it all. But, I can't do it. Not now.

I spring to my feet.

'Anyway, let's speak later, mate. I have to help Bel clean up the shit hole downstairs.'

'Well, don't blame me,' Danny says.

'Who else is there to blame?'

'It wasn't just my fault.'

'I believe you, idiot features. Thousands wouldn't.'

I ruffle his hair and exit the room, nerves pummelling my body.

The Exposer

After school the next day I'm showing Danny how to make a stir-fry. We chop, cut, chuck.

'You just bung everything in the pan,' I tell him.

'Cooking's a doddle,' he says.

'Now stir like crazy.'

He stirs like crazy.

We gorge on the food.

'I like stir-fry, Bobby,' he says, noodles snaking out of his mouth.

'Great, you can make it next time.'

I'm scooping up the remaining peppers on my plate, mouth gaping, fork on the move, but something stops me before I can snaffle it. The sound from outside is unmistakable. It's a sound that comes with its own smell. I don't need to look out of the window to see who it is; I know a vintage Vespa vroom when I hear one.

'Who's that? Who's that?' Danny says when the door goes.

'Just a pal,' I say.

'Bel?'

'No, a pal from the group I attend.'

'Why they here? What do they want?'

'I'm going to find out, Dan. You stay here.'

'You going to bring them in?'

'Maybe, I don't know.' I get to my feet. 'Wait here, I'll be back in a minute.'

'We've no stir-fry left,' Danny shouts after me.

I inflate my lungs before opening the door. It's the first time we've seen each other since … we last saw each other. How do I react? Do I smile? Go straight in for the man hug?

'Hi, Lou,' I say, going directly for the *hey-I'm-cool-as-fuck* approach.

'Bobby,' Lou says, assuming the same conduct. He stands there looking like a bloody Morrissey lyric or something. This could be a *hey-I'm-cool-as-fuck* stand-off. His snazzier clothes give him victory.

'What's happening? What you doing here?' I ask.

'I wanna talk about somethin'.'

'Oh, OK.'

'And I wanna see you.' He shrugs his shoulders almost apologetically.

Music to my lugs. I want to see him too, I really do. I hold the moment a little longer, just to plant a tiny seed of doubt in his mind. Actually, I think *I'm* winning the stand-off competition.

'Come in,' I say, stepping aside. His hand brushes my waist as he slides past. Fresh deodorant billows up my nose.

Danny's standing to attention as if awaiting royalty.

'Hey, you must be Dan?' Lou says, stretching out his hand. 'Good to meet you, dude.'

Danny sniggers. It's like the incarnation of every Netflix show he's ever watched has just entered his house.

'Is that your real voice?' Danny asks.

'Yeah, I'm not from around here,' Lou says.

'Dan, why don't you go and play some Xbox?' I say.

'You any good?' Lou asks.

'Shit hot,' Dan says.

'Cool.'

Danny sniggers again.

'Maybe you can show me some time,' Lou says. 'Probably beat my ass.'

Danny's eyes grow.

'Go, Dan.' I banish him off.

Danny heads to his room. Lou takes a seat, looks anxious. Serious. Sad.

I think I know why; since returning from the Borders I've been going through every facet of what happened. Delights and frights in equal measure. I stand in front of him.

'Everything OK, Lou? What's going on?'

'Just thinkin' and stuff,' he says.

'What stuff?'

'Stuff that happened, you know?'

DO I KNOW?

NO, LOU, REMIND ME AGAIN!!!

'I'm sorry about the Saturday,' he adds. 'I didn't know how to look at you, or how to deal with it, so I clammed up.'

'I was the same really.'

He stares at our tired carpet. Examines our discoloured walls. Judges the two Ikea prints we have hanging above the fireplace. Mum's choice. He slumps forward, bends into his knees, hands turning.

'Just haven't done anythin' like that before, that's all,' he says. 'In case you thought –'

'Me neither,' I say. 'But know what?'

'What?'

'I'm glad we did.'

'Yeah, me too, Bobby.'

'And I'm glad you felt strong enough to tell me about your mum.'

'Sorry for puttin' all that shit on you.'

'No, it means a lot actually. It's trust, isn't it?'

'I guess.'

'I'm glad you felt you could trust me, Lou.'

'I did. I can, I mean, I do. I do trust you.'

I look at the ceiling to see if I can hear Danny's Xbox. I bend to meet Lou's face. We smile. His lips move. I'm still conscious of Danny's presence.

'But can I trust *you*, Lou?'

'With your life, Bobby.'

'Because I know what watching your mum die feels like.' I stand upright, step away and leave him seated. 'I know that feeling exactly. The weight of it is attached to every garment of clothing I own – it pushes me deeper and deeper into the ground.'

'Every wakin' hour, dude.'

'And I'm struggling with it, Lou.'

'I couldn't handle it either. It sank me.'

I'm pacing. Worried about Danny interrupting. Worried about what I'm about to tell Lou.

One of us has taken the floor again, just like in the attic at the residential. But now it's my floor that awaits; it's my turn to fiddle with dangling threads. The knots in my stomach contort.

'Lou,' I say quietly. 'I've something important I need to tell you.'

'I'm here, dude. My ears are yours.'

'But this has to stay between you and me. Only you and me. Nobody else. OK?'

'Jesus, Bobby, I got it?' Lou's body is rigid, as if engrossed in a film. 'It will not leave this room. You have my word on that. You have my word.'

'I need to know I can trust you, Lou.'

'Fuck! After what I told you? The shit we've been through already – hey, you can trust me.' He reaches his hand out for me to take. 'I know we can trust each other. So I'm here for you, dude. I'm here for you.'

I look out of the window and wait for my heart's tempo to ease up. Then I begin to yap. And I tell him. It spews from me. I blurt out everything, every last morsel. Rip open my chest, expose all inner workings, slacken my burden, whatever you want to call it. I tell him about Mum's illness, her birthday, the joints, the music, John Hughes, what she wants me to do, Danny, my fears. Nothing is concealed. Nothing. And, true to his word, Lou gives me his ears and sits in utter silence. He's a good listener.

'That's why we have a strong connection, Bobby,' Lou says after I've finished. 'I felt your agony, I understood it. I saw that you were goin' through the same thing I had.'

'It's destroying me,' I say.

'But you have a choice to make now.'

'Yeah.'

'Actually, it's your mom's choice. She's the one who's drivin' this thing. You just have to agree.'

'It's not that easy though, is it?'

Lou looks confused.

'Really? I think it's very fuckin' easy, dude.'

'How?'

'Way I see it, you have a moral obligation to your mom – you have a moral obligation to free her from the torture she's livin' in. That's all she wants. You're her ticket.'

'But, what if …'

'What if what? It's what she wants. It's like her last wish. You ain't gonna take that away from her, are you, Bobby?'

I find myself staring at our Ikea prints, being sucked into them.

'It *is* what she wants,' I whisper to myself.

'And I can help you.'

'With what?'

'What your mom wants.'

'You? How?'

'I can assist,' Lou says.

I take my eyes away from the prints and fix them on him.

Cider and Black

We call it sleeping, but in reality it's flitting in and out of consciousness. She can show lucidity and is able to hold a conversation, but chatting like before drains energy and is probably painful. The raconteur in her has all but vanished, only fleeting signs here and there.

Danny's stroking Mum's head. I'm at the bottom of the bed, fighting the demons in mine. Thinking about Lou's visit, of how the conversation went from my massive revelation, to him offering to assist me. By assisting, does he mean doing it for me? Re-enacting exactly what he'd done with his own mother? Or watching over as I play executioner? Holding me tight after it's over? It's all beyond thinking. The stress and pressure is completely locked inside my mind, eclipsing everything else. I can't construct poems. My sleep is shit. I rarely smile. I eat crap, if at all. It scrapes at me like an archaeologist's trowel.

Danny and me don't speak. Carter the Unstoppable Sex Machine belt out a song called 'Falling on a Bruise'. Actually, it's not too bad. I'll definitely continue to keep her taste alive afterwards.

Mum's breathing is short and steady. There's truly a wonderful peace in the air. I think she can even sense it. I know she can.

'Her hair feels less jaggy,' Danny whispers.

'It's grown,' I say.

'Feels like fur, like a tiny kitten or a guinea pig.'

'I'll be sure to tell her that, mate, she'll be delighted.'

'It's much better than her skinhead.'

'You're not wrong.'

'She looked like a woman who likes other women,' Danny says, smiling knowingly. 'You know, Bobby, like one of those –'

'Yeah, I get it, Dan. I get it.'

'Is Bel one of those?'

'No, Danny, Bel isn't one of those. And can we stop saying "those" to describe human beings?'

Danny gently rests his cheek on the top of Mum's head, closes his eyes. Smells her hair. Kisses her. He's so content, so serene. Mum was the one who could always calm him right enough.

The song changes. Another Nineties lager-swirling classic pours from the speakers. I look at Mum and visualise the cardigan-clad Anne Seed spinning on one foot, ceiling gazing, skilfully not spilling any of her cider and black. She's a beaming, bacchanalian beauty. Who wouldn't have wanted to inhabit her world? To be loved by her? It's us who are the privileged. And now here she is with her youngest son, both dented in different ways, yet utterly connected. The true tragedy is that she's now unable to shelter him. I want to burst into tears.

'You can kiss her cheek, mate,' I say.

'Don't want to wake her.'

'She won't wake up, Dan. It's fine.'

'Will I then?'

'Yeah, you can kiss her lips if you want.'

Danny puts his lips on Mum's.

'Very dry,' he says.

'Yeah, I need to get some balm on them.'

He then kisses her cheek, mouth lingering on her skin. It seems like an intrusion on my part; I'm half thinking of leaving them alone.

'They're going to take her, aren't they, Bobby?'

'Who are?'

'The nurses and doctors. They're going to take her to the hospital.'

My head sinks, mouth tightens.

'She's not going to get better, Danny. You know that. I've told you.'

'I know, but she's our mum.'

'She'll always be our mum.'

'So she should be here with us. With you and me. You can't just go about splitting up families like that.'

'We can't give her the care and medicine she needs now, Dan.'

'But why is she going to go to the hospital if she's not going to get better? What's the point of that?'

'She's going there to be more comfortable.'

Danny nudges her pillow, fixes her blanket.

'Look at her,' he says. 'She's comfortable here.'

We take a moment to see the truth in Danny's statement.

'You're right, she does look comfortable,' I say.

'So she should stay here.'

'You think Mum would want that, Dan?'

'She'd always want to be with us.'

'Even if we can't give her the care she needs?'

'She'd not want to be away from us, Bobby.'

'You'd prefer to see her in constant pain?'

'No. Would you?'

'I just want to see her in peace. I want her to have what she needs.'

'Me too.'

I feel myself about to vault over the line, drag Danny in the same direction as me. I hear myself saying the words and his reaction to them. The tears. The snot. The punches. If anyone's going to carry out Mum's wish it's her sons, not Lou. Not anyone else.

'Danny.'

'What?'

'What if we could make the disease go away?' I say.

'What do you mean, *make it go away*?'

'We could get rid of it for good. You and me.'

Danny looks bewildered. He wants to speak, to say something, question me. He's having a torrid time formulating what I've just said. I'm having the same difficulties. Guilt pangs start to crawl over me. Even though Mum wanted me to involve him, I can't help thinking that I've betrayed her; that I'm infiltrating and corrupting my brother.

'If you had the power to stop Mum's pain, would you do it, Dan?'

'Totally.'

'Remember that game you were playing the other day and your guy was injured?'

'Yeah, so?'

'So you didn't go back for him and take his pain away.'

'Cos then I'd have got killed.'

'You just left him there to die an agonising and slower death.'

'It's just a game, Bobby. It's not real.'

'But if it was real life, would you have gone back?'

'Maybe. I don't know. Can you stop talking about that stupid game?'

'All I'm saying is that if it was real and it was someone you knew, someone close to you, would you help them if it meant making their suffering go away?'

Danny's cells are spinning. He pauses, holds me in his glare.

'You mean Mum, don't you?'

'Yeah, mate. That's who I mean.'

He looks down and puts his hand on Mum's growing hair. I notice her eyelids stutter a bit.

'I'd always help her, Bobby. Always.'

'And what if I told you there was a chance?'

'Of what?'

'Of taking her suffering away.'

'Bobby, I wish you would speak like normal people sometimes,' he spouts.

Mum's stuttering eyelids blink open. Danny doesn't see them at first. She coughs. Parts her lips. Tries to speak.

'Tell him, Bobby,' she rasps. 'Tell him what I want.'

'Mum!' I say.

'Tell him, Bobby. Tell your brother.'

'Tell me what?' Danny says. 'Tell me what?'

I look at Mum for support, which isn't forthcoming. My expression pleads with her to change the subject. My mouth tastes of sour saliva. I want to spit. Mum offers nothing, Danny's like a dog on its hind legs. I rest my hand on his shoulder.

'Everything's going to be OK soon, mate.'

'Seriously?'

'Yeah,' I say. 'Seriously.'

I'm too scared to look at Mum. I can practically smell her disappointment.

Booze and Upbeat Tunes

Bel doesn't like Lou from the off. She sits growling monosyllabic answers to his questions. It's obvious I shouldn't have invited him to our Junk Food Friday. Bel doesn't exactly roll out the red for outsiders. Yet after everything Lou and I have shared, I need to piecemeal him into my life, let him see my world bit by bit. Bel and all.

'So you guys have been friends a long time then, huh?' Lou asks.

'Yup,' Bel gives him.

'That's cool.'

'Tis.'

'You live nearby, Bel?'

'Yeah.'

'You like that music Bobby likes too?'

'Some.'

'Cool.'

'Tis.'

She tuts her disapproval when Lou snatches the last slice of pizza.

'What's that?' she asked him, shortly after he arrived.

'Oh, that?' He points out the window.

'Yeah, that thing.'

'That's my Vespa.'

'Looks like a skateboard with an engine, if you ask me.'

I know Bel's behaving like an A-list queen bitch. She's got a stick up her arse because I've the cheek to befriend other people. It's not Lou. I could've invited Ghandi or Malala and she'd have given them the mono tongue, snake-eye treatment too. Lou's accent and overt coolness don't help matters.

When she makes up some spurious excuse to leave, I'm relieved.

'Sorry about that, Lou,' I say.

'Don't sweat it, dude. The girl has eyes for you. I'm an intruder,' he says, grinning widely. 'I get why she's pissed.'

'Oh, shut up. Bel's a mate and nothing else.'

'You always lie to your mates, do you?'

'What do you mean?'

'Well, have you told her what happened at the residential?'

'No.'

'Why?'

'It hasn't come up yet, that's all.'

'Come on, Bobby. These are the kinda things you tell your buddies. Precisely why they *are* your buddies in the first place.'

'I will … I mean, I intend to, but now isn't the time.'

'Lies. Lies. Lies,' he says. 'They'll get you into trouble one of these days.'

'I'm not lying to her, I just haven't told her yet.'

'She likes you, dude.'

'As I said, we're friends, Lou. Friends.'

'You have to tell her, Bobby. She'll freak if she finds out any other way. And you have to tell her about *this*.'

Lou unfastens the top button of his denim jacket, sits forward then hauls his bag on to his knee, rummages inside. I study what he's doing, his face. I've seen that expression somewhere before.

He hasn't, has he? Tell me he hasn't brought …

'Lou, tell me you haven't brought any joints in here.'

'Come on, what kinda guy do you take me for?'

'Danny'll smell it.'

'No joints. Promise.'

Lou digs deep. Produces two bottles: Jack Daniel's and Coke, litre of.

'Look, no joints, see?' He triumphantly raises them up.

'Fucking hell, Lou.'

'Oh, come on, it's almost the weekend.'

'What are you trying to do to me?'

'Loosen your hair a bit.'

'It's my house, Lou.'

'Great. If you puke the toilet isn't too far away.'

I smile and examine the bottle of Jack Daniel's; it's heavy glass.

'But what about Danny? What about Mum?'

'Where is the little dude?'

'In his room. He plays online computer games.'

'All night?'

'Fancies himself as some sort of gamer.'

'Will he come down?'

'Not if you're here. You're still a stranger to him.'

'So we're fine. Will he crash up there?'

'He'll crash and sleep for an eternity,' I say. 'That's what he does.'

'At least we know your mom won't be joinin' us,' Lou states.

Do I detect a slight sneer in his voice? I do, don't I?

'I'll have to check on her,' I say, rising from my seat, 'before I put my mouth anywhere near that stuff.'

'Can I see her?' Lou suddenly asks. His request makes me nervous.

'I don't ...'

'Come on, Bobby. Just for a few minutes?' he says. If there's a facial expression between sincerity and eagerness, Lou has it down to a fine art. I feel as though I'm being backed into a corner.

'OK,' I say. 'Follow me.'

On the landing outside Mum's room I hear Danny talking to someone through his headphones. 'Cameron, release the hostages and meet me in the square … NO, numbsack, hostages three and four. I repeat, hostages three and four. Do it now! Now, before we're all toast.'

'Sounds like some serious computer shit your bro's into,' Lou says.

'Well, you know gamers, they live in a weird parallel universe.'

'They want to put some chill in their asses, that's what they want to do,' he says.

I move towards Mum's door.

'She's in here,' I say. 'Try to stay quiet.' I scold myself for suggesting Lou remain quiet. What an idiot.

'As a mouse, dude.'

The ten-watt bulb gives me enough light to do what I need to do, be it sorting out entertainment or something medical. Depending on my mood, Mum looks either peaceful, bloated or lifeless. Right now she looks gentle and placid. I offer no words of comfort since Lou's hovering, but I say them in my head: *You look amazing when you're sleeping, Mum. I just want to tell you that. Always beautiful.*

'She reminds me exactly of what my mom was like,' Lou says impassively.

'Yeah?'

'Completely gone.'

'Thanks for that, Lou.'

'Ain't nothin' there,' he adds, which I ignore. I don't know, I thought he'd be saddened to see her in this state, but he isn't. Where's the compassion?

'I need to change her fluid bag,' I say.

'What's this shit?' Lou says, referring to the music I'd looped for her. I created a playlist of songs, thinking the tunes might help the seconds and minutes pass.

'This "shit" is Jesus and Mary Chain, and it's definitely *not* shit,' I say.

'You do know she can't hear it,' he says.

'How do you know she can't hear it?' I snap.

'You think she can?' he fires back.

'Have you got experience of being in her position, Lou? How do you know she can't hear it?'

'All I'm sayin', dude, is that if you're gonna play some tunes, maybe you should consider an upbeat selection, that's all.'

'These are the songs she liked.'

'Point exactly.'

'What point?'

'*Liked*. Past tense.'

If my bones were violent I'd swing round and smack two rapid off his eye socket, smash my knee against his balls. Was this Lou's idea of support? Where was his compassion and kindness? You'd have thought witnessing this scene would have brought everything about his own mum flooding back. I expected tears not bloody taunts.

'Look, I need to get this bag changed. You go back down and make up two drinks,' I say through gritted teeth.

'Gotcha. I'm on it.'

'Large ones,' I say, catching him before he leaves the room. 'You'll find ice in the freezer.'

'Really? In the freezer?'

Then he's off.

I pick up the scissors from the side table, snip off the top of the new bag of fluid and replace the old. After that's done I stand looking at her for about half a Jesus and Mary Chain song, don't ask which one.

'Night, Mum,' I whisper, giving her three kisses, one on the forehead and one on each cheek. 'In case you're wondering, that was Lou. He's the one from the carers' group. The one who got us the you-know-what. He's OK most of the time, when he's not being a complete dick.' I rest my cheek on hers for ten seconds or so and mouth '*Love you*' into her ear. It's weird but I want to squash myself right into her, for us to morph into one.

I know it's probably just some sort of emotional illusion, but while we're touching skin I'm sure she moves her mouth and utters, 'Love you too.' I'm sure of it.

I've one leg out of the door when a voice in my head tells me to return. I find myself thumbing through the playlist until I come to a different selection, a more 'upbeat' group of songs. I hate myself for allowing Lou to influence me.

I've never drunk Jack Daniel's before, but coming from

Mum's room I decide that tonight's the night I'm going to introduce myself to it, sink it like a champion. Lou's waiting for me, two tall glasses in hand. Type of peace offering? A whisky-soaked olive branch.

'Here, dude,' he says, handing me the drink. 'Sorry for being an asshole up there.' I keep my silence, choosing instead to hear him out. 'It just brought everything back to me, that's all. I didn't know what to say or how to act, so I did what I do best.'

'Which is?'

'Shoot straight into asshole mode.'

'Guess that's your default setting then?'

'Seems to be,' he says sincerely. 'Thousand apologies.'

'Forget it,' I say, holding my glass out to his. 'Cheers.'

'*Salute.*'

We chink.

It tastes syrupy, burns my throat, not totally pleasant but not utter rank either. My body's unsure if it likes it. Whatever.

I know a repeat of the Borders residential is loitering, so there's purpose to the amount I guzzle down. I drink with vigour, aiming to defeat my nerves before something happens.

My phone buzzes against my thigh. I have to look at the message three or four times before it sinks in. That's what four double Jack Daniel's will do to someone's intellectual capacity. Not to be recommended.

Im such a beeeatch. U dnt deserve me ... or other way round. Speak 2mor?

I can't help wishing that beeeatch was sitting here with me now.

A cert I'm going to spew my ring if I swallow any more.

'Hey, you sure you've drunk hard liquor before, Bobby?' Lou says.

'Loads of times,' I say.

Truth: only cheap lager and cider have passed these lips before. And I've never particularly enjoyed either. The tipsy and giggly stage I don't mind, but I can't deal with morning headaches and metallic mouth.

'No need to chug it, dude,' he says.

'I like it, it's sweet,' I lie.

After sculling more Jack Daniel's it's as if I've entered another zone. I'm not me any more: I've no control over who I am or what I'm doing. Feels weird, as though I'm having one of those out-of-body experiences. Staring at myself slouched on the chair chatting to Lou, my mind revisits the past few weeks: how I've increased my booze intake, puffed joints and strived to piss school away. I don't want to be a waster. I don't want to be a mangled drunk. I'm so detached from my body with these thoughts, yet all the while I'm still in deep conversation with Lou. Maybe my brain functions that way. You know, I'm able to do things simultaneously.

'Remember what happened, Bobby?' Lou says.

My face burns with the blush.

I slug more booze.

Definitely heating up.

'Course I remember, Lou. God, how could I –'

'No, not that shit,' he says. And I could've chucked the glass at his head. A nine-stitches forehead job. 'The stuff we spoke about the last time I came here?' Lou raises his eyes.

Does he wink?

'You know what I'm on about, Bobby … the stuff?'

'About your mum?' I ask.

'No, *your* mom.'

'Erm … yeah, I remember.'

Lou sinks his drink, wipes his mouth. Sits forward and locks me in. Signs of the booze apparent: eyes raw, certain words slurred.

'It's a tough decision for you, Bobby.'

'Tell me about it.'

'Your mom's fightin' spirit must be shot.'

'I guess that's what her type of MS does,' I say.

'But you're also lucky.'

I snort. We drink.

'Yeah, dead lucky, Lou.'

'No, hear me out.'

'All ears,' I say, tipping my glass to him.

'You get to have the conversation with her, absolve yourself from guilt because it's not entirely somethin' of your doin'. You're just the water carrier. Doin' someone a favour, deliverin' them to the well.'

He is drunk.

'See, Bobby, when I released my mom I'd no time to plan

or prepare – it was a now or never choice I had to make. And I guess that's what saved me.'

'What? Doing it without planning it?'

'Yeah. I wasn't consumed by all that fear and guilt shit that thinkin' about it too much does to you.'

'All I do is think – my brain's laughing at me now.'

We drain our drinks and pour more ... like we need them.

'Know what I think, Bobby?'

'What?'

'Now is the right time to do it,' he says.

My heart sneezes.

'Now, like *now*?' I say.

'Exactly.'

'Now, tonight?'

'If we don't do it tonight we'll never do it, Bobby.'

I'm bladdered drunk.

Unsure if my nodding head is agreement or involuntary.

The other me, the guy watching everything unfold, is saying: *What's this 'we' crap? I don't remember a 'we' in this house.*

Lou is trying to appear unaffected by the alcohol. He's all sense and ideas, the self-appointed leader.

'The conditions are perfect, dude,' he says, as if talking about skydiving or fucking fly fishing.

One voice tells me Lou's trying to be helpful and supportive, yet another suggests he sounds scarily excited, lusty at the possibility, as if he's getting a perverse buzz out of this.

He's done it before, hasn't he? He knows what it feels like. I'm unnerved.

'This is our time, Bobby.'

'We' to 'our'.

'You think so?' I say.

'Think? No, I don't *think*, dude. I *know*.'

He finishes the final drops of his drink, rises to his feet. 'Come on,' he says. 'Let's go have another look.'

He's on the move before I can remonstrate. I stagger to my feet and follow him upstairs. Two three-legged donkeys climbing stairs. No noise from Danny. No doubt he's gunned and exploded himself to dreamland.

In Mum's room Lou stops dead. Tilts his ear to the music.

'These beats are more like it,' he says. 'She'll be happier listenin' to this.'

'I changed it earlier.'

'Yeah, well, that other shit was musical terrorism, if you ask me.' He moves towards her bed. 'She looks finished.'

He leans down to examine her. My mum. My glorious mother. While I have the ability to breathe she'll never be finished.

'How old you say she was again?' he asks.

'I didn't.'

'She looks about eighty.'

'You should go back downstairs, Lou,' I say. 'I'll make sure she's comfortable for the night.'

'Downstairs? Fuck you talkin' about, dude?'

'Just until I'm sure she's settled for the night.'

'Dude,' Lou says forcefully. 'We should do it now.'

'Lou!'

'It's time, Bobby. This is what she wants.'

We're standing by her head. How I get so close is an absolute blur, total time lapse. Lou's down low, ear to mouth, checking her breathing.

'She won't feel a thing, Bobby,' he says, without removing his eyes from Mum's face. 'She won't be able to prepare herself, so it's perfect. She'll have no fear.'

He reaches behind Mum's head and gently caresses out one of her pillows.

'Here.' He thrusts the pillow towards me, into my stomach. 'Promise you, Bobby, she won't have a clue. Promise.'

'Lou ...'

'What you're doing is called mercy. Liberation.'

'Lou ...'

'You're a goddam freedom fighter, Bobby.'

I'm drink-dazed, booze-fuelled. Paralysed. My speech is alien to my ears. I'm not Bobby Seed. I'm an automaton. Is this the ethics Lou spoke about? Through the fuzz in my head I want to ask him if it's the right thing to do, because from where I'm standing it sure as fuck doesn't feel like anyone is gaining their freedom. Will it bring freedom, Lou? Will it? Where is all the love and kindness? This feels like cruel coercion.

'Could we change the music first?' I ask.

'What?'

'She can't go without one of her favourite songs playing.'

'Go for it, dude.'

I search for The Jesus and Mary Chain's *Darklands*, begin to cry as soon as the sound kicks in. Like, really sob. I know that song backwards.

'I know how you're feeling, Bobby. I know.' Lou strokes my face. 'Go ahead, free her now. Free her now.'

'I don't ...'

'I know it's hard, Bobby. It's so hard.'

'Lou, it's my mum. I can't. I don't have the strength.'

'This is the time to be strong, Bobby.' He kisses my cheek, holding his lips tightly on my wet skin. 'Your mom needs you to be strong now.' He breathes into my ear. 'She needs to feel your strength.'

'I'm so scared.'

'We're all scared. Everyone is.'

He thumbs tears away from my face.

'Will you help me, Lou?'

'I'm here for you, Bobby.'

'Promise?'

'I ain't going anywhere.'

I grip the pillow tight against my stomach, so tight my body tries to demolish itself; I step towards my mother. Everything smears. I heave. Think about vomiting. I see her face. She is perfect – at peace. I can't do it. I can't. I bury my head deep into the pillow, not to muffle my scream, but to catch any vomit if I puke. She wanted to record a goodbye message for Danny. She hasn't done it yet. Let her do it. Give her those last few words.

'I can't,' I say. 'I can't. I can't do it.'

Lou steps in, takes the pillow from me. I've stopped it. It's all over. He cradles the pillow too. We hold each other's eyes. I wipe more tears away.

'Don't worry, Bobby. I can help you. I'm willin' to do it for you. I'll help your mom find her freedom.' He enters my space; I smell his boozy breath. His lips stroke mine, tongue roaming tenderly. It's the gentlest kiss I've ever had. Intoxicating almost. I keep my eyes closed for the longest of times, touch my lips with two fingers afterwards.

When I open my eyes, Lou's hunched over Mum, full weight of his body pressing on the pillow. I stand rooted for seconds, trying to process it. I can't see her face. Only her limp hands. Lou's body quaking with the force. Her face completely concealed. Mum's face. I am powerless. Feet nailed to the ground. My eyes nippy, blurry. Focus fuzzy. The other me is watching it all unfold: he can't see Mum's face either.

Over there, the other me says.

Over there, Bobby.

WHERE?

On the table.

I look at the table. Their shiny little blades glint my way. Their sparkle compels me to pick them up. I just can't see her face. Know I might not see it again. I panic. Lou's body stops vibrating. Has he done it?

Not yet, Bobby. Just wait before you pounce.

Total terror. Total fear.

His body relaxes.

Has he done it yet?

Ask him.

'Lou, what have you done?' I say. He doesn't hear me. Ignores me?

He examines his deed.

Picks up the pillow again, squeezes it hard as if it's betrayed him.

SHE'S STILL ALIVE.

I can't allow him to finish off the job. He's an expert. But it was *me* she asked. Is it too late to intervene? I'm her carer; I'm the person she wants to do this. I need him to stop. It needs to be me. Do something! Be her carer, Bobby.

Panic, fear, yes. But it's rage that scoops me up. Rage hits like a double-barrelled blast. I grip the shiny metal. Knuckles ghost white.

Now, Bobby. Now!

Shiny metal scissors in my hand.

Frenzied. I run. Lunge.

Charge with bison strength. I drag Lou off her, shove him against the wall and thrust the scissors towards his throat. Indent his skin. I want to rip the muscle. Chop his apple. Hear this piggy squeal. See *him* fight for breath. I want to hear the floor thud when he drops like a sandbag from the rafters. Scud!

'What the fuck, dude!'

'Get fucking off her!' I scream.

'Bobby ...' he mutters. His eyes full of fear.

'Don't you ever fucking touch her again.' I press harder on the scissors. 'OK?'

'OK. OK. Easy. Take it easy.'

'Now get the fuck out of my house.'

'Bobby ...'

'Get out or I swear I'll plunge these into your fucking neck,' I spit at him.

'Dude.'

'Go, and stay the fuck away from me and my family.'

It's a moment of drunken clarity. But it's not me, it's not Bobby Seed. And suddenly I'm alone with white noise ringing in my ears until I hear the front door crash shut.

I lie down beside Mum, check her breathing. Shallow, but still there. I take her arms and wrap them around my neck.

'I love you so much, Mum,' I whisper.

I know you do, son.

'I miss you more than you know.'

And me, my darling. I miss you both.

'Goodnight, Mum,' I breeze into her ear.

Afterwards I sit in the hall and polish off the remaining Jack Daniel's.

A peaceful moment.

The Last of the Normal Things

I wake on the warm carpet. Slept in the hallway. Must have. It hits me straight away. My head is thunderous. Fully hungover, half panicked. There's no space for peace: the events play out as soon as my eyes focus on the ceiling; flashbacks in speedy montage absorb me. My very own ceiling cinema.

I need water. I roll on to my knees and crawl to the bathroom, grasp on to the toilet bowl as if driving a porcelain bus. A violent torrent of puke exits that almost takes my jawbone with it. Brown and pungent. Snot and old tears plunge inside the bowl too.

'Bobby,' Danny says from behind me. 'You OK?'

'Danny, go back to bed, buddy,' I manage to mutter.

'It's getting-up time,' he says.

Next thing I know he's crouching down beside me.

'I'm OK, Dan.'

But I'm not. My body's convulsing.

'Bobby, what is it? What is it, Bobby? Why you being sick?'

'I'm fine.'

'You're not fine. Why are you crying?'

'I'm not.'

'I'm scared, Bobby.'

'Don't be, I'll be fine in a minute.'

Danny reaches around my waist and hugs me tight.

'Please don't be ill, Bobby. I don't want you to.'

Then *he* begins.

I take his body on top of mine, shaking, wailing.

'Please be OK, Bobby.'

'I'm just feeling a bit sick, Dan. It's nothing serious, mate. Honestly.'

'Will I make you some cereal? Rice Krispies?'

'Yeah, that sounds good.'

'That'll definitely make you feel good again.'

'Thanks.'

He's a weighty lump, but I don't tell him to get off. I don't want to get aggressive or frighten him. I need him to go downstairs, away from the carnage that is Mum's room and any remnants of struggle.

'Cereal works every time I'm feeling shitty,' he says. 'Are you feeling shitty about Mum?'

'Always, Dan.'

His arms compress my bones. God love him, he thinks he's

comforting me, but his human-snake routine only encourages the aching in my bones.

'You can release me now, mate. I'm good. Need to wash.'

He unleashes me. We both sit against the wall in the toilet.

'Bobby?'

'Yeah?'

'Can you tell me something?'

'What?'

'What did Mum mean when she said, "Tell him, Bobby, tell your brother"? Remember she said that?'

'I do.'

'You told me something that was a lie …'

'When?'

'When you said everything would be OK soon.'

'It wasn't a lie, Danny.'

It was the only thing I could think of telling him when Mum put me on the spot; in my heart it wasn't a lie, I truly believe that everything will be OK. I need to believe it.

'I knew it was a lie because you didn't look me in the eye. You just stared at Mum, then the duvet, and you didn't look at me at all. That's how I knew it was a lie, but I didn't say anything because I didn't want to get on Mum's goat. I wanted to stay mature for everyone. But I want to know, Bobby. I want to know what she meant. I'm mature as anything. I'm not stupid, not any more.'

'I know you're not stupid. Nobody said you were.'

'And I can prove to you I'm not.'

316

'How?'

'Because I think I know what Mum wanted you to tell me.'

'Oh, you do, do you?'

'More than a hundred per cent.'

'I'm listening.'

'And I can read. I can read really well, Bobby.'

'What's that got to do with anything?'

'I've read about this stuff on the internet, that's all.'

'Danny, my head feels like it's been in a skiing accident. You're not making much sense.'

'When you have a person close to you, someone you really love who's ill, it's all over the internet.'

'What is?'

'What you should do with people like that.'

'Danny, I need water quick, so please speak English.'

'The internet says these people make their own decisions when to die.'

'Is that right?'

'Yeah, they don't wait until the pain's poker painful. No, they say when it's going to happen and sometimes how. It's called ... it's called ...'

'I know what it's called, mate.'

I don't know whether to laugh or cry. I've misjudged my brother, thinking he'd crumble if I even gave him a sniff of what Mum wanted me to do. I feared I'd lose the two of them with one thrust of a cushion and that Danny would be taken from me. I lied about the severity of Mum's illness and what she'd asked me to do because I didn't know if I had the strength to care for the emotional needs of a fourteen-year-old; even though, I suppose, that's what I do now. I certainly know I don't have the strength to be without him.

I rest a hand on his knee.

'Mum wants *you* to stop all her pains that way, doesn't she, Bobby?' I cover my face with my free hand. 'Doesn't she?'

My mind fizzes back into the room. I can't remember if I pierced Lou's skin. I wonder if I'll see him again. What did he do wrong exactly? Oh yeah, he tried to take my mother's last waking breath, that's all. NOT HIS JOB. A mother listens to her child's first breath, sees their eyes open for the first time; naturally we repay that debt by being present for our mothers' last breath, be with them when their eyes close for the final time. That's the way it goes. It just does.

'Doesn't she, Bobby?' Dan says again.

'She does, yeah.'

'And if you don't, she's going to die anyway, but in a more horrible way, isn't she?'

'Something like that.'

'Because she has the right to die, doesn't she?'

'Dan, where …'

'It says so on the internet. I don't just use it for playing games.'

'So it seems.'

'I've read all about it, Bobby. There's tons of stuff online.'

'Well, it's a bit more complicated than that,' I say.

'But Mum shouldn't be in a hospital with tubes and strangers – she should be with us. We can't put her with the strangers.'

'I agree.'

Danny pulls himself up, glances down the toilet, grimaces and flushes.

'So, when will we do it, Bobby?'

'Do what?'

'What the internet says. When will we do it?'

'What do you mean, *we*?'

'She's my mum as well. I love her too. She loves me loads. Just the same as you. We need to do it before they take her to hospital.'

'Dan ...'

'So?'

'Listen, mate, I understand it's mega important, but can we talk about it later, when I've cleaned myself up?'

Danny's jaw sags in disappointment, but he can see by my greyness that I'm in no state to continue.

'Roger that,' he says.

I stretch out my hand so he can yank me up.

'Thanks, Dan,' I say, and I really mean it.

'Maybe we can have cereal together. Sit on the couch and watch TV. It's Saturday. Saturday TV is always good.'

'Good idea. You go on down. I'll be with you after I've had a quick wash.'

My head is still on fire from the Jack Daniel's as I watch him bypass Mum's room and bound downstairs. I need to check in on her, praying she's zero recollection of being near suffocated to death last night.

Last night!

My brain's a melting candle.

*

I can't contemplate putting anything near my mouth. Danny's on his second bowl of cereal, slurping and crunching his way through Saturday morning television. The sound amplifies and batters my skull.

'We can't tell anyone, Dan.'

'I know.'

'No, Dan. I need you to understand this. This is more than important.'

'I know, Bobby. We can't tell anyone.'

'No matter where you are in life or who you're with or if you think you're being safe. No one ever knows. OK?'

'OK.'

'This is ours and ours alone, Dan. Right?'

'Right.'

'Our safe secret, got it?'

'Got it.'

'No, Danny. Look at me. Look at me. Have … you … got … it?'

'Yes … I … do.'

'So, tell me again, who knows?'

'You and me …'

'And that's it! If anyone ever finds out, they'll separate us, you understand?'

'Roger ten four.'

'If we tell them Mum asked us to do it, I doubt they'll believe us.'

'It's just you and me, Bobby.'

'Exactly. And you're going to be strong afterwards, aren't you?'

'I'll try.'

'Because this is what Mum wants, always remember that, Dan. We're doing this for Mum. Our mum.'

'To make her pain go away.'

'And we're going to be there for each other, right?'

'Always.'

'Good man, Danny.'

'Good man yourself, Bobby.'

Failed Poet

I know it's a Sunday night but I wouldn't mind one of Mrs Sneddon's little chats. It would be nice to feel her fingers tapping on my knee with the words 'love', 'sweetheart' and 'darling' bolstering me. Or Bel, just to chew the shit, chat, talk clothes, tunes, nonsense. Maybe she could've helped if I'd confided in her. Another regret to add to the glut. When the dust settles I'll make it up to her.

Bel, I've something to tell you blah blah blah.

Bel, I need you blah blah blah.

Bel, you're the only one who blah blah blah.

When this is over it's going to be time to yank thy head right out of thine arse. Knuckle down, study for my exams. Apply for university courses. Pursue some dreams. Complete that bloody poetry topic in English. How I love that course. I get lost in the words, devour whatever I can, pour my soul into it.

I'm used to Mum's rusty breathing; her chest is the sound of an internal brawl. Lips soft again after some balm application, her skin a moonlit lake. Her voice is slow and gruff, worse than ever. Thankfully she has no memory of Lou's action: the drugs *do* work. Lou swims around my mind with the rest of the madness living there.

I'm calm.

She's calm.

'We're going to do it together, Mum. Dan's going to help. We spoke about it yesterday,' I tell her.

'I want to do it now,' Mum mumbles.

It feels like my blood goes into hyperdrive, surging through my veins. Adrenalin rushes happen so rapidly that the brain fails to process the body's shock: the flick of a switch, the flash of a lighter, that's how quick we're talking. As soon as Mum says, 'I want to do it now,' I'm practically convulsing.

'No, wait. Mum, we haven't …'

'That's not what I mean, take the stuffing out your bra.' If sandpaper could talk it would sound like my mother. It's as though she's got a sixty-a-day smoking habit. I puff out my cheeks, dodged-a-bullet fashion. 'Do you have your phone?' she asks. The space between the words are lengthy and measured, like her vocal cords have been replaced by some old crone's.

'Yeah, I got my phone.' I take it out of my pocket.

'I want to record the message for Danny now, that's what I mean.'

'Oh.'

'Can your phone do that?' she asks.

I do that teenage facial scoff thing that empowers us against the middle-aged and over: *Can my phone do that? Ha!*

'No one likes an arsehole, Bobby.'

'Yeah, my phone can record,' I say. 'You want me to hold it up to your mouth? Or will I leave you alone?'

'No, you stay.'

'Right.'

'I want you to let him hear it when I'm gone, maybe when he needs to remember me or just needs to hear my voice.'

'That's a lovely idea, Mum.'

'Keep it safe.'

'I'll drop it into my cloud.'

'Well, I might see it up there myself.'

I feed her some fluids then hold the phone up to her mouth.

'Ready?' I say. She nods.

I press record.

She begins to speak:

'Danny, this is your mum ... No, no, start again.'

I press stop.

She nods. I touch record.

Go!

'Danny, I want you to know that ever since you came

324

out of me … Oh, Jesus, no,' she says. 'Did you record that?'

'Every bit. Very inspiring indeed.'

'Right, let's go again,' she says, closing her eyes. I put my thumb on the red record button. There's nothing for the first ten seconds.

Then:

'Danny, when you're feeling like the world's against you and you're hating everyone in it, I want you to think of me. See me smiling at you, hear me say the words "I love you, Daniel" over and over again. That's because I do. I love you more than anything on this earth.

'When you feel scared because there's things you can't do, listen to that voice in your head. It'll be me, your mum, telling you how utterly brilliant and gifted you are. And it's true, you're such an amazing person, Daniel Seed.

'Some days you'll be feeling all alone and isolated. When that happens I want you to look over your shoulder – you'll see your mum standing there. I'll be waiting with open arms, Danny. You'll need a hug. And so will I. Many nights the pain will be so bad that you'll be crying into your pillow. Well, think of me as that pillow, son. Your beautiful tears will fall on to me and I'll squeeze you as tightly as possible. We can fall asleep together. Deal?

'One day, Danny, you'll meet someone special and you'll fall in love with each other. I'll be with you every step – in front, behind and beside you, the proudest and happiest mum ever. No day will end that you're without me. Let our hearts always connect to each other. Deal?

'Danny, show them the exceptional man I know you are, and the remarkable man you're going to become. Show them all how you glisten and let the world see how you shine. Speak soon, my brightest diamond. Speak soon, my angel.'

I let the recording roll until I'm sure she's finished.

Nod.

Stop.

Return phone to pocket.

I take out a used hanky. I pick up the book that's been sitting there and fiddle it around in my hands. Turning. Turning. Turning.

This is my time with her. Danny will have his too.

'Look after each other, son,' she says, reaching out her hand. I take it. She still hasn't reopened her eyes.

'We will, Mum. Promise.'

'Bobby?'

'What?'

'Don't tell me when you're going to do it, just do it. I don't need to be prepared. It's better this way, for everyone.'

'OK,' I spurt out.

'Can you read those poems again,' she says, indicating towards the book in my hand. 'You read so beautifully.'

'Thanks.'

'For an illiterate.'

Here's a woman about to close her umbrella and she's still cracking jokes, still wanting her voice to have significance. All she wants is to see her child smile.

'Go on, Bobby. Read it again.'

And I do, I read again. And again.

I read Plath, Pound, Parker.

I read her Heaney, Hughes – Langston and Ted.

Bob Hicok, Bob Hass, Bob Seed.

WAIT. WHO?

Lately she likes me to sit with her, poetry book in hand, a collection of the greats. Occasionally she's sleeping, drugged or off somewhere else. My mission never wavers: I want to transport her.

I read.

'Who wrote that one?' she says.

'Some guy called Ezra Pound.'

'I liked it.'

'Yeah, he's good.'

'And that first one?'

'Dorothy Parker.'

'She's funny. Read me her again.'

It doesn't really matter who's written what. It's simply the words, images, stories and anecdotes that she craves. Nothing wrong, nothing right, nothing to dissect. But above everything it's simply the sound of my voice that's enough. I could be reading anything, back of a cereal box, anything. It's all about the security of the voice, nothing else matters.

'Who wrote that one?' she asks.

'Allen Ginsberg, he's called,' though I'm tempted to tell her the truth, reveal the poet's *real* name.

'Not too bad. You're good at reading him.'

Fact: I'm mortified to tell her the truth. No way can I let her know that the poet is none other than her very own son. Of course, we all know that Bobby Seed is no poet. Bobby Seed is only a schoolboy doing his schoolboy assignment for his schoolboy poetry course. Most definitely Bobby Seed is no poet, that's undeniable.

'Read me it again,' she says.

'Erm …'

'One last time. Please.'

I take a sip of her water, clear my throat and open my mouth.

'What's it called again?'

'"Sail Through",' I say.

Her eyes open, lips sprawl across her face.

'OK,' I say. 'Here goes. Ready?'

'As ready as I'm ever going to get, Bobby.'

I clear my throat and begin:

> *Soon you will locate your light*
> *and it'll be time for others to find their delight in you*
> *be it gods or darkness*

a new flame shall ignite the skies

and down here we will be your force

I'll follow cracks on the ceiling
he'll watch dust dance in the rays

I'll eat without hunger
he'll sing without pleasure

I'll wash in the afternoon
he'll blink at the glinting TV

I'll speak to myself
he'll yak to the skies

I'll buy only essentials
he'll wear wrinkled clothes

we'll both dream of the silence of another ...
and keep dreaming

we'll both cry

so locate your light
greet the gods
thrill the spirits

and see us
as we sail through.

I look at Mum for some validation or mouthed applause.
She's asleep. The day has defeated her. Aw well, next time
maybe, with a new poem. Romantic. Weighty. Better.
   Next time?
   Really?

The Night of

Danny's on the floor, meditation position, glued to *Horrid Henry*. He's not really watching. He's elsewhere. I want to weep for him.

'You OK, Dan?'

'Yeah.'

'You sure?'

'Yeah, sure.'

I usher him to me. 'Come here,' I say, holding my arms out.

I grip the back of his head: it's moist. I've no words. All I can do is reassure him with my body. We're like a couple of connected paperclips dangling off one another. Forever linked until rust to rust. I don't want to let him go.

'I can hear your heart,' Dan says.

'It's fast, eh?'

'Like being stuck to a music speaker.'

'Sorry about that.'

'You nervous, Bobby?'

'Terrified.'

'Me too.'

He releases himself from my grasp, stands tall again. His face is blotchy.

'Bobby?'

'Yeah?'

'I was reading something on the internet ...'

'What this time?'

'That some people, after they die, give their heart and lungs and kidneys and kneecaps to people whose heart, lungs, kidneys and kneecaps are crap. Is that true?'

'Yeah, it's called donating your organs, Dan.'

'Should we give Mum's organs to someone who's got crap ones then?'

'You want to do that?'

'Well, I was thinking that if we maybe gave her heart to someone, then we could ... we could ...'

'Spit it out.'

'We could visit that person and listen to their heart beating, but *really* it would be like listening to Mum again, because it would be *her* heart that's beating.'

'O ... K.'

'That way it would be like listening to Mum still. When I think that she's beating away in someone else's chest, keeping them alive, it makes me happier inside, Bobby. I've done tons of thinking about it.'

I swallow my saliva. I'm sick to death of crying, living in a body that's emotionally charged all the time. Oh, to be stoic, calm and poker-faced. I tense my abdomen to halt the gush. God, I even tense my throat. All I manage to say is:

'I think it's a brilliant idea, mate.'

Cos it is.

#10 ... complete

don't blame jack daniel
don't blame lou
don't blame mum
don't say it was for danny
don't speak of such things
I take full responsibility, mother
I decided, mother
I did it, mother
I did, mum
me

mother, see my tears, caress them
mother, feel my heart, it's your image
mother, how could you ask?
mother, how could I say yes?

forgive me
mother, see my future, see it
Mother Nature, why couldn't you have acted sooner?
there is no WE
I
hands up, head down, guilty
I need you to still love me
mum?

Funeral

Ever since Friday I've basically been squatting inside my own head, thinking about Lou, a lot. That night: Mum's room. That night: the Poztive residential. I can't unhappen them. They smother. God, that night in the Borders! It occupies me, it's airtight. I'll share it one day, every last thrilling detail. That's a promise. But I've got to cast Lou aside, leave him in the past, escape his energy.

So many nights I've lain motionless on my bed, imagining Mum's funeral.

Who'll turn up?

Who'll not turn up?

Who'll carry her coffin?

Who'll cry the hardest?

Whose eyes will be dry?

Who'll come out of duty?

Who'll come out of want?
What memorial words will be said?
Who'll be honest?
Who'll be false?
Where will it take place?
Will the sun shine?
Will it rain?
What songs will be played?
Will anyone blame me?
Will anyone know the truth?

Not Being Macbeth

Patsy Cline plays. Not my choice, DJ request. Reminds Mum of being a little girl; her own mother's favourite apparently. Patsy's voice has this raw velvet edge to it that was once reminiscent of my mum's.

It's just after midnight. Tuesday morning now. A week to go until I turn eighteen, but who cares? Who remembers? Danny and me are submerged in a crippling fear, but we're resolute. We sit on her bed. I tap my fingers. He taps his feet. We're in sync. I think about that scene from *Macbeth* we read in English class. Act 1, Scene 7: 'If it were done when 'tis done, then 'twere well it were done quickly.' Macbeth, riddled with guilt and regret after his murderous spree, became grotesque in his suffering. Suffering, that's the thing I must put a stop to. I am NO Macbeth.

Her hair has grown a bit, much better than the neo-fascist look she sported.

Danny is ashen. We look at each other. I'm first to crack.

'Danny,' I say.

'Yeah?' he says.

'Do you want to go there now?' I indicate where I want him to be. We've already discussed how it's to play out. Danny knows the drill.

'OK.' He doesn't move. He just doesn't move.

'Danny!'

He dives on me, flings his arms around my neck. I jolt. The bed rocks. Mum bounces. Danny hugs so tight it feels like he's trying to crush the love right out of me.

'It's going to be OK, Dan,' I say.

'I know it is, Bobby.'

'You know I love you, don't you?' I tell him.

'I know you love me more than anyone else in the world,' he says.

'And when this is over I'm going to take care of you.'

'And I'm going to take care of you too,' he tells me.

'We'll always look after each other, OK?'

'Promise?' Danny says.

'With all my heart, Dan.'

'Roger that?' he says.

'Roger that,' I say.

He withdraws and stretches out his hand so I can cement the pact. Our hands meet. I try to breathe slowly; soothe myself a touch. A primal feeling of pure love rises within me. It's a burning desire to care for and guide my brother. My little brother. He's no burden, no weight. He's part me. I'm part him. If our mother could see how everything's going to pan out for us, she'd nod her approval, post a smile and, likely, make some sarcastic remark.

You've done well, boys.

Thanks, Mum.

For a couple of eejits. Seriously, my heart's bursting with pride.

You should see a doctor about that.

I love you more than the distance between us.

And we love you too, Mum. We love you too.

I tell Danny again where he needs to be. This time he moves into position. We both do. Mum doesn't move: she knows. I know she knows. Too busy enjoying Patsy Cline to join in. I look at him.

'Ready, Dan?'

'I'm ready.'

If it were done when 'tis done, then 'twere well it were done quickly.

'OK then,' I say.

'Can I kiss her?' he asks.

'Of course.'

He leans down and kisses Mum's mouth. He then whispers something to her. I turn away. She definitely knows.

'Do you not want to kiss her, Bobby?'

I press my lips to Mum's. They have warmth in them. I

move to her ear and whisper: 'I'll speak to you every day, Mum. My story will be yours too. I'll do everything you've wanted me to. Be in peace now. Tonight's a good night to fly. Love you.'

Finally I straighten up. Look at my little brother. 'It's time, Dan,' I say firmly.

'Bobby ...'

'Don't be scared. Look at me.'

'Is it really time?'

'Look at me, Dan. Do the things we spoke about,' I tell him. Danny puts his hand over Mum's nose, closes it. 'Keep looking at me, Danny.' I place my hand over my mother's mouth and hold firm. 'Danny, keep your eyes on me, don't look at anything else.' He's blurry in my vision, like looking out of a fast car in a downpour. 'Danny, I'm your brother. You keep your eyes on me. Feel Mum's suffering piss the fuck off. Take a big breath, buddy. You can feel it all going away.' Danny's face is broken. Our hands press harder. 'I'm here, Dan. It's me, Bobby. Your brother. Keep looking at me.'

Our hands rigid.

'Make it be over, Bobby.'

'Keep looking at me. Please, Dan, look at me.'

#11 ... complete

mum soared away last night
roared into this place
full of melody
while we
     fell
        to
            pieces

Candy Crush

The day before the funeral we're in the living room. Danny's playing Candy Crush Saga while I consider where we should place Mum's ashes, wondering if the mantelpiece is too precarious or morose. It might be a bit awkward for visitors. *Hi, come in, say hello to Mum. Biscuit?*

The house is dark and gloomy, feels as if it's in mourning too. The place is spotless though. Gleaming kitchen and full fridge. Danny even did some hoovering.

When the bell rings, I'm busy focusing on the mantelpiece, visualising our ornamental Mum plonked on top. Danny's concentration is intense. The door chimes again. I take a breath and climb to my feet.

'I'll get it, Dan,' I say.

'Who is it?'

'Why don't you go up to your room?'

'I want to stay here.'

'What's up with your room?'

'Nothing. I just want to be here with you, Bobby.'

I stroke his hair and kiss the top of his head.

'Right, stay here then,' I say. 'I'll make whoever it is vamoose.'

'Think they know what's happening tomorrow?'

'Who knows.'

The bell tolls once more.

Danny labours to his feet.

'If they keep ringing like that they're going to break it. Who d'you think it is, Bobby?'

I don't reply. But I think I know.

At the door my heart performs GBH on my chest. I put one hand on the wall to steady myself, willing oxygen into my system. Place the other clammy hand on the door handle. For some reason my fist is clenched. I open the door.

It's not him.

I'm wrong.

Beautifully wrong.

I didn't hear any vintage vroom, so why did I think it would be him in the first place? Paranoia. Obsession.

A dishevelled-looking Bel stands on the step. A sight for puffy eyes. I want to pull her to me, cry into her neck, tell her everything. But I stand in the doorway all nonchalant and dickish.

'Bel!' The next bit should have been, *It's so good to see*

344

you, but she'd have thrown that phrase at my crotch.
'What are –'

'I'm so sorry, Bobby. I'm so, so sorry.' And she pounces on me. Her grip is so tight her arms attempt to squeeze fresh blood from my veins.

'It's fine, Bel. We're fine.'

'I don't know what to say, Bobby,' she sobs.

'Hey, don't cry or I'll take a photo and post it on Instagram.' She slaps the back of my head.

'Dick!'

She wipes her eyes. Her cheeks streak with tears and mascara lines: reminds me of a distressed clown.

'She was peaceful,' I tell her.

'Is Danny OK? How is he?'

'You know Dan, give him a piece of technology and he's as happy as a best man in a brothel.'

'We're still talking about your mum passing away here, aren't we?'

'Dan's in there,' I say, standing aside so she can enter. She remains rooted.

'I'm also sorry for being such a Kardashian lately,' she says.

'We've all had our moments, Bel.'

'I get overprotective at times, or maybe I'm just not a big fan of people with flashy modes of transport and sacks of confidence.'

'Lou, you mean?'

'Yeah.'

345

'Well, your instincts might have been spot on there.'

'Something happen?'

'Tell you another time.'

'Right.'

'Come in,' I say, but still she's rooted.

'I wanted to see you before tomorrow to do the face-to-face thing and apologise in person. So, here I am!' I let her ramble. 'But feel free to jump in at any time or I'll go on about how much you mean to me and how I don't want to fuck up what's going to be a lifelong friendship, which, let's be honest, fills us both with a fear beyond any we've ever known.'

I say nothing, just so happy to see her.

'You're enjoying this, aren't you, Seed?'

'It's good to see you, Bel,' I say. 'Please, will you come in?'

'I can't stay,' she says, pushing past, which means she could be here for hours.

When we enter the living room Danny runs my way, cowers timidly behind my back. As if it's the first time he's laid eyes on Bel.

'Why are you here, Bel?' he says.

'Hey, Dan,' Bel says. 'I just came to see how my favourite guys were doing.'

Bel gives me the eyes. I shake my head and mouth, '*It's just Mum.*'

'It's OK, Dan, she came to speak to me about something.'

'What something?' he asks.

'Nothing.'

'You said "something".'

'I meant "nothing".'

'Wow! This is actually like being in an episode of *Horrid Henry*,' Bel says. Danny sniggers. 'OK, I know when I'm not wanted, Danny Seed. I'm out of here.'

And just as quickly as she entered, she makes to leave. I don't stop her.

'Bel, I didn't mean to be rude,' Danny says. 'It's just that Bobby didn't tell me you were coming.'

'No sweat, I need to head anyway, promised the old man I'd boil him some rusty nails for dinner. My work's done here.'

'*Rusty nails for dinner*,' Danny imitates.

'I'll text you later, Bel,' I say. 'We can organise something for this Friday. Noodles maybe?'

'Is that junk enough?' she asks.

'Chinese then?'

'Can't wait.'

We frisbee a smile.

'After tomorrow I'll show you this new game I found online, Bel,' Danny says. 'It's stonking.'

'This day just gets better and better,' she says.

'See you later,' Dan says.

'Laters, Brothers Seed.'

*

A week after the funeral I return to Poztive. I feel like a virgin all over again: everyone's eyes cut through me, staring and sussing. Heads twist, faces fix on floors. All the gang back together; all the gang except our lead singer. I knew he wouldn't be here. He hasn't got that amount of gall. That's not to say I hadn't thought about seeing him again. I'd played out several scenarios:

1.
Me: Lou!
Lou: Nice to see you, Bobby.

2.
Me: Lou!
Lou: Bobby, about that time, let me explain.
Me: No need, honestly.
Lou: Kiss me.

3.
Lou: Bobby!
Me: What the fuck are you doing here, Lou? (SMACK!)

4.
Lou: Bobby!
Me: Lou, about that time, let me explain.
Lou: No need, honestly.
Me: Kiss me. (SMACK!)

The Poztive crescent is getting smaller.

'Hey, Bobby,' Roddy says. 'It's so good of you to join us. Great to see you, really is. We didn't expect …'

'Good to be here,' I say.

'I just want to say on behalf of the group –'

'I received your cards. Thanks,' I say, looking around me. 'Appreciate it.'

'We want you to know we're here for you, Bobby,' Roddy says. Everyone nods in agreement. 'If ever you want or need to talk about –'

'I'm good at the moment, Roddy, but thanks.'

'OK,' he says.

'I'm just here for the karaoke anyway,' I say, and everyone laughs … and keeps laughing. Even Cal, who never laughs, laughs.

What I can't tell them is that I'm faking stoicism; my gentle, warm expression is false. My mind's addicted to thoughts of Mum. I can't tell them how much I miss even those godawful final days. I miss reading to her, snipping her hair, running the shower over her head and following the soap trickle down her back. I can't think of anything I don't miss. I never think, *Thank fuck I don't have to do that any more.* It's surprised me how much I actually grieve for the struggle: all those energy-sapping days and nights. But fundamentally it comes down to one thing: I simply miss my mum. I'd wager she isn't pining for those humiliation and dependency times. Not a chance she'd crave a return to the days when son number one wiped her down while son number two lived in abject terror at the thought of losing her. Mum's better now; she's healed, and me and Danny are satisfied about that. But, hell's fire, how I miss it all.

'You're welcome any time,' Roddy says. 'Right, I'll give you guys a five-minute chill thrill and then we can get started.'

I'd kind of forgotten how bizarre and brilliant Roddy is. I park next to Harriet, who throws me a cosy grin.

'Good to see you, Bobby,' she says.

'You too,' I say. 'Like the T-shirt.' She looks down at her attire, awkwardly straightens herself out a bit.

'Yeah, well, not everyone's cuppa, but I like them,' she says.

'No, I quite like Jesus and Mary Chain myself.'

'You know these guys?'

'Just a bit,' I say. 'Mum was a huge fan.'

In that beat I whip out a giant grey cloud and kill the conviviality. But I don't mean to. Harriet's face falls.

'I'm so sorry, Bobby. I am,' she says.

'Don't be, Harriet. Time to look forward, eh?'

'You coping with everything?'

'As best I can. Just adjusting to new routines, isn't it?'

'Suppose.'

'Getting into a different flow, different patterns of life.'

'Yeah.'

One day she'll be standing in my shoes, they all will, obviously without lugging this secret boulder around, but they'll certainly know what sorrow in the sack of the stomach feels like. Empathy, indeed.

Where is he?

I'm dying to ask the question, I am.

Where?

'Well, I never thought I'd say this,' Harriet adds. 'But this place might be good for you.'

'What, here?'

'Yes, here. Why not?'

I scan the crescent. Cal and Tom are in deep chat: Tom looks confused. Erin and Clare are phone fawning: they're blossoming into each other, striking up lasting friendship. Roddy is trying to set up a type of noticeboard: he's whistling. It all seems oddly familiar and comforting.

WHERE IS HE?

'But you've always hated it,' I say.

Harriet leans into me.

'Can I tell you something, Bobby?'

'Sure.'

'I only pretend to hate it,' she whispers.

'That's OK. I won't tell a soul,' I whisper in return. 'It's nice to see everyone again, actually.'

'Really?' She screws up her face, grins.

Probably best just to spit it out, Bobby.

'But where's –'

'Hey, did you hear about Lou?' she says.

'No. Something happen?'

'We don't really know. He blew in one night and spouted something about leaving.'

'He didn't like the meetings, I don't think,' I say.

'No, not the meetings – he was leaving.'

'Like, leaving leaving?'

'Exactly.'

'To where?'

'America, I think.'

'He said that?'

'Yeah, just walked in, blabbered something about how he didn't belong here and that he was going back to America. Then he left.' Harriet shrugs her shoulders. 'Best place for him, if you ask me. He was fucking bonkers that one.'

I don't disagree or ask any other questions. Don't want my feelings to be known. I'm grateful there'll be no explanation or confrontation. Gratitude tinged with sadness. Just a tiny tinge.

'Yeah, probably best place for him,' I say.

'Pin the tail on the donkey!' Roddy howls. 'Who's heard of that before?' Zero hands go up. 'Right, this is a variation of that …'

Choral groans.

It's good to be back.

#12 ... complete

I get further away,
        but I still see you

I don't want to feel again,
        but I'll touch you forever

I yearn for that time,
        but you darkened it

I yearn,
        do you?

New Dreams

'Don't hurt me, Bobby. Please don't hurt me.'

He says this over and over again, not every night, but it's getting close to it. I allow him to wake up. Wipe sweat from his brow. I need to be there when he opens his eyes. He has to understand that the person he sees would never hurt him.

'It's me – Bobby. I'm not going to hurt you, Dan.'

Hurt you?

Hurt HIM?

These words set me alight. Whenever I hear them I almost buckle in a combined wave of agony and grief. Every time. The very notion that Danny would be scared of me never once crossed my mind.

I maintain distance between us.

'I'll never hurt you,' I say.

'Promise?' Danny says, half dazed.

'I promise you. It's me. I'd never do anything to hurt you. Come, sit up a bit.'

He shifts upright, still looking scared and exhausted. A new routine for me, short-lived, I hope.

'Hey, buddy,' I say. 'I'm here.'

I detect a semi-smile on Danny's face. Not a hundred per cent sure though.

He groans. It's torture trying to appear undefeated all the time.

'If you want me to leave, Dan, that's all right too,' I say. 'It's all good.'

'Don't know,' he mutters.

'If you think that might be best.'

He lets out a whimper.

'But I'd really like to stay, I really would. We could have one of our chats. Remember how we used to chat? I'd really like that, would you?'

He picks up a spare pillow and sinks his face deep into it, crushing all those feathers. This is the intimate version of grief: it attacks every sense you have. When you're not hearing it you're seeing it; when you're not seeing it you're feeling it. And on it twists. It becomes your new worst friend, always there, always prodding to remind you of its presence; you know, just in case you have the gall to momentarily forget.

'But if you decide I should go back to my room, Dan, I want you to know how much I love you. You're my little brother. I'll always love you.'

He dunks his head in the pillow. It's funny: he looks like he's a giant marshmallow head.

It's not funny.

'I'm very proud of you, Dan. I know Mum would be as well. You're doing brilliantly,' I say, trying to coax him out of the feathers. 'I'm so happy we have each other.'

His body dances with sadness.

'You mean the world to me, Dan.'

He tightens the pillow around his head. I watch. His crying is distressing, makes me feel so helpless, weakened because I can't do anything to soothe him; I've no words. It's like being punched repeatedly in the lungs; it's excruciating to witness. My own body begins to judder and spasm. I didn't rock this hard at Mum's funeral. The liquid that pours from my eyes, nose and mouth flows on to the duvet. Nothing tempers it.

'Don't cry, Bobby,' Danny says.

'Yeah, sorry, mate. It's just, you know.'

'I do know. I'm sorry too.'

'Hey, don't you be sorry. You've no reason to be sorry,' I say.

Danny launches the pillow off the bed. His face is bloated, as is mine. We're like a couple of crash victims.

'Were you serious?' he asks.

'About what?'

'About Mum being proud of me?'

I compose myself, clear my miserable throat.

'Dan, she'd be so proud of you, proud of us both.'

'Really?'

'Totally.'

'I miss her so much, Bobby.'

'Me too.'

'I didn't think it would be this hard.'

'You can still hear her. You have the voice message she made for you, don't you?'

'I listen to it all the time.'

'That's good. You should always listen when you're feeling sad. It'll help,' I say. 'Does it help?'

'Not now, but maybe tomorrow it will.'

'I think we just need to try harder, Dan.'

'How?'

'Get out the house more, talk about our feelings, do things together ...'

'With Bel too?'

'Yeah, Bel can always do things with us.'

'Bobby?'

'What?'

'Can I come to your Friday takeaway night tomorrow, instead of playing computer games?'

'Junk Food Friday, you mean?'

'Crap name, but yes. Can I?'

'I'd be disappointed if you didn't.'

'Great,' he says.

'I'll give Bel a call.'

'I'll get up.'

I look around his room: place needs a paint job, a complete makeover. I'll do it in the summer holidays, give the entire house new energy. Flash thought: maybe I'll move my stuff into Mum's old room. It's bigger. I'm bigger. Plus it's rammed with laughter and happy memories. I'll just paint over the others that linger.

'See you downstairs, Dan,' I say.

'Bobby?'

'Yeah?'

'Can we search for Mum's heart one day?'

'Sure we can.'

'I'd like to listen to her beating.'

'That's a good idea, mate.'

'And, Bobby?'

'Yeah?'

'It's all going to be all right, I think.'

'I know it is, Dan. I know it is.'

Press Play

When we get back from the cinema he corners me. His look could crack your bones, deadly serious. Shuffles through his pockets.

'Bobby, Mum wanted me to give this to you.' He holds out his hand.

'What?'

'She said to give it to you when you were feeling better.'

'What is it? A phone?'

'And I think you are feeling better now, so here, take it.' He hands me the phone. 'She said you'll know what to do.'

Danny leaves me alone.

Course I know what to do.

I wait until I'm in my room, her old room. In my bed – her

old bed. I rest my head on the pillow (new one), plug in my earphones, scroll to recordings and press play. Close my eyes and wait for her to arrive.

'*Hi, Bobby. It's your mother here. Remember I told you that you weren't adopted? Well …*'

About the Author

Brian Conaghan was born and raised in the Scottish town of Coatbridge but now lives in Dublin. He has a Master of Letters in Creative Writing from the University of Glasgow. For many years Brian worked as a teacher and taught in Scotland, Italy and Ireland. His first YA novel for Bloomsbury, *When Mr Dog Bites*, was shortlisted for the 2015 Carnegie Medal, and his second, *The Bombs That Brought Us Together*, won the 2016 Costa Children's Book Award. *We Come Apart*, a verse novel co-authored with Carnegie Medal winner Sarah Crossan, won the 2018 UKLA Book Award, and his fourth novel, *The Weight of a Thousand Feathers*, won the 2018 Irish Book Award for Teen & Young Adult Book of the Year.

@BrianConaghan

a story about life, death, love, sex and swearing

'Funny, foul-mouthed, fantastic'
CHARLIE HIGSON

when $#!+!

**$€!

mr dog

bites

SHORTLISTED
CILIP
**Carnegie
Medal
2015**

brian conaghan

BLOOMSBURY

SHORTLISTED FOR THE CILIP CARNEGIE MEDAL 2015

A routine visit to the hospital turns sixteen-year-old Tourette's sufferer Dylan's life topsy-turvy. He discovers that he's going to die next March. It's only August, but still – he has THINGS TO DO. So he makes a list – *Cool Things To Do Before I Cack It* – and sets out to make his wishes come true.

'So surprising and charming it would be hard not to feel a little uplifted'
Observer

OR THE BRILLIANT

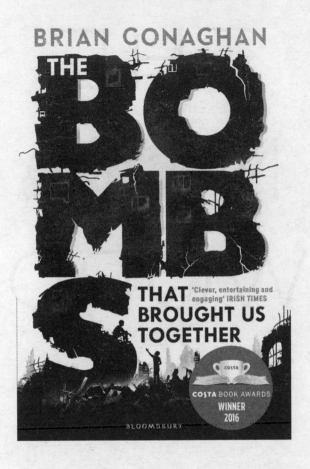

WINNER OF THE COSTA CHILDREN'S BOOK AWARD 2016

Charlie Law has lived in Little Town all his life and he knows the rules. The most important of which is to never to get on the wrong side of the people who run Little Town. But when he meets Pavel Duda, a refugee, rules start to get broken. Then the bombs come, and the soldiers, and Little Town changes for ever …

'A dark, powerful tale of survival, morality and loyalty'
Scotsman

AND DON'T MISS

THE

M ~~████~~

WORD

The unforgettable new novel
from Brian Conaghan

Publishing September 2019